"I think we should shake on it," Nick called after her.

The thought of touching him caused a fluttery sensation deep inside Becky. "Of course," she said.

When his large, warm hand captured her small one, she almost gasped. A charge like summer lightning ripped through her. He studied her, his brilliant gray eyes staring through her. His straight black lashes shadowed his cheeks—or was it the trick of sunlight on this glorious day?

Becky stood, lost in the smoky depths of his eyes. She felt as though she was peering at an ancient rock wall. Light and dark sparkles glittered from the depths of his soul.

"Agreed." He released her hand.

Her mouth felt as dry as hay. She nodded, afraid to trust her voice. She wiped her hand on her skirt, then strode back to her horse, forcing herself not to run like the devil....

Dear Reader,

In *A Wish for Nicholas* by Jackie Manning, a young widow who has been draining the income from her profitable land to improve the lives of the crofters is dismayed to learn that the crown has given away her estate as a prize to a handsome young naval hero, a man determined to uncover her secrets and win her heart. Don't miss this delightful tale.

Margaret Moore's popular WARRIOR SERIES is still going strong, as you will discover with *A Warrior's Bride,* the wonderful tale of a peace-loving knight and a fiery noblewoman who make an unlikely match in a stormy marriage of convenience. And we are very pleased to have *USA Today* bestselling author Merline Lovelace back in our midst with her new Western, *Countess in Buckskin,* the passionate story of a Russian countess who falls in love with the rough-hewn American lieutenant who has been forced to escort her through the untamed mountains of California.

Cassandra Austin also returns this month with a ranch story, *Hero of the Flint Hills,* about a woman who is engaged to an aspiring politician, but finds herself drawn to his rugged half brother.

Whatever your tastes in reading, we hope you enjoy all four books.

Sincerely,

Tracy Farrell
Senior Editor

A Wish for Nicholas

Jackie Manning

Harlequin Books

TORONTO • NEW YORK • LONDON
AMSTERDAM • PARIS • SYDNEY • HAMBURG
STOCKHOLM • ATHENS • TOKYO • MILAN
MADRID • WARSAW • BUDAPEST • AUCKLAND

ISBN 0-373-28998-7

A WISH FOR NICHOLAS

Books by Jackie Manning

Harlequin Historicals

A Wish for Nicholas #398

Previously published under the pseudonym Jackie Summers

Harlequin Historicals

Embrace the Dawn #260

JACKIE MANNING

believes in love at first sight. She and her husband, Tom, were married six weeks to the day after they first met and he proposed, many happy years ago. Home is a one-hundred-and-fifty-year-old colonial in Maine, where they live with their two dogs, a Shih Tzu and an Aussie Terrier. When Jackie isn't writing romances, she's researching and visiting interesting places to write about. She loves to hear from her readers. You can write to her at P.O. Box 1739, Waterville, ME 04963.

A Wish for Nicholas is dedicated to a true hero—a man whose love, gentle strength and quiet wisdom mean more to me each day. Bear, you're truly the wind beneath my wings.

My special thanks for the love and support from my writer's group. Mechele Cooper, Terri Hibbard, Carole Lambert, Prudy McMann, John Wells and Meg Wickes. Thanks for making Monday and Thursday nights so marvelous.

And to my three guardian angels, Vicki Hinze Barrett, Elizabeth Sinclair and my special sister, Kim Kowzlowski. Love ya, guys.

Prologue

London, England
July 1666

"**H**e looks dead," said Barbara Villiers, the countess of Castlemaine, as she watched the royal physician remove the black leeches from Captain Nicholas Sinclair's brawny chest.

"He should be dead for what he's been through," King Charles replied, leaning over the doctor's shoulder and peering at the wounded man.

Handsome devil, Barbara mused. The loss of blood from the mortar wound hadn't diminished his rugged good looks. When Sinclair recuperated, he'd make a decidedly fresh addition to the royal court.

If he lives.

The king's dark brows knotted with worry. "England needs him alive, William. You mustn't let him die."

"Of course not, Your Majesty." The court surgeon choked on the words.

Barbara smiled. If the doctor thought differently, she knew he'd not dare speak his mind in the monarch's presence. Her attention returned to King Charles, the man she had known intimately for more than six years. Why had he insisted Sinclair be brought to a suite in the palace when the other wounded officers had been sent to hospital? And why had the king personally kept a vigil over him? Never had she seen His Majesty so concerned, except when his own children were ill.

Feeling ignored, Barbara moved to the other side of the canopied bed to stand beside the king. She teasingly brushed her breast against his velvet sleeve. "Come, Your Majesty. Why don't you retire to your bedchamber? You must get your rest, too." She winked, then gave him her most inviting smile, charged with anticipation.

Charles never glanced up from the patient. "You go, my dear. I want to stay with him."

Barbara bit back her irritation. She forced a sweet face. "If you want to stay, then I'll keep you company," she replied, her voice silken.

The king rewarded her with an appreciative smile. She exchanged an intimate glance with him, then took a seat beside the bed.

The patient moaned. The king held his breath.

Barbara studied the young man who drew such royal attention. His thick black eyebrows and black hair contrasted sharply with the cream satin pillows behind his head. An appreciative glint brightened her blue eyes as her gaze lingered over the man's sun-bronzed face. Were his eyes brown or blue? The thought struck her that she might never find out.

"I think he's coming round," cried the physician, his voice openly relieved.

The king clapped his hands. "Sinclair, can you hear me?"

His eyes opened, and Barbara noticed they were gray as the Thames on a January morning. And just as cold.

"My, God, where...where am I?" The baritone voice caused a flutter of feminine response in her.

"You're with His Majesty, King Charles, at the royal apartments in Whitehall Palace." The physician drew in a loud sigh. "You're a very lucky man, Captain."

Nicholas Sinclair sat up, and the silk sheet slid from his bare chest, pooling in soft folds at his waist. "My men! Where are my men?"

A breath caught in Barbara's throat. She had noticed his broad shoulders before, but until he sat up, she hadn't been aware of how perfectly molded his body was. She felt the king's gaze upon her, and she averted her glance to the floor.

"We'll talk of your crew later," the king said finally. "Now, you must rest—"

"No. I—I've got to…my men." Sinclair grimaced as he pushed the physician aside with surprising strength. As his bare feet touched the floor, the gray eyes locked with Barbara's for the first time. He stopped, as though suddenly aware of his nakedness. He groped for the sheet that almost slid from his lap.

Barbara smiled, aware from his expression that he recognized her as the king's mistress. He met her bold stare, making no embarrassed move to glance away.

As if Sinclair realized that Barbara wasn't offended by his state of undress, he pulled the sheet around him and tried to stand. He staggered back, and when the physician helped ease him against the pillows, Sinclair didn't resist.

"You've cheated the devil this time, Sinclair," the king said. "I wouldn't tempt him again too soon."

"Aye, you may not be so lucky next time," the doctor added.

Sinclair clenched his jaw against the pain. Then he shouted, "Where are my men?" The veins in his neck distended when he yelled.

The physician paled at Sinclair's insubordinate tone in the king's presence.

The king ignored the outburst, his swarthy face solemn

as he studied the man. "Very well, Sinclair," he said finally. "I fear you'll not rest until you know."

Sinclair winced as he drew a breath and waited. "They're dead, aren't they?"

The king closed his eyelids and nodded. "Most of the lads." When his hooded eyes opened, they were bright with moisture. "Your ship took a direct mortar. You were knocked unconscious, and the few men left brought you to safety. The physicians believe your leg can be saved."

"My leg!" Sinclair's bandaged fingers clenched at his sides. "I don't give a damn about my leg." He thumped his fists on the bed, his biceps bulged with the effort. "I should be dead with my crew." He writhed back and forth against the pillows. "Damn it to hell! Damn! Damn! Damn!"

The king took a fortifying breath, then straightened his shoulders in reluctant resignation. After a moment, he stared back at the officer. "The Dutch have beaten us bloody, Sinclair. England needs a hero, and you're that man.

"When your ship chased the Dutch fleet, saving the *Royal Charles,* you salvaged England's pride. Think what joy the Dutch would have had if they'd sunk my royal yacht." The king's black eyes snapped with pride. "You're the hero England needs, Sir Nicholas Sinclair."

Sinclair's eyes rounded and his black brows arched in surprise. "Sir Nicholas—?"

"Aye. I've awarded you the title of baronet as well as the country manor that goes with it." Barbara kept the surprise from her face. Usually the king shared everything with her, but this was the first she had heard of it. Something strange was at hand; her curiosity edged up a notch.

Sinclair shook his head. "It's a ship I want, not a manor! My life is the sea. I'm not some sheep farmer—"

"Indeed you're not," the king said, trying not to smile.

"But Thornwood Hall is now your property and your responsibility. Besides, I have a special favor in mind." He paced back and forth by the bed, then turned to face Sinclair. "Before the Restoration, Thornwood Hall was awarded to one of Cromwell's generals." The king hesitated a moment. "Decent man, even if his politics were misguided. When I regained the throne, instead of removing General Forester from the estate he had made exceedingly profitable, I made a bargain with him. I offered the old man a special condition of taxation. He and his wife could remain on the crown's property providing they paid taxes based on the estate's annual profits. They readily agreed."

"What does this have to do with me?" Sinclair asked, obviously in much pain.

"The general died several years later. Since then, Thornwood Hall hasn't shown much of a profit. I want you to find out why. Besides, it's a lovely estate. An idyllic spot to convalesce while you're discovering what's wrong with the place."

Barbara wondered if the king had noticed her interest in Sinclair and wished the handsome officer away from court during his recuperation. The thought gave her a race of pleasure.

"I'll recover at sea, fighting the Dutch, Your Majesty. I'll go mad watching sheep." Sinclair's voice grew weaker, and Barbara knew he had overtired himself.

The king's face grew serious. "I wish England had the money to give you a ship, Sinclair. But the royal treasury is bankrupt due to these damnable Dutch raids. Unless the treasurer can secure a loan from our allies abroad—"

"The Dutch won't wait." Sinclair grimaced as he raised himself on one elbow. "De Ruyter must be stopped...."

The king stepped closer. "I agree." His black eyes snapped. "That's why it's vital that England gain a war hero. We can't let the Dutch or our allies know how seriously they've beaten us. We must put on a brave show, then our friends abroad will lend us the funds we need.

"Meanwhile, you'll recuperate at Thornwood Hall, overseeing your new estate. Once it was the most flourishing estate in the shire. Now it's so poor, the crofters can't pay their rents." He shook his head. "Something foul is afoot, Sinclair. It's your mission to find out why." The king scowled. "Once you discover what's ailing the place, you can sell it for all I care. But not before then."

Sinclair sighed and fell back against the pillows. Although the officer said nothing in rebuttal, Barbara thought his appeasement was more from exhaustion than obedience. Dark circles ringed his gray eyes, which did nothing to diminish his appealing masculinity.

"If you're up to it, Sinclair, one of your crewmen is waiting to see you," the physician said. "Michael Finn. That is, if you're not too tired—"

"Finn?" Sinclair's mouth lifted in surprise. "Finn is here, at Whitehall?" he asked, struggling to sit up.

The king smiled. "He's one of the men who saved you, Sinclair." He glanced at the physician. "William, keep me informed."

The doctor bowed. "Of course, Your Majesty."

"Then we'll leave you, Sinclair." The monarch's voice gentled as he took Barbara's hand. "Come, my dear."

Barbara gave Sinclair a wry glance as she swept past.

Nicholas Sinclair said nothing as he folded his arms, impatient for them to leave. Thank God, Finn was safe. He couldn't wait to see him.

His head throbbed as he fought to remember the order of what had happened. The screams of his gallant crew still rang in his ears. He remembered the mortar blast ripping the ship apart, then the cold water engulfing him. Nothing after that.

Sinclair squeezed back the tide of sorrow that threatened to overwhelm him and glared at the physician, who stood collecting his medicines. "How long before I can ride a horse?"

"A horse?" The doctor barked with laughter. "At least a month before you're strong enough to walk, let alone ride."

A jolt of pain shot down Sinclair's leg. "Bloody hell," he mumbled under his breath. "We'll see about that."

"What's your hurry, Sinclair?" The doctor tucked the herb packets back into the drawers of the medicine cabinet. "You have every luxury while you're at Whitehall." He grinned at him. "And the pick of the loveliest ladies at court."

"Beautiful women are in every port," Nick replied dryly. "All the luxury I want I'll find on board a warship."

The doctor shook his head and chuckled. "I'll be in later to see you, Captain." He gathered up his things and strode toward the door.

Nick barely heard the physician leave as he pondered how to raise the necessary capital to buy another ship. Maybe Finn could think of something. Between the two of them, they'd find another vessel if it were the last thing they did.

A few minutes after the doctor had left, the door flew open and a blond-haired man with ruddy features burst into the room.

"Captain!" The lumbering Irishman placed his arm on Sinclair's shoulder in a manly salute. "A damn feast for these ol' eyes, y'are, Nick."

Very few men had ever called him Nick, and the familiar name felt comforting. "So are you, Finn." His throat tightened and he feared his voice would betray his emotions. "Are you all right?" he managed. "The last time I saw you, you were reloading cannon near the stern."

Finn's smile faded and he lowered his blue gaze. "Right after that, we took a direct hit. You were knocked out by the blast. Smitty, Morrah and I brought you to shore, then I brought you here, the king's orders." Finn's gaze lifted to meet Nick's stare. "Do you remember how you led the *Hesper* against the Dutch fleet?" He took a step back. "You're a hero, Nick. All of our ships were saved except the *Hesper*, and everybody who survived that night has you to thank, lad."

Sinclair squeezed his eyes shut. "Damn it, Finn. I'm no hero. The true heroes went down with the *Hesper*." He swallowed back the lump in his throat. "I'm their captain. I should be with them."

Finn shifted uneasily. "You've had a shock. It's natural you feel like that now—"

"No. I've got to go back. I've got to get another ship, Finn. You've got to help me."

Finn's jaw dropped and he looked aghast. "How?"

"I've got an idea." Nick told Finn about the King awarding him the estate and the mission he had to do. When Nick had finished, Finn shook his head. "A baron with your own estate. Lord be!"

Nick rubbed his scraggly beard and studied his friend. "You're the one man I can trust, Finn. The king said I can't sell Thornwood Hall until I find out why the estate doesn't make a profit," he said, "but he didn't say I couldn't secure a loan against the place." The idea filled him with hope.

Finn's ruddy face darkened and he swore.

Nick ignored Finn's surprise. "The land must be worth something. I'll wager Thornwood Hall will provide enough collateral to buy a ship." He reached out and tapped Finn's shoulder. "I want you to negotiate it for me."

Finn scratched his fair head. "But we don't know anyone in London who would—"

"No, but I think someone at court will help us." Nick thought of the chestnut-haired mistress to the king, Barbara Villiers. "Perhaps the countess of Castlemaine might be persuaded to find a moneylender for us."

"The king's mistress?"

"Aye."

"And why would she do that?" Finn asked skeptically.

"Because I'll offer her a share of the profits," Nick answered.

"But what if the king finds out?"

"He won't find out. I'll leave for Thornwood Hall as soon as I'm able and solve the riddle. That's the least of our worries."

"Damn it, Nick. I'm not so sure—"

"Finn, I'm depending on you. Get a message to Barbara Villiers that I want to see her, then leave the rest to me." Through the pain, Nick forced a smile.

"All right, lad." Finn strode toward the door, then paused. "Luckily, I've made the acquaintance of one of her ladies-in-waiting. Ye can count on me, Cap'n." He winked as he shut the door.

Nick sighed as he leaned back against the pillows. His body throbbed; hot sharp pain traveled from his hip to his toes. He fought it away with the vision of his hands on the ship's rail, while he barked orders to his crew. Somehow, he'd find a way to get another ship and avenge the death of his men.

A mockingbird flew from a tree outside the open window and landed on the sill, bathed in sunlight. Suddenly, the room was filled with the bird's melodious song. Nick closed his eyes and drank in the sound. He hadn't heard a bird sing since he left for war, more than two years ago.

He took it as a very lucky sign.

Chapter One

County of Surrey, England
One Month Later

A high-pitched squeal pierced the humdrum stillness of the country lane. Sir Nicholas Sinclair shifted in the saddle, gauging the direction of the sound. The stand of sycamores near the bend ahead? Aye, the perfect place for robbers to hide, ready to lift a purse or to steal a horse from an unwary traveler.

Nick's hand hovered over his pistol holster. He almost hoped a highwayman would charge. Anything to break the tedium of the long ride since leaving London.

A feminine giggle, more distinct this time, alerted him to the dense elderberry bushes growing near the river. Drawing the seaman's telescope from his pocket, Nick brought it to his eye.

A trail of scattered clothing led from the riverbank to the thicket. A man's patched leather breeches and faded shirt poked through the reeds. The tangle of russet skirts billowed atop a mound of wild daisies, and a black corset lay momentarily forgotten amid tufts of grass.

Nick recognized the russet skirt as similar to the one

the tavern wench wore only last night at the Seven Swans. While serving him venison pasty and ale, she'd winked and brushed her mountainous white breasts across his hand. When he refused her offer, she sniffed scornfully. He'd have followed her gladly, but he had no time to linger. The sooner he settled his matter with Thornwood Hall, the sooner he'd be at sea where he belonged.

But if he arrived at the estate dressed as the king's dandy, the locals might not trust him enough to tell what he needed to know about the estate. Not one to miss an opportunity, he dismounted and strode toward the garments half-hidden in the weeds. A low passionate moan drifted from the elderberries. Nick chuckled as he saw the moon-shaped elder blossoms shake and the bushes rustle in the familiar age-old rhythm.

Nick snatched the man's breeches and shirt and assessed the owner's height and size. Grateful the man was tall, as well as randy, Nick quickly undid the ribbons at his neck and cuffs. Within minutes, he had discarded his ruffled silk shirt, robin's-egg blue velvet breeches and jacket, and dropped them upon the grass beside the other garments.

Before the lovers' cries ceased and the thrashing stopped, Nick had changed into the man's clothing and mounted his horse. He tossed his wide-brimmed hat—the last evidence of the court clothing he'd been given—and watched it sail through the air and land atop the strewn garments. With a sense of freedom, he galloped down the lane toward Thornwood Hall.

Fancy clothes meant nothing to him. He much preferred his naval uniform, but until he was back at the helm of the new ship, he'd settle for comfort. *His new ship!* Thank God for Finn, who had managed, with the help of the king's mistress, to obtain a loan for the new ship, using Thornwood Hall as collateral. Now, all Nick needed was a buyer for the estate so he could pay back the loan from the moneylender.

He'd set himself a new course: to find out what ailed the estate, then sell the damn place and repay the moneylender. By then, his ship would be built and he'd return to war, the king none the wiser.

A short while later, Nick found the lane had dwindled to a well-worn sheep run. The overgrown hedges grew so tangled that even the devil would have trouble gaining foot. From what he could see as he peeked through the rare openings, the land lay barren. Spindly corn stalks choked with weeds fought for their place in the sun. In the distance, the crofters' shacks, like untidy hay bundles, dotted the wildflower meadow.

He stared at the holding in dismay and growing irritation. Obviously Thornwood Hall had fallen into neglect after the general had died, but who could imagine such a pile of beetles and weeds? Apparently the king hadn't known; otherwise he couldn't have kept a straight face when he'd awarded this run-down pile of brambles as a reward for Nick's bravery.

A string of loud curses broke his thoughts. Nick wheeled his horse around. Unable to see anything through the fence of brambles, he dismounted and crept to the hedgerow. He tried poking a hole through the fence, but a stout sweetbriar thorn snagged his arm. With a growl, he jerked free.

"Damn!" he muttered. Remembering his telescope, Nick extended the tube and thrust it through the hedge like a sword.

He gazed through the lens. In the meadow, a tall whip of a man, his shirt stained with splotches of sweat, flailed an enormous black bull with a switch. The man yanked on the rope attached to the ring in the animal's nose, shrieking oaths that would have raised a blush from the crew of the *Hesper*. The bull snorted, pawing the ground. Then the man whipped the beast again.

In the distance, a rider sped hell-bent toward man and beast, the horse's hooves tearing up clumps of sod as she sped across the meadow.

Aye, the rider was female. Nick's fingers squeezed the spyglass. Ebony ribbons of hair whipped behind her head as she swooped upon her target, like a Harpy in Virgil's *Aeneid*. She brought her mount to a stop and slipped from the saddle in one fluid motion.

The girl charged at the bully, her blue skirts billowing behind her. She tore the whip from his fist and cracked the strap across his back.

Damn, if the man struck her back, Nick thought, how would he cut through the damned hedge in time to save the plucky lass? But instead of shielding himself, the bully cowered like a boy.

As though satisfied, the girl threw down the switch, then whirled to face the animal. Nick blinked. For the first time, he noticed the monstrous bull in detail. Long horns poked out from the wide brim of a hat lying atop its head. A Cavalier's hat, by God! A red-feathered plume curled along the band.

What the hell was she doing? Fascinated, Nick watched as the girl gently stroked the animal's chin. Then she began to sing. Or was he hearing an angel? High, lilting tones, like harp music, floated on the summer breeze.

The king had said that General Forester was in his eighties when he'd died. Now, his widow ran the manor, with the help of the general's bastard son. Maybe this lass with the siren's voice was the old man's granddaughter.

In less than a wink, the bull moved from standstill to trot. The girl, holding the rope, ran alongside, as if they were one. The man took up beside them. Finally, she relinquished the lead, flinging the rope back at the man. With an arrogant toss of her head, she mounted her horse, then watched at a distance.

The bull kept its pace. The red feather bounced jauntily with each jerk of the animal's ponderous steps. The man bobbed up and down, his arms and legs windmilling at his sides, laboring to keep up. Nick couldn't help but laugh.

He moved his telescope back to the amazing girl. Woman, he corrected. Through the scope, Nick watched her pert breasts lift and drop with her laughter. Her lovely face flushed with amusement as she watched the man and beast trot off.

She was not more than twenty and some, he decided. From her plain dress, she was a servant, but her bearing was that of a queen. Only when she turned and rode in the other direction did Nick realize he had been staring at her longer than necessary.

A while later, Nick continued riding, periodically ducking his head under the low-hanging limbs. The path had dwindled to a trail of dense weeds.

Ahead, stood a three-story, Tudor-style stone monster of a house. Knee-high twitchgrass grew to the entrance. Shutters hung askew from most of the windows. Nick shook his head and swore.

Irritation curled along his spine. Damn the king for thinking that Thornwood Manor could be brought around to the profitable estate it had been under Cromwell. A magician couldn't turn this pile of stones into a gainful venture again.

Nick swore under his breath. There was no excuse for unkempt buildings. Run a tight ship, he always proclaimed. No wonder the estate lost money year after year. The king had best forget any thought of receiving tax monies from this dung heap.

Thornwood Hall. Remembering the ghastly hedgerows, he realized that whoever named it had a rich sense of humor.

"Come, Rex, let's find a grassy spot by the river, where I'll hide you until dark." The horse nickered in answer.

Yawning, Nick remembered that he hadn't slept last night at the Seven Swans. The drunken singing drifting from the taproom would have wakened the devils in hell. His gaze fixed on a small stone outbuilding attached to the barn. The perfect place to grab a few winks and rest his leg before he began exploring his land.

Nick dismounted, his thoughts going back to the black-haired beauty who had taken the man to task for whipping the beast.

Why hadn't the king mentioned her? he mused.

Still flushed from her ride in the meadow, Becky paused to glance up from her planting and take in the familiar sight of her favorite flowers. Bees buzzed amid the blue delphiniums in front of the open window of the hay barn. The exposed earth waited for the seeds of verbena, lavender and coltsfoot she had yet to plant.

Why was she wasting her time planting seed? She and her sister and brothers wouldn't be at Thornwood Hall to see them flower. She brushed back the wrench of anger and loss that sometimes threatened to overtake her. The bees' buzzing drew her attention as they hugged the blossoms. She had no time to squander on such thoughts. She had work to do, for God answered those who tried solving their own troubles.

"Ah-ah-ah-a choo!"

Startled, Becky jumped. Her basket slipped from her lap, seeds scattering along the ground. Pox and calamity! Who was in the haybarn? She grabbed her husband's sword, which she always kept close to her side, and got to her feet.

She leaned into the open window and peeked inside. Shielding her eyes, she peered against the darkness. All she could see was her shadow, casting a wide-brimmed silhouette upon the sunlit patch of golden hay strewn about the floorboards. A few feet away stood the bulging hayrick; a man's leather boot stuck out between the wooden slats.

So that was where the lazy arse had hidden himself, Becky mused, remembering that Molly's son was to have shown himself this morning for the first honest day's work since he returned from God knew where.

Becky charged into the barn, her sword drawn. "Get your lazy arse out of that wagon or I'll run you through!" She thrust the sword's point an inch above where the dusty leather boot poked through the straw. Bits of golden chaff burst into the air.

"What the…" The man leaped up in the hay wagon, his legs shot under him like a marionette at the Punch and Judy show. "Watch that sword. You'll do some damage—"

"Aye, I will, an' that's a promise, Ben Twaddle. Now, out from that rick and show yourself. On your feet. Let me see what sort of an ill bargain I've bought myself this time."

Instead of obeying, the man stared at her with sharp gray eyes. Sly, cunning eyes. She hesitated a moment as their gazes locked.

In the half-light of the barn, he appeared older than she thought Ben to be. She was barely six years old when the nine-year-old Ben had left home. Aye, left his mother to bring up all the children when his father, the thief, went to jail.

She eyed him cautiously. He looked more like thirty and five than the twenty and seven he would be. She sniffed. Years on the road had aged him, no doubt.

Yet she hadn't imagined Ben to be so…Becky took in

the tousled black hair, strong jaw and high, arrogant cheekbones. The arched black brows gleamed like blackbird's wings against the sun-burnished face. She stopped and mentally shook herself. Sun-burnished from lying in the weeds with the barmaids from the Seven Swans Tavern, no doubt. Not from scything hay or weeding turnips in honest man's toil.

Aye, Molly's troublesome son didn't have his father's weak chin, or low forehead. No, this pigeon was most handsome. Cocksure of himself, too, by his outright gawk. No wonder he'd given Molly such fits since he showed up on her doorstep last week.

"Up, up, I say." Becky whirled the sword in a menacing arc. "I haven't all day, Ben Twaddle."

"Who the hell are you?"

Becky stopped dead still. Molly had said her son was shiftless and crafty, a man who'd put more struggle into getting out of a decent day's work than if he'd settle straight to the task. But Molly never said Ben was stupid.

"Surely you remember the scrawny, pigtailed lass, whose pet pig you stole and sold to market?" She narrowed her eyes. "The years have changed us, Twaddle. Today, I'm mistress of Thornwood Hall, and you're the same worthless bag of bones that ran off all those years ago with my pig." Becky blew a black wisp of hair from her face. "Surely your mum told you that I married General Forester, God rest his soul. I'm your new employer," she answered, wondering which of his artful tricks he would ply her with. She watched as the look of surprise spread across the planes and angles of his face.

Just let him try to play stupid with her. She poked into the hay, about where she imagined his hip to be.

"Ouch, you little..." He glared at her, his left hand rubbing his hip.

She couldn't hide the smug feeling of satisfaction as she poked him again. "This little nudge will sharpen your wits, Twaddle. Now, do you remember your promise to your mum to work off her rents in exchange for your labor?''

The gray eyes frosted over like icy steel, and for a flash, she thought he might be dangerous.

''You're a peppery little spit, I'll give you that, but if you don't put down that sword, you'll damn soon regret it.'' His square chin hardened into a stubborn wedge as he pulled himself to the cross rails of the wagon and peered down at her.

Becky could only gape at what was none other than blasphemy. In the seven years since her husband had died, she had never been shown disrespect by the servants—who were mostly kin—or the crofters, whom she thought of and treated as her family.

''How dare you speak to me like that!'' She glared at this giant, who had probably never broken a sweat in honest toil. Becky felt her temper boil. ''It will be my pleasure to break your spirit, you shiftless waste of skin.''

The man climbed down from the wagon and stared at her. She glanced at the familiar shirt with the wooden buttons that she remembered Molly sewing when she had last visited her. The breeches and shirt had belonged to Ben's father, as well. Ben was taller than his father and much more well-developed. His arms almost bulged the seams.

He limped toward her, favoring his left leg, then stopped a few feet from where she stood.

She studied him, then sniffed. ''Playing for sympathy with the game leg trick, aye?'' She threw back her shoulders as she decided how best to teach him a lesson. Despite his rumpled shirt and breeches, he loomed with attractive masculinity.

''I'll teach you to respect your betters, Ben Twaddle,'' she said, feeling suddenly unsure of her words.

His black brows knitted into a scowl as he glowered down at her. "What sort of fool are you, woman?"

Fueled by his outrageous lack of respect, Becky tightened her fingers through the sword's hilt and whirled the blade around his ear with record speed. A black lock of hair sailed to the barn floor. His mouth slacked open with surprise, then he shot her a look of inflamed, disbelieving shock.

"Now, who's the fool?" She couldn't help but smile when she saw the open astonishment on his face.

He leaned over her, hands on his hips. "Put the sword down this instant, or I'll—"

Becky lunged toward him. He sensed her move this time. He shot out of her way with lightning speed, the tip of the blade missing the top of his sleeve by inches.

His hand shot to his shoulder, his face open in amazement.

Becky's laughter rang out like crystal bells. "What a pity the maids at the Seven Swans can't see you now, Twaddle." Her blade whirred in the air as she spoke.

His steely eyes held a warning as they locked with hers.

"Oh, Twaddle," she cried, "I see your hose needs changing." The tip of the sword whirled to take aim at the fasteners tied to the sides of his knees. In a wink, he moved, but not soon enough. The fastener below his knee gave way, the hose disappearing into the wide cuffs of his boots, exposing a few inches of hairy leg.

She giggled. "Perhaps now you'll remember who I am?"

His eyes glittered dangerously like live, burning embers.

"I'm afraid I've taken too much off one side of your hair," she said, unable to keep a straight face. "Let me straighten the other side for you." Laughter almost doubled her over.

"You'd better think carefully, woman, before you best a defenseless man." The cold threat in his voice caused her to pause. The man's arm slid behind him and he withdrew a light saber from the hay wagon. In a motion so quick only the rush of air fluttering the drawstrings at her neckline gave warning, the arc of steel sliced through the blue ribbons of her bodice, releasing her gown as it slid from her shoulders.

His mouth curled in a sardonic smile. It did nothing to relax the steely jaw or the dangerous glint in his eyes.

Becky gaped as the blade sang through the air a second time. With a snap, the glint of steel sliced again, this time, releasing the delicate ribbon tied in a prim bow at the neckline of her chemise. The soft muslin fell from her shoulders and slid down her arms. Her hands flew to her bosom, covering herself with the loosened fabric.

"How dare you!" Only when she heard her sword clang to the floor did she realize she dropped it.

"Not giving up so soon?" He smiled, his saber tip playing about the hem of her skirts. "I'm just beginning to enjoy your little sport."

"You...you..." Becky steamed as she watched his enjoyment grow with her outrage. "Your mother praises you when she calls you a shiftless..."

"Shiftless waste of skin?" he offered, cocking a brow.

"Exactly."

"I'm much worse, I'd wager." Amused interest replaced the anger in his gray eyes. The tip of his sword hovered in the air, waiting. "Give up?"

"Never!" Becky's fingers tightened the loosely gathered fabric at her breasts while she whirled around and picked up the sword with her right hand, exposing her bare back to him.

"What an interesting birthmark you have, mistress."

Ignoring his comment, she positioned her sword in her right hand and lunged it at him. But he moved so quickly,

she didn't even see his blade. Only the soft whoosh sound
below her right arm drew her attention in time to see her
outer skirt fall to the ground.

"How—?" She stared in disbelief.

"Did anyone ever tell you that the birthmark on your
back resembles a golden butterfly?" His mouth quirked
with arrogance.

"I'll have you shaved bald for your insolent tongue!"
Becky lunged again, but he stepped out of her way, just
in time.

"I think I'll remove the red underskirt first, or perhaps
the white..." She gaped in horror to see the point of his
sword lifting her skirts as he peeked at the hems of her
undergarments. "Or should I just flick all of them off—"

She jumped back out of the reach of his sword. "I'll
see your arrogant hide tied to the fence, and your mother
and I will watch as—"

"Mum?" He lifted a questioning brow as he stepped
to within a foot of her and appraised her lazily. "What
will Mum think when I describe your birthmark on your
enticing lower back." His mouth twisted in a grin. "A
golden butterfly, I'll tell her."

"If you tell anyone about my birthmark, I'll say
you...you tried to take advantage of—"

"Now, now, now." A playful twinkle lit his eyes.
"I'm sure you know what Mum and the others will
think?" He returned his sword to the sheath at his side.

Becky narrowed her eyes and drew the loose fabric
closer. "What do you mean?"

His chiseled mouth lifted in smug exaggeration. "If
my reputation is so dishonorable, fair lady, are you not
afraid that my mum might believe you'd fallen for my
charms?"

"That's absurd! Molly would never believe such a
thing."

"Then how will you explain my knowledge of such a

personal matter as your birthmark?'' His bold eyes met hers with a warm, intimate look.

She felt a blush creep to the roots of her hair. She stepped back, but the horrible realization hit her that what he said was true. Damn Ben Twaddle's cunning. He was the sort to scrounge off women, and most women would be all agog over his handsome face.

Even though she was innocent, her reputation would be ruined if a whisper of scandal were to touch the Forester name. Sinclair would never allow her to manage Thornwood Hall for him.

Sir Nicholas Sinclair. No, she'd not think of that creature. One revolting scoundrel was enough to deal with at a time!

Becky drew in a resigned breath. ''I gave my promise to Molly that I'd stiffen your spine with honest toil, and I aim to keep that promise, Twaddle. You'll not be getting out of work this time, regardless of your brazen tricks.'' She glowered at him. Despite her words, nothing would pleasure her more than to send this dog packing.

He answered her with an amused smile. ''Brazen, dear lady? It's not brazen for a man to defend himself. After all, you flew at me. An unarmed man. I was only protecting my...virtue.''

''Your virtue?'' She laughed. ''Twaddle, you don't give up, do you? Playing daft won't lose your job. Nothing you do will keep me from breaking my vow to your mother!''

He took a step closer.

She'd wipe that expression from his face before the month was out. She sniffed disdainfully as she picked up her skirt from the hay-strewn floor. She gave it a shake, then glared at him over her shoulder.

''You can start by grabbing that pitchfork and mucking out the stalls in the livery stable. Geer will be in later to see if you've finished. Only then will he give you your supper."

In an attempt at dignity, Becky lifted her chin and strode toward the door without looking at him, but he moved to her side in three long strides and barred the door with his arm. "And what if I don't want to?"

"What *you* want has nothing to do with it, Twaddle." She moved past him but he took her arm.

"Very well, I'll do your tasks, but we have one thing to settle, first."

Becky thought to run, but she knew that was what he wanted. He was used to having his way with women. She wouldn't show that his charged masculinity and dangerous presence affected her. She forced herself to meet his gaze.

Thick black lashes fringed his silver gray eyes. She was reminded of the silver of April rain upon the river as it flowed along the gaming fields. Vibrant, changeable eyes. His black hair fell in loose waves, touching his broad shoulders. She blinked. "What do we have to settle, Twaddle?"

He held her close, and she wondered why she didn't break away. What was he going to do?

"You said I was bold." His metallic gaze fell to her lips and her stomach clenched. "*This* is bold...."

His mouth took hers in such haste she could only gasp. Her body trembled as the kiss deepened. Her fingers squeezed the fabric in front of her, her heart beating double time. His arms tightened around her, and she felt herself swirl helplessly into exciting sensations.

When he pulled his mouth from hers, she blinked back into consciousness. "How dare you—" Becky recovered quickly. She drew back, wanting to slap that grin from his face, but her hands were full of the gathers at her bodice. Repressed anger coursed through her at the pompous audacity of the man and her own blatant reaction to him.

She kicked open the barn door. "Out!" she screamed. "Get off my property and don't ever let me see you again!"

He threw back his head and laughed. "Very well, little butterfly, I'll go. But I'll take the thought of your sweet kiss with me, its memory warming my heart."

"Out! Out! Out!"

He bowed with a flourish, then walked into the sunlit yard, his rich laughter filling the air.

Becky clutched her dress to her. Pox and calamity! How would she explain to Molly that she had let her son worm himself out of the first honest position that was ever offered to him?

Besides, if Twaddle didn't work off the money Molly owed, how would the poor woman pay her rents?

She held her fingertips to her lips, the warm feel of his mouth still upon hers, and she felt herself blush.

Ben Twaddle was another scourge on Thornwood Hall, and she'd had more than enough of scoundrels. There was no way she'd hire that blackguard. A man like that was dangerous.

Now, if only to find a way to explain it to Molly.

Nick was still smiling when he brought the pail of water from the river to his horse, staked in the secluded glen nearby. Becky Forester was nothing like the wizened old woman he had imagined. Decidedly beautiful, with those flashing violet eyes and heavy mane of shining ebony hair.

He wondered why she hadn't married again. Surely the lively widow had given up trying to squeeze a profit from the overgrown, weevil-ridden rubble known as Thornwood Hall. The king had said the estate hadn't made a profit in years, and the Widow Forester had paid little in taxes for want of a good harvest.

Nick rubbed his scraggly beard. Odd. The hay in the wagon where he had bedded down was rich and fresh. The orchards, away from the path, hung heavy with green fruit. The cows in the back pasture had full udders waiting for the milkmaids. Yet the roadside fields lay untended or bore nothing but stunted crops.

Nick unwrapped the cheese that he had taken from the sack that hung from the saddle. Becky Forester didn't expect him for another fortnight. Perhaps he should have accepted that job she had offered, or rather ordered him to take. His lips curved in a rakish grin at the memory. It might have provided just the opportunity to find the answers to his questions.

He smiled again, and he was reminded that he had smiled more today than he had in a very long time.

Chapter Two

The pleasant aroma of freshly baked bread and blackberry tarts that Becky had brought did little to dispel the gloom that pervaded Molly Twaddle's croft. The old woman sat in front of the fire, and her frail shoulders, wrapped with a thick woolen shawl, shook with muffled sobs.

"Molly, please try to understand..." Becky's voice faded, her hands twisting in despair as she paced a tight circle in front of the hearth.

Molly wiped her cheeks with the edge of her apron, then gazed at Becky with a look that said it was Becky who didn't understand. "Maybe if ye'd ask Ben to work for ye again." Her lips pressed into a brave line that caused her chin to quiver. "Give 'im a week t' show ye what 'e ken do." Her sweet face beamed with the eternal hope all mothers have for their wayward offspring.

Becky groaned and twisted her hands again. She should have told Molly about yesterday's encounter with Ben. But would she have believed that her wild son had removed almost all of Becky's clothing with two swipes of his blade, then brazenly kissed her?

Perhaps, but for the moment she preferred to keep the incident to herself. Her throat went dry as she remembered his commanding presence and the way she felt when he held her in his arms. Was it the man who filled her with such exasperation, or her foolish reaction to him?

"We can't force Ben to do what he doesn't want to do." Becky swallowed, gaining her composure. "It might be best if he went back to where he came from and never returned."

Molly's squall of fresh tears brought a tug of guilt to Becky's heart. Kneeling beside the old woman's chair, Becky wiped a tear from Molly's dumpling cheek. How she'd like to tell Molly that her son would probably rob her blind and bring trouble from the sheriff, just like his father. But she bit her words. Loyalty was the strength that bound families together.

"I know how you feel," Becky said instead. "But it's—"

"Nay, ye don't know how I feel." Molly's chin quivered, but her voice held steady. "'Cause ye don't know 'bout Nelda."

Becky rose to her feet. "Nelda?"

"Aye, Nelda." Molly lifted her white-capped head, her blue eyes brimming with tears. "I was ashamed t' tell ye before, but now I see I must. Ben wasn't alone when 'e came home last week, Becky. Me son 'ad a lass with 'im. Nelda's gonna 'ave 'is babe." A watery smile brightened her face. "Me first gran'babe."

Becky's understanding mixed with disgust. She thought of his kiss and rage fired within her. She wiped her mouth with the back of her hand. The man was a rutting goat!

Becky reined back her anger. "Where's Nelda now?"

"Next door with me sister, Clara. I 'ad no place fer 'em to sleep, an'..." She tugged on Becky's skirt like a hungry tot begging for a crust. "Please, Becky. I ain't askin' ye this time. I'm beggin' ye to give Ben a job."

A lump formed in the back of Becky's throat.

"If ye don't, I'm afeared Ben'll turn to thievin'. If the sheriff catches 'im, then what'll Nelda and the babe do?"

Becky glanced at the dear woman, and her heart melted. Besides, she had no choice. The crofters knew it was her duty to provide for them and their kin. "Very well, Molly. When Ben comes home, tell him to see Geer about a job weeding in the turnip fields." At least she could keep the rogue a safe distance from the womenfolk. Besides, who knew what might happen to all of them when the new owner of Thornwood Hall arrived in two weeks? Everyone might be out on their arses.

The old woman beamed. "You're a saint, Mistress Becky. A blessed saint for not forgettin' yer promise to yer mum an' da. How proud they would've been to see 'ow ye take care of us."

The mention of her parents brought the familiar tug of sadness to Becky. It had been almost a year since they were stricken by the plague, along with her older sister, Betty. "Of course I'll take care of the crofters. You're my family. I'll never forget that I was a crofter's daughter."

"Botherin' with us, when ye 'ave yer 'eart full of yer own troubles." Molly tucked back a gray strand under her white cap, her expression serious. "What 'ave ye figured to do when Sir Whatsis 'ighness comes t' take over 'is property?"

"It's not *his* property, Molly. Sir Nicholas Sinclair's been awarded *my* property. I don't care what the king dictates. In my heart, Thornwood Hall will always belong to me, Peter, Baby Harry and Aphra."

"Aye, but yer brothers and sister will be grown one day. Ye should remarry and have yer own babes. Peter's almost a man. Aphra will be leavin' the nest 'fore long. Ye don't want t' end up like me in yer old age."

Becky chuckled. How she loved this dear soul, who

had been like a second mother to her since her parents' death. "You're hardly lonely with your growing family," she teased, thinking of the added grandchildren Ben would surely breed for Molly to raise.

Molly shook her head, as though she knew she was talking to a lost cause. "You need to marry a man who'll take care of ye."

"That's why my mother wanted me to marry the old general. Poor man was dead in less than a year, and I still have to manage on my own. Besides, no man will marry me with a baby brother and a sister who's unable to speak. He'd insist they be turned over to an orphanage, or worse. Marriage isn't the answer, Molly."

Molly's brows knitted together. "I 'eard Willoughby knew of a gentleman offering to buy the estate from Sinclair."

Becky had heard the rumor, too. Willoughby had a keen business sense, almost as astute as her own. He leased the river rights for his livestock from Thornwood Hall, but that was no guarantee he'd continue to do so unless he made friends with Sinclair. But there was no reason to worry Molly about it.

"Sinclair might keep the property and ask me to manage it," Becky answered with confidence, despite the wrench of fear in her stomach. She dared not reveal her plan to frighten any prospective buyers away, including Squire Willoughby. Not yet, anyway.

"You and the other crofters have nothing to worry about, Molly. I'm taking care of everything." She winked, then put on her riding gloves while she strode toward the cottage door.

"I'll see that your sister has extra bedding brought around for Nelda, and I'll tuck in a basket with a ham joint and an extra bowl of eggs," Becky said.

She was rewarded with Molly's broad smile. "God

bless ye, Becky. Yer mum an' da would be so proud of ye.''

No need to upset Molly with the facts. If Becky's plan failed, the new owner would throw out the old, frail crofters who couldn't pay their rents, thus forcing them to join the bands of paupers who went on the tramp for food, only to be greeted by scorn and little charity.

Becky forced a smile as she waved goodbye to Molly, then strode purposely toward her mare, waiting at the fence.

A few minutes later, Becky rode along the hedgerow path, her thoughts tumbling around the greatest challenge of her life—Sir Nicholas Sinclair. For whatever reason, she couldn't push back the threat from her mind.

She chewed on her lip. Aye, she'd be thrown in prison, if Sinclair knew all the facts. What if he discovered her duplicity with the business ledgers? What if he found out she kept two sets of accounts? One ledger recorded the true profits, the other—kept for the tax assessor—registered only a tiny sum of the manor's true bounty.

But Sinclair wouldn't find out. The servants were family, and the merchants who purchased their goods were related to her in some way. Furthermore, they were paid handsomely for their loyalty.

She was safe. Besides, hadn't Squire Willoughby's wife said that Sinclair was a navy man who'd return to sea when his wounds healed? Aye, he'd only remain in the country long enough to see Thornwood Hall for himself and to find a buyer.

And he wouldn't find a buyer. For what man would purchase an estate that was haunted by the avenging ghost of her late husband, Ol' Winky? Crops would be stunted, cattle would drop in the fields, all manner of bad luck would follow. Or so word would spread.

Usually, thinking of her plan to invent her late husband's ghost raised her spirits. But not today, for some reason. She needed to go to the one place that always brought her peace.

Becky pressed her heels into the mare's sides and rode across the field toward the wildflower meadow. She needed to talk to *The Family.*

A short while later, Becky brushed aside the sun-dried flowers from her mother's gravestone that the wind failed to blow away from yesterday's bouquet. Then she laid the freshly picked buttercups and blue larkspur at the foot of the stone cross.

Head bowed, she prayed silently. Afterward, she adjusted the sash, which held the general's sword she always carried, and stepped back. Her gaze swept the tall, hand-carved headstone.

"Mum, you'd be so proud of Baby Harry. Yesterday, Aphra dressed him up in Da's Roundhead uniform. He paraded around the study, grabbed the poker like a sword and marched like a glorious little soldier." Her throat felt thick and dry.

"Sally is teaching Aphra to sew. Aphra tried to stick her with a pin, but I think it was because Sally had taken apart your yellow silk gown and was fitting it to her...." Becky bit back the sting of tears. To see her mother's favorite gown in pieces had triggered a jolt of sadness in her.

Becky squeezed the hilt of her sword. "I keep praying Aphra will speak again, Mum. It'll be a year next month since..." Her bottom lip trembled.

Becky paced back and forth. "This morning, I told Peter he could try his hand at repairing the old boat that Da had built. He gave me one of his rare smiles...." She grinned at the memory. "When Peter smiles at me like that, Mum, he reminds me so much of you. His warm brown eyes light up like yours when he's happy." She swallowed hard to fight back the tears while she poked at the grass with her sword. "Next month, Peter will be ten and two, and already he's as tall as I am." She smiled as she thought of her quiet, sensitive brother. "Remember what fun we had when Da took us to market in that boat? Peter says he remembers, but he was too young. He was Baby Harry's age, then."

Becky closed her eyes, the sun warming her face as the memories comforted her. "So many years ago. I wasn't much older than Aphra, myself."

The sun hid behind a cloud, and Becky opened her eyes. She stepped to the next grave, a massive stone cross and circle.

Her dear da. She laid a few yellow wildflower sprigs on the tufts of green grass beside the stone column. "Geer and I sold the best pieces of furniture at market last week, Da. Got three times what I had hoped for them. You'd have been proud at how I wrangled the bid. Told the story of how Cromwell, himself, had lain on the table while his aide dug a musket ball from his arm."

She chuckled. "Those royals will believe anything." She rubbed her hand over the carved letters on the marker. The stone felt warm in the July sun.

"Don't worry, Da. I'll find a way to send Sir Nicholas Sinclair back to sea before he sells our home. I'll keep my promise to take care of everyone."

Becky strode past the shady rise to the three distant headstones. Her older sister, Betty, lay beside their grandparents. Betty had been taken ill within a fortnight before the plague had claimed their parents.

Becky scattered the buttercups among the remaining graves. Memories rushed at her like an unsuspecting gale. She could hardly put her feelings into words.

"God help me, I'll take care of Aphra, Peter and Baby Harry, just as you took care of me." Her eyes stung with unshed tears while the memory of her sister's high spirits rang on the soft breeze of the sunlit meadow. Her heart wrenched with loss.

A few minutes later, Becky climbed the steep hill near the cemetery fence. Scattering flowers onto the bright green blades of grass surrounding the older headstones, she moved to the last marker. She released the remainder of the wildflowers at the bottom of the stone of her late husband.

"General," she said, addressing him by the title she had always used in his presence, although she referred to him since his death as Ol' Winky, as he was affectionately known by everyone. "I'll stand fast against this Sinclair fellow. I won't give up Thornwood Hall without a fight."

She wondered what the old general might have done if he were alive. Ol' Winky had been almost seventy when she'd married him. Even in his dotage, his iron will and feistiness earned him respect among the shire.

She rubbed her fingers across the rough stone. "I'm sorry for the lie I'm about to tell, General. But I thought if you knew that a Royalist was taking over your estate, you'd tear off on one of your rides, like you did on the anniversaries of the great battles, your shouts echoing throughout the valley." She smiled. "So loud even Squire Willoughby and his wife will hear you."

For a moment, she thought she heard his low laughter on the breeze. She turned and faced the wind, the hay-scented air drying her lashes. She shook her head. No, she had only imagined it. But the idea was real.

If Ol' Winky's ghost were seen racing across the fields, surely the sight might give pause to a prospective buyer.

Becky smiled. "The plan will work, General. Keane has agreed to dress in your uniform and ride the fields as your ghost. He's been as upset as I have with the king awarding Thornwood Hall to a Royalist. We'll see how Sinclair likes owning a haunted manor."

Her smile faded when she thought of Keane. Did he truly believe he was Ol' Winky's son? The two men were so different in so many ways. But if Keane thought so, perhaps he felt he should have a part of Thornwood Hall, too.

Picturing Keane in her mind, on Ol' Winky's charger in the dark of night, even she might be fooled that the ghost of her late husband had come back to seek revenge against the new owner.

Her hand patted the gray stone, then she loosened the ribbons of her straw hat and wandered along the path toward the fence row. The wind lifted her hair on the breeze. Her eyelids closed while she delighted in the small pleasure.

She hoped to find her courage among the silent counsel, and she hadn't been disappointed. She knew her duty. When Nicholas Sinclair arrived, she'd spread the word that Ol' Winky's spirit rode the fields, and when the neighbors saw his ghost, no one would dare offer for the estate. Sinclair would return to the sea, she and Keane would manage Thornwood Hall. The crofters and her siblings would be safe, and all would be well with the world.

Her horse whinnied, and she glanced up.

Although the man was more than several furlongs away, she immediately recognized the slant of broad shoulders and the limp. He ambled along the path toward her, and she wondered how long he had been watching her.

"Mistress Forester," he said a few minutes later. Doffing his hat, he gave her a sweeping bow that was exaggerated with sarcastic ardor. "We meet again."

"I see you remembered my name." Her gaze fell to the blue glints of sunshine on his black hair. "Are you on your way to visit your mum?"

"I was hoping to see you, actually." His gray eyes glittered mischievously beneath black arched brows. "I thought it best that I apologize for my...outrageous behavior."

Becky couldn't believe what she was hearing. "Are you up to one of your tricks, Twaddle? Because if you are—"

"Fair lady, I have no tricks up my sleeve. I ask for the job you had so kindly offered. For how can I face my dear mum if—"

"And best you not forget Nelda."

Surprise darkened the gray eyes as though he were truly caught unaware. If Becky hadn't known better, she'd have believed he didn't know Nelda. The man was a cunning devil!

"Forgotten Nelda so soon?" Outrage flared with disgust as she remembered how he had boldly kissed her, and her foolish response to it. Now that she had her good sense again, she'd straighten the matter out.

"Nelda, who's big with your child, in case you're suffering from another bout of scattered wits," she said.

His mouth pursed carefully, but he remained silent.

"Aye, I know all about Nelda." She wrinkled her nose. "It's because of Nelda that I'm giving you another chance."

"You've pointed out the error of my ways, dear lady. I'm here, begging you for a job."

Becky almost laughed. She'd seen trickery by experts, and this performance was pitiful. The mischievous glint in his vibrant gray eyes told her he was no more chagrined than she was.

No, there was more to his ruse than a change of heart. If she stood here until All Souls' Eve, he'd never tell her what had changed his mind. It didn't matter. She'd find out from Molly.

"So you're wanting to labor under the July sun from morning to night, a hoe handle breaking the soft skin on your palms?" She tried not to smile.

"My hands are hardened to work, mistress." He opened his fists. Hard calluses covered the insides of his handsomely shaped long fingers and hands. She felt her breath catch. Her reaction was only surprise, she decided as she met his gaze.

"Very well, but I'll never believe you weathered your hands by honest toil."

His smile told her she was right. "I'll take you on," she said. "With a condition." She thought of Molly, alone all those years, longing for her son to return. "You'll spend the Sabbath with your mum, take her to church and do whatever she chooses to do for the day." She watched his expression. "Agreed?"

His mouth moved as though he had tasted something bitter. "Aye," he said finally.

"And you'll provide for Nelda and the babe. Make plans to marry her, for a start."

He almost choked. Becky tried not to laugh.

"Marriage is a big consideration." He glanced back at her, his eyes like diamonds. "I'll need more pay if I'm to become a family man."

"Should have thought of that before you—" She stopped herself, ignoring the blush that warmed her cheeks. "Do you agree to the terms?"

"Aye."

Something strange was afoot. Becky had dealt with sneaky devils before, but this rogue was planning something devious. The fine hairs on her arms stood up in warning. "You'll make an honest woman of Nelda, you'll work from dawn to dark, you'll spend the Sabbath with your Mum?" She raised a brow, waiting.

"I've seen the error of my ways, and I'm here to make amends." The corner of his mouth lifted, and the glint in his gray eyes told her he was lying through his handsome white teeth.

"One more condition." She held his gaze. "Till the end of the month, you'll have no credit at the Seven Swans Tavern, and you'll stay away from Lily."

"Lily?"

"Don't play simple with me, Twaddle. You've only been back a few days, and already the servants are buzzing with tales of you and Lily and who knows of how many others?" She stiffened her spine and folded her arms in front of her. "I've your promise?"

He folded his muscled arms across his broad chest in mocking imitation. "Agreed."

"Very well, Twaddle. You'll meet the crew at four o'clock tomorrow morning by the cattle gate." She turned toward her horse, her sword clanging against her thigh with each step.

"I think we should shake on it," he called after her.

She stopped. The thought of touching him caused a fluttery sensation deep inside her. "Of course," she said, bounding back toward him.

She extended her arm, but when his large, warm palm captured her small hand in his, she almost gasped. A charge like summer lightning ripped through her. He studied her, his brilliant gray eyes staring through her. His straight black lashes shadowed his cheeks, or was it the trick of sunlight on this glorious day?

She stood, lost in the smoky depths of his eyes. She felt as though she was peering at an ancient rock wall. Light and dark sparkles glittered from the depths of his soul.

"Agreed." He released her hand.

She swallowed, then put on her hat, tugging at her hat brim to cover her nervousness. Her mouth felt as dry as hay. She nodded, afraid to trust her voice. She wiped her hand on her skirt, then strode back to her horse, forcing herself not to run like the devil.

The late-afternoon sun filtered through the alders as Nick curried his horse by the river. For the past half hour, since he had seen Becky Forester again, he couldn't get the picture of her out of his mind. Her manner was regal, despite the faded gown she wore. Running through the buttercups, she had held her skirts as she ran, revealing the flash of shapely ankles amid her underskirts. Her hair flew behind her like black silk.

Her face reacted with surprise when she saw it was he. More than startled, had he imagined she was somewhat glad to see him?

Damn, it wasn't like him to show conceit with a woman. She doubtless thought him some impossible rogue. It was dismay, not attraction, that had brightened her cheeks so becomingly.

Ducks quacked as they swam past, diving for their dinner amid the last lull before twilight. Nick's thoughts returned to his task at hand. "You're growing fat on this rich grass, Rex." He smiled as he swept the currycomb along the animal's back.

For a moment, Nick sensed that he wasn't alone. Rex lifted his head, ears twitching, as though sensing something, too. Nick slipped the curry rack in the saddlebags and pulled out his pistol from the saddle holster.

"Stand and deliver," came a shout from behind.

Nick dropped the pistol in the holster and lifted his hands above his head. A man stood a few yards away, dressed in the familiar velvet breeches and frilly shirt that Nick had been wearing before he exchanged them with the ones he found beside the river this morning. Nick guessed the robber was Ben Twaddle.

Ben Twaddle's eyes widened in surprise as he appraised Nick's clothing, obviously confirming the same conclusion.

"Yer the one who took me clothes?"

Nick lifted a brow. "Aye, and you'd never come by a better deal, Twaddle."

"'ow'd ye know me name?"

Nick watched Ben's right hand shake as he waved the

pistol. He would guess that Ben was new to the occupation of thievery. "What do you want from me? Your clothes back?" He couldn't quite hide a smile.

Ben frowned in bewilderment. "Why'd you do it? Yer' a...a gentleman, by the look o' yer clothes."

"Ben, my arms are getting tired. Put that damn thing down or use it."

Ben blinked, then lowered the weapon. "I want yer horse."

"I've given you my clothes, do you think I'll just hand over my horse, as well?" Nick sat down by the tree and glanced up.

"I'm taking yer horse, so it don't matter what ye think." Ben kept his gaze on him. Obviously mistaking that Nick wouldn't mind, Ben took several steps toward Rex.

"You could hang for stealing a man's horse," Nick warned.

"I'll be gone before they find me. Besides, who'll believe a rogue like you, dressed as y'are?" Ben narrowed his small pig eyes. "How'd ye get a 'orse like this? Steal 'im?" The idea brought a light to his eyes. "Aye, I'd wager ye stole this 'orse and clothing from a wealthy man. Then ye tossed 'is clothes to me so I'd be caught for the act." Ben glanced at the horse again, as though he were reconsidering taking the animal.

"You're a sharp lad," Nick said, trying not to grin. "You're much too smart for me." He shook his head. "If you steal this horse, you'll be caught before you ride past Ferry's Crossroads."

"Then ye did steal 'im?"

"I'll forget you asked me, lad." Nick lifted a brow while he pretended to study the matter. After a considerable pause, he spoke. "Let me make you a deal, Ben Twaddle."

The young man looked surprised. "Tell me 'ow ye know me?"

"I know many things about you, lad. Many things." He rubbed his chin thoughtfully. "I know about Nelda and the babe. About your poor old mother, Molly."

Ben's long, thin face paled. "'ow'd ye know 'bout them?"

"I know *everything*."

Ben looked as though he'd seen a ghost. "Everythin'?"

Nick nodded. "I know your soul's going to hell, lad."

Ben's eyes bulged. He ran a finger around his velvet collar.

"I've been sent as a messenger from above." Nick rolled his eyes heavenward. "And I've a message for you, lad. A last chance to save your soul."

Ben's black eyebrows knotted, his hands trembled. "A message, sire?"

Nick forced the amusement from his face. "Make it up to yer poor mum. Take her to church on the Sabbath and spend the day with her. Stay away from Lily at the Seven Swans. Spend time with Nelda, and help with the chores." He narrowed his eyes and grabbed Ben by the collar. "Because if you don't—"

Ben's Adam's apple protruded in his bony throat as Nick's fingers clenched tighter. "I'll come after you. I'm faster than the west wind. You can't hide from me."

Ben's white face froze with terror.

"Disobey me and I'll snatch you up, and you'll never be heard of again."

Ben's arms and legs shook at his sides. Nick lifted him up off the ground and gave him a shake. "All that'll be left of your miserable body will be the low howl in the pines when I'm through with you. Do you understand, Ben Twaddle?"

Ben bobbed like a duck. "Aye, sire. I—I promise, sire."

Nick released him. The lad stumbled to his feet.

"Go home to your mum, and beg her forgiveness." Nick's voice was stern. "Off with you, now." He strode to his horse as the scurried footfalls of Ben's huge feet sped down the path.

Damned superstitious lot. Nick couldn't keep from laughing as he watched the sight of Ben Twaddle running across the cornfields toward the crofters' shacks.

He wondered what Becky would think when she heard of Ben Twaddle's sudden reformation. He smiled again. Aye, she wouldn't be fooled. Suspicious, perhaps, but he didn't think the lovely lady believed in miracles, if he was any judge of women.

Chapter Three

The following morning was hot, with no promise of a breeze to cool the coming swelter. Nick stood up from hoeing and wiped the beads of moisture from his forehead. Across the meadow, he noticed Becky on the sorrel mare, galloping along the hedgerow.

He'd hoped she'd ride out to check if he'd shown up for work. He'd enjoy seeing her again, if only to observe if the dark shards in her lovely eyes were as violet as he remembered.

Damn, what the hell did he care what color her eyes were! He'd best find out as much information as he could from Geer before Becky discovered that he wasn't Ben Twaddle.

But he'd like to see her again, because she was nothing like any other women he'd known. His fascination was only business, he decided, pushing back a rush of unwelcome arousal. She knew the answers to the questions about the estate that he needed to know.

Nick watched as Becky and the mare vaulted gracefully over a stone fence. She controlled the sorrel with the same mastery of skill that she had shown yesterday with the bull.

After a few moments, Nick grasped the hoe and was

bending over the next row of turnips when a voice called out to him.

"'ey, Twaddle." Geer came up behind him with a water pail and tin cup. The old man squinted at the long, neat row of dark green leaves Nick had finished hoeing. "This ain't a race, lad." His wrinkled face creased when he smiled. "Save some of that muscle for this afternoon's toil."

Nick took the offered drink of water and drained the cup. Geer's smile faded. "Noticed yer limp. 'ow'd ye hurt the leg?"

"Nothing serious." Nick hoped to deter the man's curiosity. If Geer were to see the red zigzag pattern of scars along the length of his thigh and calf, he would pry all the more.

"Put yer hoe down, Twaddle. I've a better chore fer yer strong muscles."

Nick hesitated while Becky brought the mare to a sharp halt in front of them.

"How's the work going?" Her gaze was fixed on Geer, but Nick could tell that she was aware of him by the faint flush that rose from her neck to her cheeks.

"We've got an able worker, here, Mistress Becky." Geer said. "Ben hoes twice as fast as the regulars."

A tinge of surprise flitted across her face.

Taking advantage of her refusal to glance his way, Nick drank in the sight of her. Her eyes were truly as violet as he had remembered. Her plain blue gown contrasted brilliantly against the riot of cascading black curls that fell unbound across her shoulders. In her unadorned dress, she appeared more lovely than any of the over-adorned women he'd seen recently at court. Her rounded bosom lifted and fell as she caught her breath. He tried to imagine what the dark cleft between the soft mounds would look like—

"Twaddle! Get in the wagon," Geer ordered. Then he

glanced up at Becky. "I'm takin' Ben to where the crew's fixin' the crumblin' rock wall. No need wastin' his strong back on weedin' when those rocks need movin'."

"Just see that Twaddle keeps out of trouble." Becky wheeled the mare around and took off across the field, her black hair whipping behind her straw hat.

"Mistress Becky isn't 'erself of late," Geer said as he trudged beside Nick toward the wagon. "Her mind is full o' troubles."

"Because Sinclair is arriving to take ownership of the estate?" Nick asked uneasily.

"That bugger!" Geer sputtered the words. "What kind o' man takes away a poor widow's livelihood?"

Nick's interest grew. "What are her plans when she leaves here?" He curbed his step to the older man's slower gait.

"Our Becky won't leave without a fight." Admiration, pride and loyalty filtered through Geer's words. "It's Sinclair who'll be runnin' with his tail 'tween his legs before our Becky is through with 'im. Just wait an' see."

Nick's curiosity edged up several notches. "How will she manage that?"

Geer shot him a silencing look. Nick knew that he'd have to be more tactful if he wanted further information from Geer.

"It must be hard for a woman to manage alone," Nick said into the growing silence.

"Keane oversees the manor for 'er, 'though I'm not sure how much of a help 'e is." Geer wiped the beads of sweat from his brow with the back of his sleeve.

"Keane?" Nick didn't recognize the name.

"Ye remember Keane, surely." Geer squinted at him. "Some say he's Ol' Winky's son, born on the wrong side of the blanket."

"Ol' Winky?" Nick asked carefully. Although he remembered Becky saying that Ben Twaddle had left Thornwood Hall when he was nine years old, Nick didn't want to alert Geer by asking questions about things that Twaddle should have known.

"You remember Ol' Winky." Geer crinkled his brow as though Nick should have remembered. "General Forester, God rest 'is soul." Geer shook his head. "Ol' Winky never admitted if Keane was from his own seed or not. Don't rightly blame him none."

Nick was more interested in Becky Forester. "Why hasn't the widow remarried?"

Geer chuckled. "No man's good enough, I'd say."

A few minutes later, they arrived at the horse-drawn farm wagon. Climbing next to Geer on the driver's bench, Nick asked offhandedly, "Does the estate make much profit?"

Geer only grunted. His mouth remained as tight as his grip on the leather reins. Nick knew better than to ask any more.

The wagon creaked and wobbled as they traveled along the back fields where wheat and corn grew tall and green. Nick wondered about the spindly crops growing beside the lane he'd first seen on his way to the manor. Had the untended fields, unkempt hedgerows and falling-down fences been neglected for a reason? Had someone purposely wanted Thornwood Hall to look unproductive? And if so, who and why? The first things he'd insist upon reviewing were the account ledgers. But another thought bothered him.

It's Sinclair who'll be runnin' with his tail 'tween his legs before our Becky is through with 'im.

Something in the way Geer had said those words. Nick sensed that the lovely Becky had a plan to rid him of Thornwood Hall. Damn, he could feel it.

Ten minutes later, the wagon rumbled to a stop in front of a crofter's shack. A tall, wiry man stood overseeing a group of men loading stones on a skid. Nick recognized him as the same man who had tried to lead the bull from the pasture yesterday.

"That's Keane, the overseer," Geer said. Before they had stepped from the cart, the man approached them.

"Who's this?" Keane asked.

"Twaddle, Molly's son," Geer answered. "I thought he'd be best used to load stones for the cutter."

"Yer not paid to think, Geer." Keane's attention remained fixed on Nick.

"Ye look nothin' like yer mum." Keane's mouth twitched, then his face lit with an idea. "Twaddle, stay in the wagon. I've got just the chore fer that strong back of yers."

Geer's mouth drew tight. "But Mistress Becky says—"

"Git back to the fields, Geer, before I take me whip to ye."

Nick had all he could do not to put an end to this charade and call this clodpoll out. He hated bullies and never tolerated such behavior aboard ship. He decided to wait and see what Keane had in mind.

Geer climbed out of the cart and lumbered back toward the fields. Keane said nothing as he climbed into the wagon and picked up the reins.

For the next ten minutes, the men didn't speak until they reached the other side of the crest.

"Let's see what yer muscles can do with Tumbledown Dick," Keane muttered as he climbed from the wagon.

Nick glanced at him with curiosity. "Tumbledown Dick? Who's he?"

Keane sneered. "Mistress Becky's pet bull." He rolled his eyes. "She's mighty fond of that animal." He spit on the ground.

Nick said nothing for several minutes, then he asked, "What are your plans after Sinclair arrives, Keane?"

Keane's mouth dropped open, then he shot him a sharp look. "Ye know a lot for only bein' back a few days, Twaddle. Who filled yer noggin about Sinclair?"

Nick knew he had said too much. "My mum, who else?"

Keane snorted. "From what I 'ear from Lily at the Seven Swans, ye 'aven't been 'ome enough to hear much from Molly." Keane lifted a black brow and grinned knowingly.

Nick decided to press the subject. "So what will you do when Sinclair takes over?" Nick asked, climbing down from the wagon.

"I'd worry about yerself, Twaddle." Keane ambled toward a grove of sycamore trees. "I want ye to bring Tumbledown Dick back to where Geer and the lads are filling the skid."

Nick glanced around. "I don't see—"

Suddenly, a piercing snort shattered the stillness. The enormous black bull Nick had seen yesterday lay in the shade of the tree's umbrella of leaves. The bull's eyes bulged as he glared at them.

Nick swallowed. "That's Tumbledown Dick?"

"Aye, 'e is." Keane smiled at Nick's apprehension. "Ye'll find the way back by the wagon's tracks in the weeds," he added, barely keeping a straight face. "And don't be long, Twaddle. The lads will have the skid filled with stones within the hour."

Keane flipped the reins, and the horse lunged forward. The wagon wheeled around in a tight arc toward the direction from which it came.

Nick glanced back at the bull. Tumbledown Dick tossed his head and snorted. Noticing the sharp horns, Nick swallowed hard.

Keane's dark laughter echoed across the meadow as the creaky wagon disappeared behind the rise.

* * *

The sun had barely reached the ten o'clock position in the morning sky when a black-lacquered coach rumbled up the weedy lawn of Thornwood Hall. Chickens, pecking crickets from the grass, flew in the air, cackling in annoyance.

From the study, Becky glanced up from her account books to peek through the lace-curtained window. "Pox and calamity! It's Willoughby." She turned to her cousin Sally. "Quickly, help me hide these books—"

"It's not Willoughby, it's his wife, Hazel," interrupted Sally, who stood beside Becky at the window.

"Saints! What does Hazel want now?" Becky watched as the liveried footman helped a short, stylishly dressed woman from the vehicle.

"She must want it pretty much to fussy herself up in this heat." Sally wiped a bead of sweat from her brow. "Well, we'll soon find out. She's practically running to the front door."

Becky glanced back at the pile of gold coins from the sale of furniture Keane had taken to market. "Show Hazel into the withdrawing room, Sally. I don't want her to see what I'm doing." Becky yanked the floral scarf from the back of the sofa and covered the desk with it. The coins and ledgers were safely hidden from view.

Satisfied, Becky straightened her gown, patted a few wisps of hair from her face and strode into the withdrawing room as though she hadn't a care in the world.

"Hazel, what a lovely surprise." Becky greeted the older woman with a dazzling smile. If Hazel had come to see how Becky was enduring the loss of Thornwood Hall, she'd be damned if she'd show her.

Sally hovered uncomfortably, unsure whether to stay or leave. "I'll bring a tray—"

"Oh, stay, Sally, and hear my plans, too." Hazel began most sentences with "oh" as if it gave importance to everything she said. Becky also thought it made her face look like a trout's.

"Oh, wait until you hear about the social!" Hazel fluttered her hands in her lap.

"Social?" Becky hoped to get rid of her so she could finish posting the accounts. "For what occasion?"

Hazel's pink cheeks flushed with heat and excitement. She pulled out her beaded fan and waved it dramatically. "First, please tell Molly Twaddle how sorry we are for what happened to her son."

"Her son?" Becky felt a prickly sense of unease. "Ben Twaddle? What happened to him?"

"Oh, an unfortunate accident last night." Her round mouth pinched in sympathy. "Ben was running through our gaming fields and fell into the ravine. His howling woke the gamekeeper's dogs, who woke the gamekeeper, who woke Mr. Willoughby." She rolled her eyes. "Imagine a grown man bolting through the fields in the dark of night, jabbering on about being chased by the devil." She closed her eyes dramatically. "Poor dear Molly. What is she to do with a son like that?"

Becky and Sally exchanged glances.

Hazel shook her head. "Thought his back was broken, for sure."

Becky listened skeptically. "Was he deep in his cups?"

Hazel shook her head. "Stone sober." She made a face. "Oh, Ben Twaddle's a rascal, they say." Hazel's thin brows knitted together. "But he won't be rustling the skirts at the Seven Swans for a while, from what Dr. Rivers said."

"You sent for Dr. Rivers?" Sally asked.

"It was our Christian duty, dear. Twaddle was howling like he'd seen the devil." Hazel whirled the fan in her lap. "The doctor said Twaddle should remain abed for a week or two. Then Mr. Willoughby ordered our lads to lift Twaddle into the wagon, and they drove him to Molly's croft, this morning.''

The back of Becky's neck prickled with alarm as she listened to Hazel's tale. Something wasn't right. She'd just left Ben Twaddle in the turnip fields, a little more than two hours ago. And from every indication Geer had given her, Twaddle had been hoeing since sunup.

But if Ben Twaddle was the lad found tripping through the Willoughby fields last night, then who was the man hoeing her turnips?

An ominous thought crossed Becky's mind, and she almost gasped. "What did Ben Twaddle look like, Hazel?"

"Covered with dirt and twigs, it was hard to tell. But he had the Twaddle chin. Aye, he takes after Molly's husband.''

For a moment, Becky couldn't move as Hazel's words sank in. Why hadn't she realized it before?

"Becky, dear. What's the matter?" Hazel leaned forward and fluttered the fan in Becky's face. "You're white as a cloud.''

"It's the…heat," Becky said, the terrible truth crashing around her with the weight of an anvil.

She should have known by his commanding presence. His skill with the blade as his sword whirred through the air, touching the ribbons at her bodice with chilling exactness. The muscular strength of his warrior build, the callused hands, the arrogant challenge in those gray eyes.

Sir Nicholas Sinclair!

She had aided him in his intrigue as easily as if she were his willing accomplice. Pox and calamity! She'd let the fox in the henhouse, now what was she to do?

Becky glanced at Hazel and Sally, who were both watching her with a worried frown. "I—I'm sorry, Hazel.

I don't know what came over me." Becky took a fortifying breath and moved near the door.

"Thank your husband for me, and for your time, Hazel." Becky opened the door, waiting for Hazel to take
the hint. "I'll see to Molly and Ben immediately."

Hazel frowned. "But I haven't had the chance to tell
you of my social."

Becky forced a smile, then reluctantly shut the door
and took a seat beside Sally, who offered her a sympa-
thetic look. Despite her best efforts, Becky couldn't keep
her mind on Hazel's droning monologue.

Why had Sinclair tried to fool her into thinking that
he was a common laborer?

"Dear Becky, I don't think you've heard a word I've
said."

Becky sat up with a start. "Of course I have, Hazel.
You were talking about your social." Becky's lips froze
into a smile.

"Aye, for Sir Nicholas Sinclair, of course."

"Sinclair?" Becky strangled a whisper. "Do I understand that you're planning a social to welcome that—"

"Oh, I know it wouldn't be appropriate, under the circumstances—" Hazel's voice lowered "—for you to do
it. Besides, your lack of furniture and..." She glanced
around the cavernous room, frowning at the few chairs
and sofa.

Becky stood, her hands flew to her waist. "I can't
believe you'd give a social for that...that stuffin'bob who
is removing me and my family from our home at the end
of the month."

Hazel stiffened. "Oh, my dear. We must remember
that Sir Nicholas Sinclair is a wounded war hero. He
distinguished himself at the battle on St. James Day, defending our country against those barbarous Dutch." She
lifted her chin. "Mr. Willoughby says Sinclair is the talk
of London."

"Humph!" Becky paced to the window and stared at the overgrown driveway. What would Hazel think of the war hero if she knew Sinclair as Becky did? Her cheeks flamed with the memory of his mouth taking hers and the riffle of feminine pleasure it had given her.

If only Hazel would leave. She tapped her foot as she gazed out the window. Afternoon sunshine glimmered off the Willoughby coach, while four perfectly matched, high-spirited black horses snorted impatiently. From the rear of the coach stepped Becky's eight-year-old sister, Aphra, and three-year-old brother, Baby Harry. The children stood wide-eyed, as they watched the magnificent coach and four.

Just then, the red-and-gold-liveried footman made a face at the children and shooed them away. Aphra scurried off with her younger brother in tow.

Becky bristled at the footman's snub. What did Hazel know of defending oneself against snobbery? Easy to talk when one is born to wealth and security.

"Oh, besides," Hazel went on, her hands fluttering like a startled wren, "Thornwood Hall is much too much work for you, Becky. My dear, you're not getting any younger. You should marry again, not worry over those crofters." She made a face as if she smelled something rank.

Sally's head bobbed from Hazel to Becky, her blue-eyed gaze finally resting on her cousin, waiting for her defense.

"Those crofters," Becky said, her voice even despite the emotion she felt, "are my family, in case you've forgotten, Hazel. My parents were crofters, and their parents, as far back as the time of King Harry. If I hadn't married Ol' Winky, I'd still be grubbing in the soil, paying my rents to the master of Thornwood Hall."

Hazel's face blanched. "Oh, Becky. Oh, Becky, I meant no disrespect, dear."

Becky sighed, immediately sorry for her outburst. She rubbed her temples. "Aye, it's I who am sorry, Hazel. This heat has me out of sorts." She smiled. "If you and your husband want to welcome the man who's tossing me out, I can't stop you. But don't expect me or my family to attend or to be festive about it."

Hazel's green eyes rounded. "Oh, I daresay I'm shocked by your words, Becky. Your dear mother and father, God rest their souls, would expect you to leave here with your pride."

"Aye, but not throw rose petals in Sinclair's path when he comes to throw me out." Becky turned and glanced out the window. Thornwood Hall stretched as far as the eye could see. She had put her heart and soul into the land since her marriage to Ol' Winky, and she wouldn't give it up without a fight.

"I'm sorry, Hazel. You'll have your celebration without us."

"Oh, Becky, it's not a celebration. It's our Christian duty to welcome a new neighbor. Mr. Willoughby says Sinclair is a war hero, rewarded by the king with a title and an estate."

"My estate," Becky shot back.

Hazel's eyes widened, and she drew back, her fan clucking like an angry hen.

Becky regretted her outburst at once. What Hazel said was undeniably true, but when she thought of that gray-eyed Sinclair kissing her as bold as sin...

"Oh, I think having Sir Nicholas Sinclair assume the affairs of Thornwood Hall is divine intervention," Hazel said.

So that was it, Becky thought, finally realizing what was behind the Willoughbys' support of Sinclair. They wanted to toady up to Sinclair in order to retain the free use of the water rights that Becky had allowed her neighbor, as Ol' Winky had done.

Becky felt the threads of her best-laid plan begin to unravel. Fear, revitalized by the threat of loss, rushed at her. She gripped her hands together. She had hoped for Willoughby's support against Sinclair.

Becky whirled back toward Hazel. "When will this affair take place, Hazel?" Her voice was so sweet, Sally glanced at her with a suspicious look.

"Oh, in two weeks. I've just now posted the invitations. Sir Nicholas Sinclair will be staying with us until…" Her voice dropped, as though she wished she hadn't divulged the fact that they had obviously offered Sinclair their hospitality until he took over Thornwood Hall.

Hazel rose to her feet, averting her gaze.

"Until Sinclair takes over Thornwood Hall," Becky finished for her.

"Oh, Becky, I wish there was something I could do." Hazel's mouth sagged with frustration.

Becky sighed. More than likely, the party was her husband's idea, and poor Hazel was only playing her required part. She moved beside Hazel as they crossed the room and paused at the door. "I understand your need to do your Christian duty, Hazel. Truly, I do."

Appreciation lit Hazel's round face. "Do give it thought, dear. With the proper attitude, Sir Nicholas might make you an offer of compassion."

Pity was more like it. But Becky bit back the scathing reply. Suddenly, she thought of the ghost of Ol' Winky. What a perfect time for the spirit of the general to appear. Besides frightening off the prospective buyers, Ol' Winky's ghost would terrorize most of the guests, and the news of the haunted estate would spread through the shire like a grass fire.

"I'll not need time to think about my duty. You're absolutely right, Hazel. It's my Christian obligation to meet my enemy with forgiveness. After all, I'm General Forester's widow.''

Sally shot Becky a look brimming with questions, but thankfully kept them to herself.

Hazel's face froze with surprise. Becky could only imagine how Hazel would try to explain to her husband this evening that she'd persuaded Becky to accept their invitation.

Becky forced a dazzling smile as she escorted Hazel to the waiting coach. ''Thank you for inviting us.''

After the footman had helped Hazel into the coach, and the rumbling vehicle clacked down the drive, Becky buckled her sword's belt to her chest and grabbed her bonnet.

''Where are you dashing off to, Becky?'' Sally asked.

''I'm off to see Ben Twaddle,'' Becky tossed over her shoulder. ''Both of them!''

Chapter Four

Nick glanced around for a place to run in case the enormous, black bull suddenly charged. He noticed several sycamore trees that might provide a few stout limbs if he needed an immediate haven. Damn Keane, he thought. He'd deal with that bounder when—

The beast bellowed, charging to his feet. For a moment that felt as though time stood still, Nick froze, not wanting to show fear as he stared at the bull. Eyeing the nearby arm of the tree, Nick held his ground, waiting for Tumbledown Dick to charge.

Neither man nor beast moved. The bull stared—not with anger, Nick decided after a few minutes, but with curiosity. The huge brown eyes were as soft as a spaniel's; the thick fan of eyelashes brushed his black curly cheeks when he blinked. Finally when Tumbledown Dick swung his massive head in the air, he swiped at a clump of daisies nearby, chomping a mouthful.

Nick's experiences with bulls were the few times cattle had been freighted as cargo aboard ship. Although this bull was enormous and sported a deadly pair of horns, Nick remembered the scene in the pasture yesterday. He doubted Keane would have browbeaten the animal before

Becky came roaring in to stop him if the bull possessed an ornery disposition.

Nick took several strides toward the beast, whose watchful eyes remained fixed on him. A rope dangled from the ring in his nose, and Nick decided that if a slip of a woman like Becky Forester could bring the beast to heel, then damned if he wouldn't do the same.

Cautiously, Nick crept toward the tree where the lead rope was tied to the trunk. He hesitated, watching. The bull returned to his grazing, a serene look on his curly-haired face.

With a steady hand, Nick reached for the rope and untied the loose knot. When he'd finished, he tried not to think that at the end of the rope was a beast that could gore him to shreds if he had a mind to.

Tumbledown Dick munched happily, seemingly oblivious to him. Nick presumed that Keane would expect him to yank on the bull's ring. Likely, Keane would wait, then drive back, making sport of Nick the way Becky had done to him.

"What a sweet boy you are, Tumbledown Dick," Nick crooned softly, ready to lunge for the overhead tree limb, if necessary. Instead, the bull ignored him, munching noisily.

The idea to sing in the bull's ear was ridiculous. Besides, although Nick's singing carried fair for the sea chanteys he'd sung with his crew, he doubted his voice would calm wilder beasts.

"Tumbledown Dick, I think you're all bluster." Nick reached to scratch the glossy curls between the bull's eyes.

The animal blinked, stretching his powerful neck closer, obviously enjoying the attention.

"Let's be off," Nick shouted, coaxing the animal to move forward.

The bull ignored him, rubbing his head among the wildflowers, chewing contentedly.

Nick moved to within a foot of the animal's ear. Glancing over his shoulder, Nick felt exceedingly foolish. But no one was around, he reminded himself.

He surveyed the pasture and the woods one more time, in case someone might be watching. Finally, convinced that no one was about, Nick knelt on one knee. In a soft baritone, he sang a sea chantey as though it were a lullaby to a babe.

Heave-o-ho, me mates. Heave-o-ho.
Hang yer gib on a crow-o.
Heave-o-ho, me mates. Heave-o-ho.

Immediately, the bull tossed his head and glanced about. As Nick continued to sing, the bull stepped forward and plodded alongside Nick's limping gait as they made their way through the fields.

A few minutes later, Nick couldn't help but laugh out loud, despite the pain in his wounded leg. He was filled with a sense of triumph he hadn't known for the longest time. How he'd relish Keane's surprised expression when he brought the bull to where the men were loading stones.

For the first time, Nick noticed the brute's excellent conformation. Surprised at such quality, Nick made a mental note to check the account ledgers to see what breed the animal was. Indeed, this beast would bring a handsome fee for stud. He wondered again who was in charge of the manor's account books.

By the time Nick and the bull had reached the lower valley, the sound of horse's hooves broke the afternoon silence. He turned to see Becky ride along the ridge toward them. Nick smiled at the look of absolute astonishment on her face when she came up alongside him a few minutes later.

"How did you get Sir Richard out from under the tree?" she asked, reining the mare to a walk beside Nick. Although her mouth held suspicion, reluctant admiration shone from her eyes.

For an instant she looked so appealing, flushed from her ride, that Nick almost forgot his thoughts. "Keane told me his name is Tumbledown—"

"The bull's registered name is Sir Richard. Keane has a singular wit, I'm afraid. He doesn't like the animal and insists upon the insulting name."

Becky had no idea how Sinclair had made her pet bull obey, but she knew it must have been with kindness. Sinclair was cocksure proud of himself, too. How she longed to ask him why he would masquerade as Ben Twaddle on his own property. And she still wasn't certain if she'd been glad or sad, just a short while ago, to have found the real Ben Twaddle, taken to bed with a sprained back, with Molly and Nelda happily taking care of him, just as Hazel Willoughby had said.

Ben Twaddle had told the same story as Hazel Willoughby—that he'd accidentally fallen from a cliff while running from the devil.

Becky couldn't help wondering if the mysterious Nicholas Sinclair had something to do with it, but at least Molly and Nelda were happy that Ben was finally home. And when they promised to keep secret Ben's accident, for a few more days, Becky was relieved. She needed as much time as possible if she was to convince Sinclair that she was a capable manager who could run the estate for him after he returned to sea.

She glanced down at the intriguing man who limped beside the bull. Suddenly Hazel Willoughby's words came to her mind:

Sir Nicholas Sinclair is a wounded war hero.

A touch of sympathy caught her unaware as she remembered the physical chores he had performed that day.

He must be in excruciating pain, but he gave no hint of it, other than his limp. Why would he toil like a peasant when he could be languishing at the Willoughby estate, being pampered as his position dictated? Why, indeed?

To spy on her, of course. A surge of anxiety welled up inside her at the truth of it. The tax officials might have reported the estate's long history of meager earnings to King Charles. Maybe Sinclair was sent here to gather evidence against her that she was skimming profits that were rightfully the crown's. What other reason could there be?

Nick noticed the blood drain from her face, and he couldn't quite put his finger on the reason. "Are you unwell, mistress?"

Becky blinked. "I—I'm…" She hesitated, then forced a smile that didn't quite reach her eyes. "I'm quite well." She glanced back toward the bull. Then, as though changing the subject, she said, "I see animals take to you, Twaddle."

"Animals, like the fairer sex, can sense if one likes them. They've always responded in kind."

Her answering glare brought a smile to his lips.

"Was it Keane who asked you to bring in the beast?" she said finally.

"Aye. He's waiting where the men are loading rocks."

"Indeed!" Her mouth lifted. "Well, let's not keep Keane waiting. Climb behind me, Twaddle. We'll both bring in Sir Richard."

Becky reached out and took the bull's lead, while Nick climbed on the horse. He put his arms around her waist. Her body stiffened in response to his touch. "Hold on to the saddle, Twaddle," she said, but the horse bolted slightly, and he tightened both arms around her waist to steady himself. He felt Becky's quickened pulse beneath his fingers with each breath she took before he gripped the saddle and held on.

She dug her heels into the mare's sides, the horse beneath them picking up speed. Her hair brushed Nick's face, the scent of lavender filling his nostrils. He didn't have to see her to know her jaw was set and her chin jutted in the air.

Cantering through the fields of buttercups, Nick felt the same sense of freedom that he had at sea. The July sun beat hot against his back. The fresh air whipped his face. For the first time since his ship had taken the direct mortar, he felt aware of being alive.

Was it because he impersonated the bounder, Ben Twaddle, that brought this brief respite from melancholia? When he became Sir Nicholas Sinclair again, would the heavy mantle of remorse clamp its weight upon his shoulders and around his heart?

Or was it the relative peace of the moment, with the magnificent beast of burden keeping pace at their side? Or was it this unique experience of riding behind the mistress of Thornwood Hall, leading him across the sea of wildflowers? Becky, so like the beautiful figurehead he planned to fashion for his new ship.

As they rode, he thought of the carved woman who would grace his ship. She'd have a mane of ebony waves that flowed to her tiny waist. Violet eyes set wide in a face of creamy ivory. Her head would meet the storms with a proud lift of her chin, and her breasts would be the size to fill a man's hands.

Beneath the pounding rhythm of the horse, he wondered if the spirited Becky would bring her zest for life to his bed.

Damn, what was the matter with him? He'd never been inquisitive about a woman before. But he was more than curious about this woman, and the thought bothered him.

Beautiful women were in every port. He'd paid for what he wanted, with no unsettling loose ends. Neat and orderly. That was the only way he wanted women in his life.

Poor Ben Twaddle. Falling for every skirt who gave him the come-hither, and look at the tangle they made of his life. And why was Becky so concerned with Ben Twaddle—the no-account son of one of her crofters? This woman, who carried a sword as easily as a man; who sang to beasts instead of whipping them; who took up the thankless chore of devoting herself to her orphan siblings instead of trading her beauty for an easier life? Each new thing he discovered about Becky made her all the more mysterious.

Aye, there wouldn't be enough days to come to understand a woman like that, so why try? And why did he care, anyway?

Damn, he was not here to be pleased or attracted to anything. He was here to get a job done, then get back to sea. He wondered if Finn had met with the shipbuilders by now. In the meantime, the less Nick thought of the secrets of the night with the lovely Becky, the better.

Keane stood in the shade beneath the sprawling oak tree and watched the other four men strain to lift the rocks onto the skid. When the sound of horse's hooves announced Nick and Becky's arrival, Keane's shoulders tightened, and he scowled as they rode up beside him. Becky dropped the rope from Tumbledown Dick's lead at Keane's feet.

"Keane, report to me in my study before supper." Her voice held none of the tension Nick saw in her stiff spine and shoulders. She had spared Keane's authority rather than demean him in front of the men, and he respected that.

Nick slid from the horse, then brushed himself off. "Here's the bull, Keane. Just as you asked."

Keane glared beneath the straw-brimmed hat he wore.

"You'll get no lady's help with the next job I give ye, Twaddle."

"That's enough, Keane." Authority laced Becky's words, and Keane's face flushed.

"For the rest of the day, Twaddle will be under my charge."

Everyone's gaze fixed on Becky. Nick wondered, as well as the other curious men, what chores she had in mind for him.

"Get back on the horse, Twaddle. We don't have all day."

"I don't mind walking," Nick said lazily.

"Let you walk alone?" She tossed her head and huffed. "You're not going to be out of my sight, Twaddle. Jump back on and be quick about it."

Nick did as he was told, but not before he witnessed the resentment deepen in Keane's face. If Keane was the overseer, as Geer had said, Keane acted as the puppet with Becky controlling the strings. Yet she cut him no slack when they were alone, as Nick had witnessed in the pasture yesterday. A man like Keane wouldn't enjoy being ordered about by a woman.

Becky forced the mare to a steady gallop, and for the next few minutes they rode silently over the fields and meadows toward the manor house.

When they came in sight of the horse barn, a small boy ran out from the bushes alongside the path in front of the horse.

Becky pulled on the reins. The animal whinnied, reared back from the child and missed trampling the youngster by mere inches.

Nick was at the child's side in seconds. He picked up the boy, who was at least three years old, by the size of him. Sandy gold curls framed the face of an angel. Blue-violet eyes, wide with surprise, stared back at him.

Becky slipped from the saddle in one fleeting motion.

When the tot saw Becky, a wide smile flashed across his cherub face. Her hands shook when she grabbed her brother and cradled him to her. "Baby Harry." She buried her face in his curls.

Nick remembered that Becky had lost her parents and older sister with the plague only last summer. No doubt the close call reminded her of the loss. The idea recalled his own memories as he gathered the reins of the startled mare and tied the animal to a tree.

By the time he came back to where Becky and her brother were, she had composed herself, and the child smiled happily in her arms.

Becky glanced around, then held up the boy's hand to Nick. "Hold Harry while I see what happened to Mary. She should have been watching him."

Nick stared at the child, then back at Becky. "You're not leaving me with this babe, are you?" As the only surviving child in the family, Nick had run off to sea as a young lad, so he'd never been alone with a child.

"You're staring at him like he's going to bite! Just hold him while I find my cousin Mary."

"Hurry back." Nick took the child, whose smile faded immediately. Nick felt more terrified than if he were staring down the barrel of a cannon on one of De Ruyter's ships.

Nick held the baby with outstretched arms, its chubby legs dangling in the air.

"Pox and calamity! I'd swear you never saw a tad before." She glared at him, then a slight smile brightened her face. "I'll be right back," she shot over her shoulder. Both Nick and the child watched Becky dash along the bushes and disappear inside a small shed beside a pink-flowered hedge.

Then Nick and Baby Harry stared at each other. The boy's pink mouth flew open, and he howled the most bloodcurdling scream Nick had ever heard.

Becky burst out of the shed, along with a flushed young girl who looked around ten and six, and a young man whose beet-colored face told a tale all of its own. The young couple headed in different directions.

Becky sailed toward Nick, cheeks the color of the pink blossoming hedge, her skirts flying behind her. He was reminded of a tall, beautiful ship, banners flying, as she made course.

"Best you get used to crying babies, Twaddle. It seems that Mary, who was Baby Harry's nanny, is leaving to get married."

Becky chuckled as she took her brother from him. Harry rubbed his eyes, the screams immediately turning into hiccups.

"So? What does that have to do with me?"

"I'll explain, but first follow me." Only the slight smile Becky tried to hide warned Nick that she was planning some devilment. He limped behind her, taking one step to her every two. Over her shoulder, Baby Harry peered at him, eyes round and distrusting.

Nick swore under his breath. He wasn't afraid of hard work, but as they approached the crumbling stone entrance to the old manor house, his sense of wariness increased.

The mixed aroma of sour milk, molasses and vinegar rushed out at him as he stepped inside the small storage room off the galley—kitchen, he reminded himself. He glanced around. Bloody hell, she wasn't going to stick him here, in the cook's quarters, was she?

But she pushed past the servants, who were busy with supper chores, and he was reminded that whatever she had in mind might be a blessing in disguise. For how else would he be able to seek entrance to the house if she didn't assign him duties here?

He trailed in her wake through several large rooms, all devoid of furniture. Only faded squares along the walls bore evidence of the missing pictures that had once hung there.

Across from the front entranceway, he spied a room that might be a library or study. He didn't want to draw back in case she noticed his curiosity. Perhaps it was where the account books were kept.

She guided him toward the back stairs, her boots brushing the bare wood as she climbed the steps that rose to the second landing.

Following her, Nick glanced around at the small bedchambers that led from the narrow corridor. "Where are we going?" he asked, his curiosity growing.

"To Baby Harry's chamber," she said, pushing open a door. The narrow room was as shipshape as a captain's cabin. Lacy ruffled curtains fluttered from the open windows that overlooked the gardens.

Becky's smile glowed with a genuine sense of delight. "You're to be Baby Harry's new nanny."

Nick felt his knees weaken. "B-but, I—I can't..."

Laughter rippled low in her throat. "Of course you can." When she suppressed her laughter, her violet eyes brightened all the more. "Besides Baby Harry, your charges will include my sister Aphra, who's eight, and my brother Peter, who's ten and two." She sat down on the edge of the bed and studied him. "Aye, the more I think of the idea, the more I like it."

Nick scowled. "Well, I don't like it." He balled his hands and put his fists to his hips. "I won't do it. I'm not some wet nurse who—"

"You have nothing to say about it, Twaddle. You'll do any chore I give you." She chuckled, unable to keep the smugness from her voice. She clearly felt she held the winning hand.

"I know nothing about children."

"You don't need to. My aunts, cousins and I give them as much attention as we can, but you saw what happened today. You must keep your eye on them at all times. If you need assistance, ask. One of the others will help you, but the responsibility of the children is yours. Do you understand?''

''You don't understand. Being a children's nanny is...well, it's...'' He sighed. ''It's not...manly.''

Her fine black brows arched. ''Manly?'' She crossed her leg and sat Baby Harry on her knee. ''I'd think any man who manages to have all the maids at the Seven Swans swooning over him has no worry with appearing *manly*.'' She pressed her pink lips together to keep from laughing.

''I won't be a nanny. I'll do anything else.''

''You'll be a nanny, and that's final. Besides, Peter needs a man's firm hand. Mary is no match for his wiles.''

''Being wily must run in the family.''

She grinned. ''Aye, it does.'' With a toss of her head, she jumped to her feet and strode to the door. ''Change Baby Harry's clout, then bring him downstairs to me in the study. I'll give you further orders, then.''

Nick stared after her, then turned at the wide-eyed child.

Clout? What is a clout?

Becky was laughing so hard when she passed Sally on the hall stairs that she almost stumbled into her. When she told her cousin that the man she had thought was Ben Twaddle was really Sir Nicholas Sinclair, and that she had just ordered him to be the children's nanny, Sally looked dumbstruck.

''What does he know about children?'' Her eyes grew round.

''Don't be foolish, Sally. I'll keep my eye on him, and so will you. No one else knows his real identity, and that's the way we must keep it. Besides, that impudent lout needs to learn a few lessons." She giggled. "Oh, Sally, I wish you had seen his face when I told him he was the new nanny." She bent over in stitches of laughter.

Sally remained skeptical. "Mary isn't the most trustworthy, certainly. She's always running off with her young man and forgetting about the children, but..." She gulped. "Hiring Sinclair as a nanny." She shook her head.

"You and I can show him what needs to be done. Besides, Mary is leaving shortly to marry." She glanced at her cousin. "It's only until the end of the week. He's sneaking around for information, and if we keep an eye on him, then we can be sure he won't find out anything."

Sally stroked her chin, considering. "Aye, Sinclair's a handsome lad. I can see why you'd want him around."

Becky rolled her eyes. "Such romantic foolishness. Sally, you must learn to appraise men as you would wild beasts. Beneath his handsome face and silvered words beats a crafty mind just waiting to take advantage. Just like dogs, you must teach men who's master, or in this case, mistress."

"Aren't you afraid Sinclair will influence their young minds?" Sally whispered. "After all, he's a sailor."

Becky laughed. "He's an officer and a war hero."

Sally gasped. "Mercy! You're defending Sinclair?"

Becky scowled at her. "I'm doing no such thing." She glanced back up the stairs toward the second landing. "Sinclair won't be influencing their minds, dear Sally. One of us will be near at all times."

She gave Sally a reassuring smile, then took a seat at her desk. "Excuse me, cousin. I must get these account books copied. Why don't you go upstairs and see how the new nanny is getting on with his charge?"

Mutiny. Insubordination. Anarchy. Aboard ship, Nick had dealt with them all and more. But he'd gladly trade a vicious crew with revolt on their minds for what he discovered Becky had meant when she told him to change Baby Harry's clout. He glanced away at the foul thing he had finally cast off the helpless baby.

"Enough is enough!"

Nick had fought and won against some of the most diabolic men under God's heavens, but as he locked eyes with Baby Harry, he felt completely helpless.

"The devil's own damn handiwork!" Nick cursed under his breath as he laid the baby's bare bottom upon the blanket on the cot. The child watched him with interest.

"Let's go tell the little queen of Tumbledown Manor that Sir Nicholas Sinclair has arrived. She can rent a damn stall and live in the livery stable for the rest of the month for all I give a damn. She and her whole damn family."

He picked up Baby Harry and tucked him under his arm like a small keg of rum. "Damn! Damn! Damn!" Nick bellowed with each step as he dashed down the stairs, not stopping to acknowledge the young woman's gasp as she stepped aside to allow him past.

Moments later, Nick spied Becky in the study, sitting at the desk in front of a broad window. He would ignore how the sun's rays cast brilliant lights through the black mane that surrounded her like a mantle of light. He'd ignore how very young she looked, bending over the work that occupied her, the serious expression on her lovely face making her even more appealing. He'd ignore her young nubile body, the yellow muslin stretching across the full feminine curves of her bodice, rising and falling with each breath she took.

She lifted her head with a start. "My, God! Where are Baby Harry's breeches?" She jumped up from the desk and gathered her brother in her arms. "See here, Twaddle. You'll not shirk your duties. If you don't know how to swaddle him, then you'll be taught." She snuggled the boy to her chest, then shot Sinclair a severe glance, which immediately turned into a smile.

Becky rolled her eyes. "Oh, Twaddle, look at you."

He glanced down at where she was staring. At the side of his leather jerkin, a dark stain marked his waistcoat.

"Damn! Damn! Damn!"

She disappeared behind a screen to the chamber cabinet and came back with a white cloth in her hands. "Wipe yourself off, then see Geer about a change of clothes." She rolled her eyes again as she placed another similar cloth on her lap, laid Baby Harry across her knees and in less time than he could knot a line, she had tied a fresh clout to the child.

"I've something to tell you, Mistress Becky. I'm not who you think I am."

"Aye, you're not." She stood up and leaned against the side of the desk, the baby clasped in her left arm. "I thought you might have a bit of compassion in your soul when I saw how you managed to move Tumbledown Dick without violence." Her eyes grew large, and he wondered if that was admiration he saw in her violet depths. He hoped so.

"I thought I saw a bit of integrity when you hoed the turnips." She riffled the curls along Baby Harry's head while she spoke. "You even convinced Geer that you've done a turnaround after all those years since you stole our chickens and traded them at market for sweetmeats."

While he listened, Nick's gaze drifted across the desk to the four thin volumes that lay open. Neat, feathery handwriting graced the pages with tidy sums entered in columns.

"But I think you're the same wily lad who ran off with my pig." She narrowed her eyes. "And I'm going to teach you a few lessons, Ben Twaddle."

As she went on, Nick noticed the papers in a neat pile

were invoices. He had interrupted her posting of the account ledgers.

An idea formed in his mind. "Surely you want your sister and brothers to have proper care? I'm a pitiful nanny. Instead, put me to good use. I've learned how to keep books while I've been away. Let me do that tedious work for you instead."

Her eyes brightened with amusement. "Twaddle doing my account books?" A riff of laughter filled the sunlit room. "What do you think Sir Nicholas Sinclair will think when I explain that the likes of Ben Twaddle records the manor's ledgers?"

"Maybe Sinclair will be more interested in an efficient result than who performs it."

She didn't answer. Damn, why did he have to say that? Her sense of amusement had fled, and she stared out the window, as though deep in thought.

He was sorry, realizing how he had enjoyed the brief respite, and he wished he knew how to bring it back.

"Do you know Sinclair, then?" he asked.

"I know the breed."

"I hear tell that he cuts a fine figure of a man." He lifted his brows in anticipation for her answer.

"A vain, arrogant man, I'd wager." Her full lips twitched. "Don't forget, a man in a uniform, Twaddle, is most impressive. But one must be wise enough to recognize the man from his rank." She smiled in a way that was becoming hauntingly familiar.

"I'm positive that you'll be successful in rankling a deal from him, Mistress Becky."

"A deal?" She lifted a brow. "Who said anything about a deal?"

"Well, my mum said..." He stopped, waiting for her to take the bait.

For an instant, she almost smiled, then the smile vanished. "Molly said what?"

He shifted his feet, hoping he gave the impression that he had revealed something he regretted. "I don't want to get my mum in trouble."

She narrowed her eyes. "I don't know what you're talking about." Her eyes glittered as though she were secretly enjoying herself.

The certainty of her attitude puzzled him. Damn! Why not confess to who he was and be done with it? He glanced at the ledger books, which were so close, yet were as far away from him as the bottom of the sea, if she had her way.

The ledger books. Within their covers lay the answer to the riddle of Thornwood Hall. By the size of the accounts and the faded covers, the records of the estate must go back to before the Restoration. If he could sneak into the study tonight while everyone was asleep…

Nick held out his hands to the child. "Come, Baby Harry. I'll take you upstairs while your sister tends her ledgers."

A flash of suspicion crossed Becky's face, but she relinquished her brother to Nick's waiting arms.

Baby Harry smiled at Nick, waving his chubby fists in glee and squealing, "Damn, damn, damn!"

Chapter Five

The shaft of moonlight shone through the lacy paneled windows of Becky's study. Nick stared into the unlit chamber and blinked. Considering the sparse furnishings, the only logical place to keep the ledgers was in the locked desk.

Thank God for the full moon. He wouldn't need a candle, which might alert a servant. He tiptoed into the room, the floor creaking with each step. The chamber held the scent that reminded him of Becky—the spicy pink blossoms in a vase on the hall table.

Nick cast the thought aside. He needed to find out how the estate operated, and if Becky was involved in deceiving the tax collectors, the account books might provide the proof. And the sooner he had the evidence, the sooner he would be back to sea.

But what would become of Becky and the old crofters who relied on her if he found that his suspicions were correct?

He knew damn well what would become of her. She'd spend the rest of her days in prison. And what would become of that family and the others who needed and depended on her? A clench of anxiety jarred him. Damn, he had no place worrying about the wench and her tribe who devotedly followed her every order, legal or otherwise. He drew in a long breath, then exhaled slowly. His duty was to the king's mission, and he'd do his duty. He always had. If she faced prison, it was her own doing.

Nick turned the knob in the desk latch, but it held firm. He jiggled the handle, but the wood remained secure. Damn! Of course she had locked it.

With an impatient thrust, he grabbed hold of both sides of the desk and lifted it off the floor. The veins in his hands and arms bulged as he shook the damn thing. The locked door rattled while the contents inside the desk clattered against the frame, the noise fueling his frustration. Finally, with a sigh of defeat, he set the furniture down with a thud.

He clenched his jaw at his own ineptness. Why hadn't he realized Becky would lock the desk? He should have brought a wire or something to pry open the lock. He would have if his thinking hadn't been so mired lately with thoughts of her.

Nick sank back in the wooden chair and rubbed his fingers over the polished mahogany desk.

Her desk.

An unexpected vision of how she'd looked that morning caught him unawares. Her ebony hair had been filled with sunshine. Dressed in that unadorned yellow gown, she appeared as lovely and unspoiled as a spring daffodil.

When she'd cuddled Baby Harry in her lap, he'd been struck, unexpectedly and without precedent, by the love in her eyes. She should be married with toddlers of her own. A home, a husband—

Nick shot to his feet. This kind of idle thinking wasn't like him. Perhaps her large, violet eyes were working their magic on him. Maybe he didn't want to find out what game she was playing with the king's profits.

Face it, Sinclair. You've been thinking of the lass ever since you first saw her. He took in a deep breath, then leaned against the edge of the desk. He'd try again. But next time, he'd bring the proper tools to do the job. Next time, he'd not let his tangled thoughts of the lovely Becky get in the way of what he'd come to Thornwood Manor to find out.

A few moments later, Nick opened the door and listened before making a dash up the stairs. When his boots scraped against the first step, he heard the banister creak above him. A circle of candlelight spilled over him.

He lifted his head to see Becky leaning down from the upper railing. A black coil of hair fell over her shoulder; her face looked golden in the flickering glow. A pink shawl was draped over her nightrail and a white sleeping cap tilted on her head.

She glided down the stairs, her shadow following along the wall. The smell of lavender soap invaded his senses.

"Can't sleep either, eh?" he asked before she spoke.

"I don't sleep well when someone's prowling around my study."

"Me?" Nick raised his hands innocently. "What would give you that idea? I thought if I stretched my legs, it would help me sleep."

"Indeed!" Her brow rose suspiciously while she sailed past him on the way to the study, slamming the door in his face.

When the bolt slammed in place, he grinned as he returned to the stairway. With one boot on the first step, his hand draped casually on the banister, he waited for her. Beneath the door, he watched the slant of light brighten and fade when she dashed about the room, searching for anything that might prove his trespass.

A few minutes later, the bolt snapped back and she opened the door. Nick saw the question still upon her frown.

"Care to join me for a stroll?" he asked easily.

Becky watched him, recognizing the challenge in his deep voice. His devilish grin dared her to accept. But the idea was improper, and he knew it.

"I-in the dark?" *Of course it was dark! What a foolish thing for her to say! What was the matter with her wits?*

He stepped to the front door and opened it. "It's bright moonlight." A rush of cool, fragrant air, heavy with the scent of phlox, swirled about them.

"Shut the door." She closed her hand around the candle to prevent the wind from snuffing out the flame. "You'll let in the miller moths." Becky's voice was sharper than usual.

Nick appeared not to notice. "Come, a bit of night air will help you sleep." The corners of his mouth lifted slightly. He stepped toward her and blew out the candle, plunging them in darkness.

The smell of burning wick spun between them. She blinked, her eyes straining to see his face in the shadows.

She heard his chuckle as he took the candlestick from her shaky fingers, then he placed it on the side table by the door. Afraid to move, she grasped the banister knob as though her life depended on it. Before she thought to turn and dash up the stairs, he took her other hand and urged her to him.

He threw open the door. In the silver moonlight, he appeared as she would imagine a pirate to be. He grinned, defying her to run back to her chamber, bolt the door and hide under the covers.

A wise woman would do just that.

Instead, she released her grip from the handrail and allowed him to pull her into the night, his large hand warm and inviting. Why she followed him she didn't know.

Perhaps it was the clumsy but charming way he had handled Baby Harry that afternoon. Or the gentle streak he'd revealed about himself when he brought in Sir Richard earlier that day. She didn't know why, but she felt safe with him.

Yet he was her enemy. She should feel nothing but loathing for this man who dared take away her family's security. And yet, she had thought of little but him all day.

"Show me where the flowers grow—the pink ones that smell like cinnamon." He flashed a reckless grin, and she felt a burst of excitement amid her uneasiness.

She lifted her free hand to the ruffles at her throat. "Since when does Ben Twaddle notice flowers?" Reminding him of his role as a crofter's son gave her a bit of courage.

"I've never smelled blossoms like the bouquets you bring into the house. I want to see how flowers grow." He glanced back at her over his shoulder. "You're not afraid one of the servants might peer out the window and see us, are you?"

"Certainly not," she shot back too quickly. Of course she was nervous, but she refused to let him know it.

He laughed, and she hoped he believed her. If only things were that simple. She could squelch any foolish gossip among the family members. But she couldn't seem to squelch what addled her senses when he was concerned.

"You refer to the gillyflowers," she said, forcing her thoughts away from him. "They grow beside the house, alongside the kitchen garden." She kept her voice light, hoping he wouldn't notice her nervousness.

"What are these flowers?" He pulled her toward the huge clumps of plants blooming on both sides of the path. "I noticed when Baby Harry and I brushed near the flowers earlier on our walk that the leaves release the most incredible fragrance."

She smiled despite herself. "Aye, that's lavender. We pick the long spikes, then after they're dried, the flowers are layered among the linens. My late husband's first wife planted that stand from seed, many years ago.''

Nick brushed off the garden bench with his hand and offered her a seat. She paused before considering, hoping her slight hesitation might suggest that it was her idea to sit. When she finally settled down, he moved so close beside her that she felt his warm breath on her face when he spoke.

''Did you love your late husband?''

The shocking question made her gasp. Moonlight silvered his gray eyes peering at her from beneath dark lashes. He appeared so sincere that she resisted a snap reply.

Instead, her gaze drifted over the weedy gardens, the knee-high grass that sprawled to the oak trees barely visible in the shadows.

Had she loved the old general?

She felt gratitude and admiration for the old man who had provided her with Thornwood Hall. But she hadn't felt love the way she sensed Nicholas Sinclair had meant.

''My husband was a great deal older than I.... The general was a brave man who fought with Oliver Cromwell against the king's army for what he believed. Generous and kind, he was respected by the crofters. When the general died, he was mourned by everyone.''

''Admiration isn't love.''

Why was she allowing her enemy to ask her these personal questions amid her own garden? No, they were seated in *his* garden, she remembered with a start.

She jumped to her feet. ''Ol' Winky's more loved than Sir Nicholas Sinclair will be when that popinjay sells Thornwood Hall and puts us out. Who'll care for the elderly and the sick crofters then?''

Sudden tears stung her eyes, and she turned away. ''If Baby Harry should wake, he'll be frightened if he's alone in his chamber," she said, reminding Sinclair of his role as Ben Twaddle.

"Harry is old enough to be sleeping alone in his chamber."

She lifted her chin. "You know more than I about babies, Ben Twaddle?"

"Harry isn't a baby. He's three years old."

"Baby Harry still suffers from the loss of our parents, just as Peter and Aphra do. You'd know that if you'd spend time with them." She reeled in her anger.

"I've offered to help Peter with rebuilding the boat tomorrow. Aphra seems very shy and I haven't spoken to her yet. But I can understand their pain." His voice held a certain empathy that surprised her. Then she remembered Sinclair's loss of his men, his ship. Perhaps he did understand.

"I believe children need coddling, especially while they're healing from their grief." Her throat felt tight and dry. "Your place as the children's nanny is to do what I tell you to do, nothing more."

"And who coddles you over your grief, Becky?"

Her breath caught in her throat. She didn't know what to say in the awkward silence.

"Don't be afraid of me, Becky."

"I'm Mistress Becky to you."

"I'm not going to hurt you, Becky." For a moment, it was as though he was speaking to her as Nicholas Sinclair. Her heart skipped a beat.

He brought her trembling hand to his lips and pressed her fingertips to his mouth. As though caught under his spell, she remained motionless, wanting to believe him.

Nonsense! He was as dangerous to her family as if he were the Black Death. She drew her hand back. "I should have Geer give you fifty lashes for your impertinence, Ben Twaddle." Her husky voice betrayed her words and she averted her gaze.

Drawing the shawl about her shoulders, she forced herself to face him. "You're a very impudent man." She whirled around and ran along the path toward the front door, not stopping until the heavy portal slammed behind her.

After she slipped inside the house, Nick cursed himself. What had he expected when he'd brought her out into the moonlight? His conscience nagged him about the way he continued to play the no-account Ben Twaddle. He'd planned to tell her that he was Nicholas Sinclair.

He almost had. But if she knew the king was suspicious about the manor's dip in profits, then she'd block Nick's every turn to find the truth.

He sighed, thinking of the stubborn tilt of her chin and the tenacious grip she held on Thornwood Hall. Whom was he fooling? She'd fight him because her life depended on it.

The account ledgers might be all he needed to show the king and to prove that she was pilfering the profits. Then, he'd be free to leave this damned ruin and never look back.

What fear and anger she must have for him—the usurper who'd been awarded her manor. No doubt she'd expected him to charge the estate, as he'd overtake a warship, throwing the enemy overboard.

A burst of conscience touched him. He swallowed back the tightness in his throat. No, Becky Forester and the crofters weren't the enemy. It would be so much easier if they were.

An owl hooted. Nick glanced up at the stars, twinkling like fireflies against the indigo night. He was out of his element in this godforsaken pile of weeds. He had no skill or patience for dealing with growing things, whether it be children, lambkins, or turnips. He missed the sea, his ship, his men.

His men. His crew of loyal, devoted sailors, gone.

A wrench of sadness engulfed him. For the first time since he woke up at Whitehall Palace and learned of his crew's fate, tears welled in the corners of his eyes. Suddenly, all the pent-up anger, bitterness and revenge tumbled into a raw chasm of grief. Safe within the night's shadows, he gave in to the pain.

Becky left the candlestick on the upstairs hall table before she tiptoed into Baby Harry's bedchamber. She bent over the sleeping child and pulled the small thumb from his rosebud mouth. How tiny he looked when asleep. Angelic, too, she thought with a grin. She kissed his satiny cheek. His soft, even breathing feathered her face. "I love you, sweet brother," she whispered as she brushed her hand over the tousled, sandy curls.

Her gaze fell to the narrow bed in the corner where Sir Nicholas Sinclair had slept. The crumpled bedsheets were creased flat from his weight. How cramped and small he must find her brother's chamber compared to the captain's quarters.

She moved beside the low cot and sat down. Her hand slid across the rough muslin, a hint of dampness lingering. A faint, masculine scent veiled the sheets. She found the pleasant aroma strangely arousing. What must his lengthy, muscled body look like, stretched in slumber?

The vision of his deeply tanned chest she'd seen when he was hoeing turnips came to her mind. Her cheeks warmed at the thought. Through the V of the shirt opening, his black hairs bristled in dense whorls. How much of his body was brushed with the curly mat, she wondered? With this illicit fantasy, her throat grew tight, and a tiny shiver coursed through her.

She had never been a wife—in the biblical sense. Her husband's bedchamber had smelled of poultices and herbs to mask the odors from the ravages of age and ill health. The general had emphatically maintained his separate bedchamber, declaring because of the differences in their ages, theirs would only be a marriage of convenience. Their union provided security for her and her family in exchange for her care in his final years.

Then, she'd thought loyalty to his first wife had kept Ol' Winky from her bed. But had he known that after his death, her chances for remarriage would improve if she was a virgin?

A man would consider marriage to a widow with her own children, but never to a woman who brought her siblings to the new household, for a wife's brothers and sisters were considered her parents' responsibility, or her uncles' or grandparents' duty. Peter, Aphra and Baby Harry would live as crofters. They had no hope for education or a better future without money.

Becky moved to the window and opened the glass. The curtains billowed with the cool evening breeze. Below, in the moonlit garden, Sinclair sat where she'd left him only minutes before.

His hands cradled his dark head in thought. Was he thinking of a woman he loved in a faraway port? Or was he worried that she might not be faithful to him while he returned to sea?

Nay. Any woman who fell in love with this man would always love him. He would never have to worry about that.

She felt a warm blush at the thought. How she wished she knew about this mystery between a man and a woman.

A few minutes ago, in the moonlight, she had been aware of something that she'd never known before. Dangerous and exciting. She had wanted to remain with Sinclair, although she knew it wasn't wise. Maybe if she had lingered, she'd have discovered what it was. Now, she felt only an emptiness and perhaps she might never know.

Chapter Six

Early the next morning, Nick left Baby Harry with Sally, who had cheerfully offered to give the youngster his breakfast. Relieved that he wouldn't have to lug the youngster with him, Nick set off to talk to Peter. As long as Becky persisted in amusing herself with his role as nanny, he would rather spend time with the lad and leave the ticklish duties concerning Baby Harry and Aphra to Sally's capable hands.

By the time Nick approached the bend in the river, the sky had turned leaden with a threat of a summer shower. Nick inhaled the scent of the coming storm. The smell rushed his senses, reminding him of the many times aboard ship when he'd relished a squall's challenge.

Ducks flew from the alders, pulling him from his pleasant reverie. With luck, he'd be at sea before long; then he could put the thought of Becky and her wide-eyed siblings behind him.

Nick traipsed through the reeds along the river where he'd remembered seeing the battered remains of what passed for a boat. He followed the sound of hammering and soon found Peter bent over the hull, intent on his work.

Nick was almost beside the boy before Peter acknowledged the intrusion with a scowl, obviously not pleased to be interrupted. For a youngster of only ten and two years, Peter's angular, tall frame gave him the appearance of a much older lad. Or was it his serious brown eyes, which smoldered with unspoken anger?

"Saw you fixing the old boat," Nick said carefully. "Thought maybe I could give you a hand."

Peter snorted. "Well, ye thought wrong." He returned to his work, scraping the wooden frame with an adze.

Nick studied the curved wooden knee—the part behind the sternpost of a boat—that the lad was trying to salvage. "You should get rid of that knee and start anew," Nick warned, pointing to the dry rot. He picked up the chisel and drove a hole through the piece.

Peter glared in horror. "You stupid lout! You ruined it."

Nick sighed. "It was ruined already."

Peter's fists tightened, ready to do battle.

"Come, lad. I'll show you how to make a new one."

"An' what do *you* know of boats, Ben Twaddle?"

Nick ambled to a large oak tree. "I've had plenty of jobs since I've been away." Peter made no move to follow. Instead, he clenched his jaw in the same stubborn way Becky often did.

"But where'd ye learn of boats?"

"Ships, not boats, mostly." Nick studied the ancient tree before him. "Shipbuilders use special limbs from hardwood trees that conform to the shapes of the pieces they need."

Scowling, Peter watched him. After a few minutes, he strolled toward Nick.

"See how this limb curves naturally from the trunk," Nick explained, when Peter came beside him. Nick traced his finger along the crotch of the tree. "See how this piece grows in a natural shape for a knee of a boat?"

"Aye, let's chop it down," Peter said with childlike excitement.

"Nay, lad. The wood's green. We need seasoned wood."

Instead of scoffing, which Nick expected, Peter waited warily for Nick to offer a suggestion.

"Is there any blown-down trees or timber that's already been cut and stacked?" Nick asked.

Peter shook his head. "We gather blowdowns and sell them at market."

Nick wondered how much of a tidy profit Becky received from the frugal practice, and he'd have wagered the money wasn't posted in the manor's ledgers. For now, he brushed the thought aside.

"I noticed a stand of oak along the west meadow. Let's go and see what we'll find there."

It took only a short while to hike the path through the woods. "There's an ol' oak blown down," Peter yelled, excited as if he'd found a gold coin. He ran toward a gnarled tree, the lateral limb broken and lying on the ground. The lad's face was flushed with eagerness, and Nick was reminded of himself at that age. "Look here, Ben!"

Nick winced. For the moment, he'd forgotten he was supposed to be Ben Twaddle. Damn, how could he justify lying to an innocent boy? He bit back the thought. The king had given him an order, and he was carrying it out the best way he knew.

"Ben!" Peter called again. He held on to the oak limb, which was as thick around as he was. A stout angular tree limb butted from the crotch.

Nick nodded. "Aye, that will do."

Peter wrestled the choice limb free. Nick knew better than to offer help unless the lad asked. Determination and hard work must be a family trait, he mused.

When they had returned to the river, Nick showed him

how to remove the bark and fashion the natural curve of the wood into the proper shape of the boat's knee. How Nick's hands itched to take the adze from the lad and demonstrate the proper way to handle the tool. After several awkward attempts, he couldn't help but offer.

"Do you want me to show you how I'd do it, Peter?"

Peter wiped the sweat from his face, then stood, scowling. But he relinquished the blade. Surprised at the change in the boy, Nick picked up the adze handle and stroked the wood with a smooth, almost loving touch. "Gently. Let the tool do the work," he said, as fresh wood appeared from beneath the bark.

Peter watched, transfixed. "Let me have a try?" he asked, after a few minutes.

Nick happily relinquished the tool. Peter's genuine smile softened the sharp angles and planes of his face.

After several hours, Nick had showed Peter how to shape and plane the wood into what would pass for a strong replacement for the dry-rotted knee. He'd filled in the morning with tales of the sea, of his early days with Finn, working on merchant vessels.

"I'd like to go away to sea," Peter said. "But with that bugger Sinclair, I'll have to take care of my family."

Nick felt a rush of regret. "Maybe things won't turn out so bleak," he said, regretting the words immediately.

Peter frowned. "Why'd ye think that?"

Nick rubbed his chin. "'Cause it's my experience that things have a way of working themselves out."

"Like how?"

"Like I think you're a talented lad, and a smart one, too," Nick added, not wanting to give him false hope.

Peter shook his head. "It's Aphra I'm afeard for. After our sister Betty and our parents died, my sister never spoke another word. Never cried at the funeral. Just stared off into space. It was when Becky made a new doll for her that Aphra hugged it, then finally started to bawl. She cried for days. We knew then that her mind was all right, even if she couldn't speak." Peter's sad eyes darkened with the memory. "Becky and Sally will see after Baby Harry, but little Aphra..." Peter's voice trailed off. "I'm the man of the family, and she's my responsibility."

Nick couldn't help but admire the lad. He thought to change the subject back to the earlier ease between them. "With your talent for carpentry, why don't you try your hand at making furniture? I don't even have a bed in my room."

Peter grunted, his gaze fixed steadily on shaping the wood.

"In fact, I've noticed there's not much furniture in any of the rooms," Nick added. "What happened to it, lad?"

Again, Peter appeared so engrossed, he didn't hear.

"The furniture?" Nick asked, his voice louder. "There wasn't even a bed for me to sleep on last night."

Peter shrugged.

"Surely, lad, you know what happened to all of the pictures and furnishings in the manor?"

"Ask my sister." Peter rubbed his hand over the fresh wood, then glanced up at him. "Will you help me whittle the wood?" he asked, anxious to return to what interested him.

"You've got the hang of it, lad," Nick said. "I've got to be getting back to my chores."

"So soon?" Peter glanced up, disappointment clearly on his face. "Will ye come back later and tell me some more of your adventures, Ben?"

Ben. Nick swallowed the lump in his throat. Peter had given him his complete trust and faith. Damn, this charade felt like a horsehair shirt. Nick sighed. "Aye, lad, later. I'll come back after I finish my chores."

Peter smiled, and Nick realized that he'd enjoyed himself as much as the lad.

Before he trudged back to the manor, Nick followed the river for several miles. The storm's threat had passed, and silver chips along the water's surface reflected the sunlight overhead. However, the brightness did nothing to lift his feeling of worry at what was wrong with the estate. The more he saw of the manor's operations, the more he was convinced that Thornwood Hall was a profitable bit of land.

Damn, he needed to sneak into Becky's study and have a look at the account ledgers. And the sooner, the better.

Later that afternoon, Becky and Sally stood on each side of Keane, who sat astride the largest trunk in the attic as if it were a magnificent war charger.

"It's hot enough in this attic to bake bread," Sally complained, patting the hem of her apron to her brow.

Becky put down her sewing basket and dabbed the nape of her neck with a handkerchief. "We're almost finished, Sally." She tucked the linen inside her cuff. "Try not to think about the heat."

"But can't we fit Ol' Winky's uniform to Keane later this evening, outside under a tree when it's cooler?"

Becky shifted the armor plates against Keane's back, his spine ramrod straight. She frowned at Sally. "It's safer to work here, during the day. Later, someone might see us."

"A-a-a-choo!" Keane shook his hands at the dust motes that danced on the sunbeams slanting through the shuttered attic windows. He sneezed again.

"Keane, if you don't hold still, I'll never fit Ol' Winky's armor to your frame." Becky buckled the leather strips that held the metal plates across the back of Keane's narrow shoulders.

"Why can't I wear my own clothes under the general's uniform?" Keane rubbed his nose. "At night, no one will notice."

"Oh, all right." Becky felt too hot and irritable to argue with him. "It's Ol' Winky's officer's jacket and hat that everyone will recognize." She stepped back and appraised the general's uniform on Keane's lanky frame. "Sally, you've done a fine job of sewing the padding inside the jacket front. But I think it needs more stuffing through the shoulders and stomach."

Sally put the sewing basket down and appraised the uniform. "I think you're right. Ol' Winky sat grand in the saddle."

Keane whipped his head around. "It's goin' to be hot ridin' in this stuffed wool uniform. I refuse t' wear the heavy armor plates. They weigh a ton."

Becky pushed back a wisp of hair from her face. "If we want the Willoughby guests to believe Ol' Winky is avenging his property from Sir Nicholas Sinclair, then Ol' Winky would wear his battle gear."

Keane scowled. "Sinclair ain't never seen Ol' Winky."

"It's not Sinclair we aim to frighten." Becky picked up the shiny steel helmet of her late husband and placed it on Keane's head. "The clanking of the armor as you charge across the Willoughby front yard will excite the guests into a frenzy." She grinned at the thought.

"Their front yard?" Keane shot to his feet. "You said their fields. I ain't goin' near the Willoughbys' manor house."

Becky removed the hat from his head. "Sally, we'll need a lining inside the headband. Ol' Winky's head was much larger than Keane's."

Keane's scowl deepened. "I said I'm not ridin' near the Willoughbys' house!"

Becky propped her hands on her waist. "Keane, you'll do what you're told. Now, I've said this before. It's important that you're seen by everyone as they leave the Willoughby social. It will be dark. Most of the guests will be deep in their cups, and you'll catch everyone by surprise. By the time they catch their breath, you'll be over the hill on your way home.'' She straightened the armor plates at his chest.

"Don't worry, Keane, I'll be there,'' Becky said reassuringly. "In a loud voice, I'll declare that you're my late husband, avenging the property from Sinclair. Then I'll swoon.''

"What if someone rides after me an' they catch me?''

"Keane, don't be foolish. Who'd dare ride off after a specter?''

"Sinclair,'' Keane replied with foreboding.

The mention of his name caused an unbidden flutter inside her. "Don't worry about Sinclair. By the time we're through with him, he'll be so ashamed for throwing out a destitute widow and her starving siblings that he won't dare show his face.''

"And what if you're wrong?'' Keane held his nose to keep from sneezing again. "These sailors are a mean breed. They throw their enemies overboard just to keep from feedin' 'em. From what I've heard of this Sinclair, he'll be sellin' our home, sight unseen.''

"You don't know that.'' Becky bit back her tongue. She knew Keane didn't want her to lose the property to Sinclair, but she also knew that Keane had his own reasons, and it had nothing to do with her siblings' future. Keane had always felt that Thornwood Hall should be his, and although he never said it, she felt he resented her position.

She felt a touch of sadness for the man. Keane's mother had been the easy skirt of the town, from what Geer had told Cook, who had told Molly. Ol' Winky had given Keane a home with the crofters, like so many other children born the wrong side of the blanket. Becky could never see any resemblance between the two men. Yet Keane's mum had put the bee in his ear, all the same.

"Keane, you're forgetting that no one will buy Thornwood Hall if they think it's haunted." Becky spun around and faced him. "Nobody."

Keane shook his head. "Ye might fool some, but ye won't fool Sinclair. Yer plan won't work, I say."

"I don't remember you providing us with a plan to save the day." Becky's voice was sharp and she immediately regretted her stinging barb. "I'm sorry, Keane. But we can't sit idly by and let Sinclair sell the most profitable venture we'll ever have."

"Becky's right, Keane." Sally's high voice quavered with loyalty. "Sinclair's the enemy, and we can't just give up without a fight."

A man's urgent cries sounded outside, and Keane dashed to the dusty window, the armor plates clanking. He rubbed a hole in the powdery dirt and peered into the courtyard. "It's Geer. He's yellin' that Tumbledown Dick broke loose."

"Saints, how did that happen?" Becky straightened her skirts and turned toward Sally. "Help Keane out of his armor. Then both of you meet me in the pasture. It'll take everyone till sundown to find him if he's decided to court the Willoughbys' cows."

Becky dashed down the stairs, her hair flying behind her. She paused for only a second as she grabbed her straw hat and Ol' Winky's sword from the table by the front entrance. Within minutes, she ran to the barn gate where Geer waited.

Hidden behind the forsythia bushes beneath the study window, Nick crouched with Baby Harry sitting on his broad shoulders. Nick grinned as he watched Becky listen to Geer tell how he'd found the bull missing, its rope dangling from the tree.

A short while later, Keane lumbered down the steps, followed by Sally, her skirts forming a bell as she dashed beside Keane to where Becky and Geer stood.

Nick checked his vest pocket to be sure he had the piece of stiff wire he had cut earlier in the blacksmith shed. When Becky, Keane, Sally and Geer had taken off down the lane in the creaky old wagon, Nick crept back inside the house.

Nick knew that Becky would never have left the study door unlocked if she had given it a thought. He chuckled, thinking how adorable she had looked, so earnest and caring, her sword clanging at her side, her hat brim flopping, as she dashed after that sissy bull. He smiled as he shook his head at the thought.

Nick placed Baby Harry down on the floor of the study. Then he fished in his pocket and pulled out the wire. When his fingers found the collapsible telescope that King Charles had presented him, Nick glanced over at the boy. "How'd you like to play sailor, Harry?"

Nick held up the glass to the child's eye. "What do you see, lad?" Harry peered into the lens, then after a few moments, he squealed with delight. Relieved that the child would be occupied for a while, Nick left him to play on the rug beside Becky's desk while he closed the door. The house was empty except for the kitchen maids, who were busy preparing supper. This time of day, no one would observe the front of the house.

Nick glanced back at Baby Harry playing happily beside him. So far, his plan was going well. By all that was holy, he'd have most of the afternoon to study the account ledgers and decipher exactly what the mistress of Thornwood Hall was all about.

Dusk had fallen by the time Becky and Sally drove the wagon to the barn. Geer and Keane had remained in the fields to finish bringing in the cattle.

"Sally, unhitch the horse while I see to the children." Becky jumped down from the wagon, every muscle in her body aching from trudging through the woods, her voice hoarse from calling for the bull.

Nick was waiting for her, with Baby Harry in his arms, as she came around the side of the buttery door.

Her brother's sandy-blond curls shone from a recent brushing. He was bathed and wore a fresh nightdress. She reached out for the child. "Baby Harry, how handsome you look," she said, lifting him with both arms from Nick's hold.

She waited for Nick to ask if they'd found the bull, and when he didn't, her suspicions that he had had something to do with the animal's escape grew.

Nick's expression gave no hint to his thoughts, either. In fact, he appeared rather subdued. She glanced warily toward him. "And how did you loll away the afternoon, Twaddle?" Becky put the boy down on the settle beside the fireplace.

"Tending the boys. I showed Peter how to rig a sail on the old boat he's repairing. Fine lad, your brother."

"And earlier?" She lifted her brows, certain she saw a flinch of guilt cross his face.

"Before or after I read to Aphra?" He looked so innocent she gave up. If he had sneaked away at dawn to where Keane had tethered the animal, untied the bull and led it several miles downstream to where she found it a little while ago, he'd surely not admit it. But why would he do such a thing? Something foul was afoot.

"You may have the evening off, Twaddle, after you put Baby Harry to bed." She needed to be alone with her thoughts. For some unfounded reason, when he was near, all sense went out of her head. "I'll be in the study if Sally should ask."

She turned and left the room. She'd finish posting the account ledgers this evening. Nothing like figures to force the foolish thoughts of Sir Nicholas Sinclair from her brain.

When she found the study door open, she scolded herself for her carelessness. She should never have left the chamber unlocked with Sinclair about. Hurriedly, she went inside, closed the door and bolted it.

She glanced around nervously. Something felt wrong. Although everything appeared to be in order, a strange uneasiness settled around her. She dashed to her desk. Her fingers trembled with the key, dropping it with a clink on the wooden floorboard. As she bent to pick up the key ring, her gaze drew to a shiny object underneath the sofa. She strode across the small rug, then knelt down to spy a long, slender metallic tube. She studied the elaborately engraved object.

Her fingers grabbed it, then she twisted the delicate instrument. Never had she seen anything like it! She slid the shaft, extending the rod. Fascinated, she studied the intricate round end, then her index finger pressed the tiny knob. The end cap opened. Startled, she held it to her eye and peered inside.

A telescope! *A seaman's telescope!*

Pox and calamity! He'd been snooping, just as she feared. She clenched her teeth as she flew to the desk. The drawer was unlocked. Inside, the fraudulent ledger books she had prepared for him to see were exactly as she had left them.

All the pieces fell into place.

Sinclair had hidden the bull so she'd go searching for it, giving him time to sneak through her things.

How Nick must have laughed, knowing she'd trudged hither and yon for Sir Richard while he snooped in her study, prying through her private affairs.

Outrage, for the fool she was, jolted through her. Thank God, she'd hidden the real ledgers. *Or had he found them, too?*

Her gaze flew to the loose brick in the hearth. Shaking, her heart pounding, she stormed across the room to the fireplace. With fingers trembling, she pulled out the heavy brick. Behind it, in the secret hiding place, were the authentic ledgers, the journal entries disclosing the true worth of Thornwood Hall. Below, the leather sack of coin—her siblings' savings—was untouched, as well.

Relief flooded her. She replaced the brick with shaking hands and whispered a prayer. For the longest time, she remained motionless, forcing herself to remain calm.

She needed time to think. Her cheeks burned as she thought of the innocent look on his roguish face when he greeted her. Innocent, indeed!

She'd been lucky this time. But she couldn't afford to trust her plan to luck. What Sinclair had been looking for, he hadn't found. She'd be a fool to think that he wasn't wise to the discrepancy he'd seen between the state of the manor and the paltry profits shown in the ledgers in the desk.

Another thought occurred to her. For Sinclair to go to such bother to see the books, there was a real possibility King Charles, himself, might suspect her. Maybe the king had asked Sinclair to look into the matter.

She had cheated the crown. It was likely Sinclair had been told of the king's suspicions. If Sinclair had seen the real ledgers, he'd have proof she had lied about the profits of Thornwood Hall.

What she had done was a criminal offense. She pressed her fingers around her throat and swallowed. Well, so far, she hadn't been caught. Sinclair had his suspicions, but he had no proof, yet. Perhaps he didn't believe the ledgers he'd seen in her desk, but they were all he'd seen, so far. Sinclair couldn't prove anything against her without the genuine ledgers.

She rushed to the fireplace and removed the original ledgers from the hiding place. Then she replaced the brick and got to her feet. Without a moment's hesitation, she took the ledger-account books, which proved her sins against the monarchy, and threw them on top of the kindling ready for the evening fire. Then, she started a fire.

Greedy orange flames licked the tired, faded covers. Within minutes, sparks flew up the chimney while the fire blackened the pages of the books. She lost track of time as she watched the heat blister and distort the thin sheets. The chimney draft pulled at the white embers, whirling them into powdery ash.

Later, she poked at the telltale remains of her transgression. She stood, for a long time before the fire. The flames warmed her face and hands, reminding her of hell, as she felt the guilt for what she had done.

Why had she continued to commit the crime Ol' Winky had begun when King Charles had forced the unusual taxation upon the estate? Was it to provide a future for her siblings, as she always believed? If she was honest, it was more. She had seen a way to strike back at all that had been taken from her.

Her youth. Her parents. Her older sister. Becky had used the welfare of her siblings and of the old crofters as the excuse. But she also enjoyed tricking the king, she realized with a start.

Before, there had never been a face to her enemy. She'd never seen King Charles, and everyone knew the king squandered tax money on his mistresses and other extravagance.

Now, the enemy was Sinclair. Although he owned what she wanted, there was something about the man that had crept into her very soul. Becky reached for the richly engraved silver telescope. The metal felt warm from the flames in the hearth. She clutched the tube in her fingers, closing her eyes.

The man in the moonlight last night wasn't the enemy. He had asked if she had loved her husband. She knew now that she had, but not in the way Sinclair had meant.

She had cared for the general, but that wasn't the same kind of love.

If a man like Sinclair would have a wife, he would love her. Truly love her.

She lost track of time as she knelt by the fire. When she finally opened her eyes, her gaze fell to the metal rod in her hands. It didn't matter how she felt about Sinclair; as long as he had the power to take away what was dear to her, he was her enemy. She held the proof in her fingers.

He had lied to her about his identity, plotted to have her leave the manor while he sneaked through her desk, searching for information with which to prove his suspicions of her. She must never forget that. She slid Sinclair's telescope into her pocket and strode toward the fireplace.

Grabbing the poker, she crumbled the telltale remains of the ashes into black soot. Then she placed the iron back into the rack.

Tomorrow, she'd confront Sinclair and show him what she had found in her study.

Chapter Seven

The next morning, when Becky went to return Nick's telescope, the kitchen maids said he hadn't come down for breakfast. Nor had his bed been slept in.

Where was Sinclair?

In her heart, Becky sensed Nick had left. Although she should be glad to be rid of him, her relief was somehow clouded by loss, yet she didn't understand why.

After checking the gardens herself, Becky ordered a room-by-room search. Geer and the men looked through the barns, corn mill and smelting houses. Keane and Peter searched the fields. When she found Nick's shaving gear and horse missing from the barn, she faced the truth.

Sinclair had come to assess his property, to assess her. She wouldn't meet him again until two days from to-day—at the Willoughby social. The next time she'd see him, he'd be Sir Nicholas Sinclair and she would no longer be the mistress of Thornwood Hall. Instead, she'd be expected to hand over the keys to him. Her future and those she loved would be in the hands of that silver-eyed devil.

The day of the Willoughby party finally arrived. Becky brushed her jet-black hair until her arms ached. Then

Sally offered to help, chattering incessantly while she arranged the curls on top of Becky's head. Save her soul, but Becky couldn't keep her mind on anything except seeing Nick again.

"You'll be the loveliest lady there," Sally said finally, her blue gaze brimming with admiration for Becky.

"Don't speak foolishness, Sally," Becky said, coaxing a wayward tendril into place. But she couldn't help feeling pleased at the charming way the bouncy curls danced about her face.

Sally sighed, laying the brush on the dressing table. "If only I had your thick, curly hair," she said, patting the thin braided coil at the nape of her neck. "Your mother always said that a woman's hair was her greatest glory."

Becky glanced at Sally's sad face in the mirror, and she guessed that her cousin was thinking herself too plain to find a husband. Without a large dowry, a woman might never marry unless a man considered her comely. Resentment rippled through Becky at the injustice.

"Sally, you're beautiful," Becky said, meaning every word. Her cousin's heart was pure gold, and she deserved so much better than the bleak future that was her certain end if Becky couldn't provide a sizable dowry so Sally might marry well.

Sally's future was one more reason why Becky needed to convince Sinclair that she could manage Thornwood Hall for him when he returned to sea.

"Sinclair will think you're the most beautiful woman at the social," Sally said.

"I don't give a damn what Sinclair thinks."

Sally's hand shot to her mouth. "Becky! You swore!"

"I'm sorry I swore, Sally." She huffed. "Sinclair's profanity has been a bad influence on us all."

"But he's so handsome...." Her voice trailed off in

that awestruck way that was becoming increasingly familiar.

Becky frowned. "Handsome is as handsome does, *your* mother used to say." She exchanged a knowing look with her cousin before Sally lifted the black taffeta gown over Becky's head.

After Becky had finished dressing, she glanced at her reflection in the mirror. The dress had been Ol' Winky's first wife's gown, found stashed away in the attic trunks. With much altering, Sally had helped Becky fashion the costume into a perfect fit. The fabric was so fragile, it had to be pieced together in many places. The result reflected modest frugality—exactly the effect Becky had in mind.

"Becky, why don't you marry Sinclair?" Sally grinned as though her idea might solve all of their problems.

Becky sighed. "Don't be foolish, Sally. First, he doesn't wish to marry. Besides, he's titled. Why would Sinclair marry an impoverished widow when he can marry into the wealthy upper class? He even said as much."

Sally's eyes widened. "He spoke of marriage to you?"

"Well, not exactly." Becky remembered the night in the moonlit garden when Sinclair had asked her if she had loved Ol' Winky. She blushed at the recollection. "Sinclair is happy with his life at sea. Besides, not every man needs a wife."

"But now that Sinclair has an estate, he might want heirs." Sally pursed her mouth in thought. "He might want to marry you—if you'd be pleasant to him instead of badgering him at every turn." She gave Becky a teasing glance.

"If he wants to marry, he has his pick of the wealthy women at court. I'm sure they're very *pleasant* to him."

Sally giggled.

Becky frowned. "You're such a romantic, Sally. In the real world, men don't raise other people's brothers and sisters. They want young, pretty, empty-headed wives who look the other way when they drink excessively, gamble immoderately and—"

Sally's long face made Becky stop. She chided herself for saying too much. "Your delicate stitching on my gown is lovely, Sally," she said, brightly. "You're so very talented."

Sally burst into tears.

Becky put her arm around her cousin's heaving shoulders. "Sally, please, what is it?"

She buried her face in Becky's shoulder. "I'll never find a man who'll love me. I'll be an old maid, taking care of other people's children."

Becky felt her cousin's frustration. "Sally, wait and see. One day, you'll meet a fine man, and you'll steal his heart." She stepped back and smiled. "You'll marry, have children and enjoy a wonderful life."

Becky held her, afraid to say anything more. Now, who was being the childish romantic? What right did she have to give Sally false hope? After all, Becky wasn't certain they'd have a roof over their heads when Sinclair returned tomorrow.

"Dry your eyes, Sally. Neither of us has the time for self-pity." Becky smoothed back Sally's blond hair and forced a smile. "In a few hours, we'll have to face Sinclair and our neighbors. You'll help me serve my last function as lady of Thornwood Hall."

Sally dabbed her eyes. Becky grinned back at her. "I have a feeling that after Ol' Winky makes his fateful ride tonight, Sinclair will be begging me to manage the haunted estate for him."

Sally managed a weak smile. Gone were all traces of her earlier tears. Becky felt a grain of hope, too.

* * *

That evening, Becky and Sally descended the front steps of Thornwood Hall to find Geer and Peter waiting to escort them to the farm wagon. Geer's hair was powdered, a blue satin bow tied around the queue at the back of his neck. "The children are waiting in the wagon, mistress." He offered his arm as elegantly as if he were the groom at the royal court.

"Thank you, Geer," Becky replied, sinking into an exaggerated curtsy. She was rewarded with his toothy grin. Geer glanced around self-consciously, then helped Becky into the wagon beside Aphra and Baby Harry. When he turned around, she noticed the seat of his breeches was patched with leather.

Becky bit her lip to keep from laughing. The brief amusement quieted the fluttering inside her stomach. Dear God, she was so nervous, how would she get through this evening?

Peter stepped toward Sally. "My arm, milady."

Sally clasped the neck of her cloak with one hand, the other arm slipping around Peter's thin sleeve. "Thank you, kind sir." Both broke into a fit of giggles.

Geer scowled at them as he climbed onto the driver's seat. "This is a serious matter," he said, disengaging the brake.

Sally tittered nervously while she settled herself beside Becky and Aphra. Peter climbed aboard, then Geer brought the horses to a trot. The creaky wagon swayed and rocked along the rutted lane as they made their way to the Willoughby estate.

Several years past, Becky had sold the general's carriage. For a brief moment, she was sorry she had.

Stuff and nonsense! Money was more practical than a frippery-bob of a carriage. What was the matter with her tonight? Her neighbors valued frugality, or at least, most of them did. Although Sinclair wouldn't see the virtue of it, certainly.

"When was the last time you looked in on Keane?" Becky asked Geer. "He was sober, wasn't he?" The worry that Keane might be tempted to take a drink was overshadowed by knowing how serious Keane knew his mission was. Besides, he enjoyed setting a sober example for the other men. But Becky knew that once Keane took so much as a man's usual daily ration of ale, he became tipsy, unlike the other workers.

"Keane was cold sober, Mistress Becky," Geer said. "I helped 'im dress in Ol' Winky's uniform, meself." Geer shook his head, the wig slipping forward. "If I didn't know, I'd say 'e's Ol' Winky, 'imself." He straightened his wig. "Gave me a start, 'e did."

"Excellent," Becky said, feeling relieved.

Aphra tugged on Becky's skirt. She smiled at her younger sister, the pretty little face gazing back at her. Aphra and Peter had their mother's large brown eyes, and both children could play on her heartstrings with a glance.

Becky slipped her arm around Aphra's thin shoulders. What would become of her dear Aphra if Becky's plan failed? What sort of life could a female, unable to speak, expect to have?

Becky shuddered to think of what might happen if Sinclair had found out about her fraudulent account ledgers. Dear God, she didn't fear prison for only herself, but what would happen to the children?

Any guilt she had felt for deluding Sinclair with her ruse of Ol' Winky's ghost faded as she hugged her little sister. Her family depended on her, and her duty was to them.

Sally shifted beside her, and Becky gave her a reassuring smile. Her gaze lingered on the familiar dusty-rose satin gown that Sally wore. Her mother's gown. The fabric had become a charming outfit for Sally. Becky had tucked remnants of satin inside Sally's braid to provide added substance.

"What if I fall with spells of giggles when I see Keane dressed as Ol' Winky?" Sally asked, barely able to keep a nervous titter from her voice as she shifted Baby Harry onto her lap.

"Do as I do," Becky said resolutely. "Never forget how important Ol' Winky's ghost is to our purpose."

"When will Keane make his ride?" Peter asked, his long legs dangling from the back of the wagon.

"He'll arrive later, when the guests begin to leave. I thought it best Keane not wait around on the Willoughby property." She brushed back a tendril of hair from Aphra's face.

"Aye," said Geer, straightening his wig. "I reminded Keane to wait until the carriage drivers pull up to the door."

Becky loosened the collar around her neck and let the evening breeze cool her flushed skin. The thought of seeing Sinclair again brought back the fluttering feeling in the pit of her stomach. Her skin felt hot. What would she say to him when she first saw him? What would he say to her?

Now, as she listened to the clip-clop of the horses' hooves, the usual half-hour ride to the Willoughby estate seemed like three days. Becky's fingers felt cold, and her insides were quaking by the time their wagon creaked past the surprised gatekeeper, who scowled at their humble conveyance.

Geer answered the snub with a jerk of his chin. His wig slipped backward. Jabbing at it with one hand, Geer reined the horses around the circle drive in front of the Willoughby mansion.

At least thirty handsome, empty coaches waited along the verge, each vehicle attended by several grooms and footmen. Torches and lanterns blazed alongside the driveway. Women, dressed in glittering gowns, and men, handsome in colored outfits, strolled the gardens among the bright borders of flowers.

Becky dared not glance at Sally. The last time she did, her cousin's face grew starchy white. Gone were the giggles; in their place was panic.

Dear God, was she making a fool of herself and her family and degrading Ol' Winky's reputation by coming tonight? For a brief moment, she thought to tell Geer to stop the horses, turn around and head for home before anyone noticed them. There was still time to stop Keane from making his ride. Panic lurched like a tight ball in her stomach.

Nay, she had to try to save Thornwood Hall for her family. She couldn't turn cowardly and run. She'd hold her own with her neighbors. She always had. *She had no choice.*

Hazel Willoughby's nasal voice called out from the green. "Oh, Becky, my dear." Becky looked twice before she recognized her, gowned in blue silk, her hair dressed in ringlets. Sapphires winked from her ears and around her neck.

"Hazel, how nice to see you." Becky turned to her hostess in time to see Hazel's gaze sweep over the rickety farm wagon. Her nostrils flared with disapproval.

Peter jumped down from the back of the wagon and tramped off by himself. Becky glanced at him, wondering if she had done the right thing by not taking him into her confidence. But she couldn't risk anyone knowing that the man they had come to know as Ben Twaddle was really Nicholas Sinclair.

As she watched her brother meander behind, she hoped she had made the right choice. It would have been too difficult to explain that she chose to treat Sinclair as a servant while she knew his real identity.

She had only told Sally. Now she wondered if Peter might think she couldn't trust him with the secret.

Becky took Baby Harry from Sally's lap while Geer helped Sally out of the wagon.

Aphra wrapped her arms around the wagon seat and wouldn't budge. Becky whispered in her ear the promise of a sweetmeat. Aphra gazed up at her with wide, trusting eyes. Her hand finally loosened its grip.

Hazel smiled patiently as she waited for Becky and Sally to be assisted down from the vehicle. By the time Geer drove off to park beside the other vehicles, Hazel had escorted them to the door.

"Oh, I—I'm so glad you had the courage to come, dear." Hazel's voice was barely a whisper. "The general and your parents would have been very proud of you, Becky."

Becky bit her tongue to keep from saying that the general must be sitting up in his grave at the thought that she would honor a Royalist, but she knew Hazel was only thinking of avoiding discord. She nodded in agreement.

Melodic violin and flute music drifted on the night air. Becky peered through the huge windows. She wondered where Sinclair was. Shifting uncomfortably, she strode toward the music.

Her gaze roved over the couples strolling beside the well-tended rose beds. But Nick was nowhere to be seen. "I trust Sinclair arrived safely?" she asked, her voice higher than normal.

"Wh-why, yes, Becky. And he's most anxious to meet you." She glanced at Aphra, who was making a sucking sound with her thumb.

"I wasn't aware that you had planned to bring the children, dear." Hazel's Christian charity appeared stretched to the limit.

She waved to a manservant, standing on the front steps. He came rushing to them. "George will assist you with the children," Hazel said, then ushered them inside like a flock of sheep.

Becky stepped inside the main hall and paused, staring. She had attended elegant affairs at the Willoughbys' while married to the general, but for some reason, this occasion seemed different. *The only difference is that he's here,* she reminded herself.

For a moment, Becky wished she could tap her feet and dance to the lilting music. But she didn't know how. As a crofters' child, she had had to work in the fields until dark. For the poor, there had never been time or money to waste with dancing masters.

Becky bit back the thought. It might be too late for her, but it wasn't too late for Sally and the other crofter children. Once Sinclair was gone and her life returned to normal, maybe she could barter a deal with Hazel to install a dancing master to teach the children. Aye, she might have a chance to mention it this evening.

She glanced at Sally, who held Baby Harry's hand while the boy hid his face in her skirts. Peter stood beside her, tall and gangly, painfully uncomfortable. She gave them a dazzling smile, full of confidence. "Are you ready to face the receiving line?" she asked, with a lilt to her voice.

Sally glanced nervously at Peter, who gazed steadfastly toward the floor. Unrelenting, Becky forged ahead. They followed closely in Hazel's wake.

A hush skirted the room when they entered the hall. Becky paused, allowing the gaping guests to recognize the proud lift of her chin. She took in the opulent ballroom, the candle-lighted crystal chandeliers, the lilting music coming from the drawing room. Clouds of silks, organzas and satin rustled. Jewels flashed everywhere, like colored fireflies on a summer night.

With a fixed smile, Becky nodded and acknowledged the guests as Hazel introduced her, along with Sally, followed by Peter, who carried Baby Harry, and gripped Aphra's hand.

Although Becky's husband had died before their first wedding anniversary, her caring for the old man, and her responsibility for her family and the crofters had earned her neighbors' hard-won respect. She was a crofters' daughter; some things would never change, but she had been treated as an equal. Tonight, the respect and admiration she saw in her neighbors' eyes made her proud.

However, Becky knew that her neighbors would never take her side against the king's award to Sir Nicholas Sinclair. These good people would show her no mercy if she refused the proper show of respect due a war hero. They expected Ol' Winky's widow to leave Thornwood Hall in the proud and gracious manner in which she had always carried out her role.

Her arrival with her family at Sinclair's reception showed this very spirit—everyone believed that she had buried her resentment at losing the estate and that she was welcoming him. Regret for this lie made her uneasy. Truth be known, she had only begun her fight to oust Sinclair from her property.

Becky's gaze drifted to Hazel as she made polite chatter. Becky's lies had forced Hazel to be an unsuspecting party to her deception, too. Along the wall, Sally and the children were seated in a quiet corner. Wide-eyed, they watched the dancers twirl across the room.

As each guest was introduced to her, Becky received praise for her acceptance of Sinclair, praise for her grace and praise for her great Christian duty. Her neighbors, her late husband's friends and several guests who had moved to the area since her husband's death all joined in her toasts. The reason for her appearance tonight was clear to everyone. She had come to pay homage to the war hero, Sir Nicholas Sinclair, who through no fault of his own had been awarded her estate. And in doing so, she had honored Ol' Winky's name, as well. The civil war was long over. Long live the king.

Compliments, all meaningless, whirled in her mind. Would this never end? The air felt hot and stuffy. How she wanted to run home, bar the door, and forget this nightmare had ever happened.

"How do you do?" Becky nodded to a feeble old woman in a high-backed chair. Several other matrons chattered endlessly. Hazel's eyes shone with pride. Becky felt like a charlatan.

Suddenly, her attention was drawn to the crowd beyond the staircase. Becky sensed Sinclair staring at her before she saw him. She turned. The challenging gray eyes fixed with hers, and for a heart-stopping minute, Becky forgot the sea of faces swimming around them.

Dressed in a dark blue military uniform, Sir Nicholas Sinclair was the most handsome man she had ever imagined. The sight of him, clean-shaven, his dark hair unpowdered, took her breath away.

She didn't hear what Hazel was saying. All she could do was stare. Compared to his commanding presence, every other man in the room appeared pale, unmannered and unrefined, although she knew they were not.

Sinclair's demeanor must bring his crew to their heels, she thought, realizing how he must appear to his men on deck. Wise, responsible, masterful.

He whispered to the circle of women fluttering around him, then they parted, allowing him to thread his way toward her.

Dear God, she wasn't prepared. She'd never be prepared for this confrontation. Her throat felt as if it were stuffed with wool.

Hazel made the introductions. Despite Becky's inward trembling, she straightened her shoulders and stood tall before relaxing into a graceful curtsy before him.

Sinclair bowed as gallantly as if she were Queen Catherine.

"I'm delighted to make your acquaintance." He took her icy hand and smiled down at her. "I've heard so much about you, mistress." His eyes sparkled with unspoken amusement.

Her pulse beat faster at the deep timbre of his voice. Why had his innocuous comments affected her so? Becky couldn't think of what to say.

Aware of the audience around them, she smiled sweetly. "Thank you," she managed. Thank God her voice didn't betray her panic.

Hazel discreetly fluttered her fan to bring attention to the several young women who flocked to her side, waiting for their introduction to Sinclair. Becky recognized the prettiest as the unmarried daughter of a baron.

The unbidden vision of Nick and the red-haired beauty brought a lump to her throat. Her words to Sally earlier came back to bedevil her. If Sinclair wished to marry, he'd have the pick of the king's court. Why would he desire a crofter's daughter?

She jerked her thoughts back to the present. What did she care who Sinclair married? No doubt the lilting music, the beautifully adorned women and elegantly dressed men were putting romantic notions into her head.

It was time to leave. She had only planned to make an appearance. "P-please, I—I must—"

"Have some refreshments, surely," Nick added. "Something for the children, perhaps?"

The children. For the moment, she had forgotten about her siblings and Sally. Becky glanced around to see Peter's dark scowl targeted directly at Sinclair. She recognized the mutinous slant of her brother's thin shoulders, and she groaned.

Peter realized that the man who'd befriended him was the very man who was taking away their home—Sir

Nicholas Sinclair, not Ben Twaddle. Besides, when he would discover that Becky had known, he'd be angry with her for not telling him. Peter moved toward them, his dark-eyed gaze boring into Sinclair, betrayal clearly etched on his youthful face.

Hazel whirled her fan, trying to attract Nick's attention back to the women at her side, but Sinclair met Peter head-on.

"Peter, I'd like to explain—"

"You bastard! You lying bastard!"

"Peter!" Becky gasped, staring at her brother.

A hush fell across the cavernous room.

Becky turned to face Peter. "Escort Sally and the children and wait for me in the—" she paused "—carriage."

Peter's jaw opened in surprise. Clearly, he had expected her support against Sinclair. Within seconds, his brown eyes darkened with betrayal. He turned on his heel, strode with a purposeful gait to the far wall where Sally, her face flushed, waited with the children.

Peter swooped up Baby Harry from her arms, and grabbing Aphra's hand, trudged from the room. Sally darted a worried look over her shoulder at Becky before dashing after them.

The room was silent except for the sounds of a few embarrassed guests clearing their throats.

"I—I must go, too." Becky stepped away from him, but Nick held her arm.

"Leave Peter be," Sinclair whispered. "I'll deal with him later."

"No, you don't understand." She jerked free of him. "Peter thought of you as a friend. He finally reached out to someone outside the family since our parents died. And I should have protected him, somehow. Please, I— I need...air."

"Certainly, Mistress Becky." Nick led her past the curious stares as the crowd parted to let them pass. When they reached the garden, the music begin again. Becky's cheeks burned with embarrassment at the gossip she knew the spectacle provided.

She took a deep gulp of cool night air. Her knees felt wobbly as she walked to the garden bench beside a water-lily pool. Becky sat down and took another deep breath.

"I felt you'd guessed my real identity when you discovered my seaman's telescope that I'd forgotten in your study," Nick said, sitting beside her.

She kept her gaze on the glittering torchlights mirrored in the surface of the pond. "Aye, and I should have told Peter your real identity, then. He's thought of you as a friend these past weeks. But—"

She heard his deep sigh. "Aye, and I of him."

Becky glared at him. "Then why did you lie about your identity?" She sniffed. "As Ben Twaddle, no less."

His mouth twitched. "It was you, my dear, who presumed I was Ben Twaddle, if you remember." He leaned back and studied her.

"You did nothing to clear my mistaken notion, as I remember. You can't deny your behavior was anything but fraudulent."

"Speaking of fraud, I read the account ledgers you'd left for me to find in your desk." Nick folded his arms in front of his chest. "Do you really expect me to believe them?"

Her heart hammered. "What do you mean?"

"If you want to play games, then I won't disappoint you." His voice lowered to a chilling depth. "I've given your situation a great deal of thought these past two days, and I've come to a decision. But this is neither the time nor the place to discuss our differences. I'll make the announcement tomorrow."

He spoke as if she were to be hanged at sunrise. She averted her gaze. "I must say, Peter expressed our family's sentiments about you, exactly."

He grinned. "My manners fail me. I forgot to say how very enchanting you look. The last time I saw you, your hair cascaded down your back and your face was flushed from chasing your pet bull." A corner of his mouth lifted. "I think I prefer your hair as I last saw you. Loose and flowing."

She started to protest, but words failed her.

"I'm certain that Peter would find quite a few who'd agree with his assessment of me, dear lady. And I can be, if the occasion so arises." He grinned at her growing irritation. "By the way, I trust your pet bull is well?"

"Yes, thank you. But I should remind you, he's your bull, now, isn't he, Sinclair?"

"Call me Nick."

"That's not quite the word I'd like to call you." She rose. Her family was waiting, and she knew if she remained any longer, she'd lose her composure and tell him what she thought.

She turned to leave, but he caught her arm. "I'm going with you."

"Where?"

"To Thornwood Hall."

"You can't leave now. Hazel will be aghast. The social is in your honor."

"I'm responsible for your family and the crofters. After all, Hazel would expect me to take care of you, under the circumstances." He took her arm and led her along the path. "We're going to Thornwood Hall together. It's my home now, or until the Prescott family arrives from Hampshire to look at the property." He paused when he saw the look of surprise in her face. "Aye, Willoughby knew of a friend who's eager to settle closer to London. The Prescotts will be here within a fortnight, and I'm certain I can convince them that Thornwood Hall has the makings of a valuable estate."

"That's none of my concern," she said, frightfully

aware Nick knew that nothing was further from the truth. "Furthermore, I don't consider it decent for you to stay with us."

He threw back his head and laughed. "Would you prefer to live under the same roof with Ben Twaddle or Sir Nicholas Sinclair?" The deep baritone laughter reminded Becky of when she had first met him in the hay barn and she took a blade to him. How she wished she wore Ol' Winky's blade at her side now. She took a deep breath. But she gained nothing in arguing with him. He held all the cards.

She forced a serenity that she didn't feel. "If you wish to return to Thornwood Hall, I have very little choice about it."

He took her arm. She shook free of him. "Let's hurry. I'll wait for you in the wagon while you say goodbye to the Willoughbys and your guests."

She didn't wait for his answer as she dashed along the path toward the verge alongside the gardens. She must speak to Peter. Maybe he'd calm his temper before Sinclair saw him again in the wagon.

In the shadows beyond the torch lights, she saw Geer sitting on the driver's seat. Sally, with the children, waited inside the wagon. Peter stood outside, leaning against the wooden side, his expression grim.

She strode purposefully, her footfalls muffled in the soft dirt. Torchlights blazed along the road, and Becky could plainly see the fresh anger in Peter's face.

Geer appeared restless as he wrapped the reins around his hands, disengaged the brake and glanced around before urging the team toward the center of the drive.

Becky stood beside the wagon, wondering if she should try to speak to Peter. She glanced helplessly at Sally, who sat on the floor of the wagon, Baby Harry already asleep in her arms. Aphra, eyes heavy, leaned against Sally's shoulder.

The warm, moonlit night brought half a dozen guests out into the gardens. Several couples strolled nearby, giving her only a cursory glance.

Becky gazed back to see Hazel Willoughby and a circle of admirers cling to Nick's arm as he tried to make his way out of the front door. Finally, he bade farewell, then hurried across the green toward Becky and the wagon.

Nick had almost reached them when a loud commotion rose in the distance.

"Aaaaaaaaaa!" yelled a tall figure riding a warhorse. The soldier, dressed in full battle gear, galloped noisily across the lawn. Another bloodcurdling howl at the top of the man's lungs shrieked into the night.

Becky screamed, forgetting for the moment that Keane was due to make his arrival as the ghost of Ol' Winky. Instead, she felt only terror at the sudden specter. She screamed again.

The horses reared wildly. Geer pulled back on the reins, to no effect. Becky jumped out of the way before the wagon bolted forward, jarring everyone inside.

"What the hell was that?" someone shouted from the garden. Several men ran toward the vehicles to try to calm the horses. Nick was the first to arrive at the wagon, grabbing the horses' bridle, and if he hadn't, Becky knew that the wagon might have stormed down the road, out of control.

Becky stared back at the manor house. Faces peered from the downstairs windows. People huddled in frightened knots all along the gardens.

"It's the ghost of Ol' Winky, General Forester," Geer shouted to the men gathering around them. "The ghost of Ol' Winky, ridin' to avenge his estate from that bastard, Sinclair!"

Becky felt like crying. Geer had recited his lines like a schoolboy repeating his sums.

Keane appeared as foolish as a dressed-up shill, as phony as the rest of them. She wanted to hide. No one would believe such a foolish idea. Why had she ever thought of it? She didn't dare look at Sinclair.

"Damn, but it was Ol' Winky," shouted a portly man in a crimson waistcoat. He pointed in the direction where Keane had ridden off.

"Ol' Winky! I saw 'im, too," another man yelled.

Becky's gaze darted to Nick. His eyes glittered dangerously. The accusation was on his face as clearly as if he had openly charged her with masterminding the trickery.

"Get in the back of the wagon, Geer," Nick shouted. Then he glared at Peter. "Jump in the back, and not a word out of you."

Peter's eyes widened, but he obediently climbed into the vehicle beside Geer.

Nick didn't wait for Becky. Instead, he lifted her by the waist and set her upon the driver's bench. He took the seat beside her, grabbed the reins, then shouted to the team of horses.

The wagon took off with a jolt, the creaking wooden wheels jostling them as Nick drew the team into a tight turn and headed back along the road.

Becky glanced over her shoulder at the faces in the wagon. In the flickering glow of the lantern, Geer, Sally, Peter, Aphra and Baby Harry scowled back at her.

Beyond, the twinkling lights of the Willoughby estate disappeared around the bend in the road. Over the creaky wagon's rumbling wheels, she could still hear the raised voices floating on the night's breeze, recalling the ghost of Ol' Winky.

Chapter Eight

No one spoke during the ride back to Thornwood Hall. Nick's arms ached from gripping the reins in his tight fists, but his ire and outright stupefaction at Becky's disgraceful attempt to scare off buyers with the ghost of her late husband still rankled him.

He cursed under his breath. Ah, she'd dare anything, remembering the account ledgers he'd found in her desk—left for him to see, no doubt. She will face prison when she was found guilty of tax evasion. Damn, if she wasn't the biggest obstacle to selling the estate, he'd feel sorry for her.

He drew the team to a halt at the front door and jumped down from the driver's seat. "Geer, take the horses to the barn and bed them down. You help him, Peter."

Geer climbed onto the seat, taking the reins in his hands, while Peter sat silently, refusing to acknowledge Nick.

Nick glanced at Sally, who clutched Aphra and Baby Harry to her like two shields of armor.

Nick sighed. Damn, he'd rather face an unruly crew of men than one timid female. "Sally, take the children and put them to bed. Then get a good night's rest, or what little that's left." He raked his hair with his fingers as Sally and the children scrambled from the wagon.

"Tell the staff that I'll meet with them in the morning," he added after Sally had the children in tow. "I'll speak to everyone about my plans for the estate."

Sally's face blanched with uncertainty, her gaze darting to Becky. Becky gave her a confident, don't-worry expression. Without another word, Sally ushered the children inside.

Nick frowned at Becky. "You, mistress, will come inside with me. Our differences can't wait." He took her arm to help her from the wagon.

Becky jerked her elbow free, then climbed gracefully over the wooden slats, coming to stand before him. "It's much too late for discourse." She brushed at her skirt. "I'm going to bed."

Nick grabbed her elbow and spun her around. Geer and Peter gasped from the wagon.

Nick paused, then scowled at their shocked faces. "You've had your orders," he snapped. "Be off with you."

Geer shouted to the team, the wagon jolted forward. Peter's hands clenched the seat as the vehicle bounced over the grassy clumps on their way, finally disappearing into the barn.

Nick turned to Becky. "Thornwood Hall has but one owner, mistress. You'll make this easier on everyone if you accept that."

"I accept it." She raised her chin a notch. "Good night."

"We have something to discuss that can't wait."

"*You* have something to discuss." She narrowed her eyes. "*I* can wait." She wrestled her elbow from his grasp. "Unhand me, Sinclair. I'm going to bed."

"I said—"

"I said," she interrupted, matching his tone. "You can

stand out here till the rooster crows, but I'm exhausted, and I'm going to bed."

"You'll take orders from me, you little—"

"Not until tomorrow, the first day of the month, when you legally own Thornwood Hall." She exaggerated a yawn. "Saints, I can hardly keep my eyes open."

He couldn't believe one slip of a lass could hold so much courage. He scowled at her. "Larceny. Theft. Imprisonment. Maybe those words will shake you awake."

For a moment, her eyes widened with fear, before she quickly recovered. The change almost took his breath away. Damn, he almost wished he could take the words back.

He let go of her, staring at her in silence. Why the hell couldn't he control himself when she was near? He took a deep breath. "We need to talk. Do you want to discuss this outside for the servants to hear, or shall we go into the study?"

Becky's shoulders stiffened. Without looking at him, she marched up the steps and went inside. She removed her cape and hung it on the hook, then lit a fresh taper from the burning candle, while he removed his hat and sword belt. A few moments later, he followed her into the study.

When he closed the door and turned to her, Becky was seated in the chair by the fireplace. Her head bowed, her hands folded in her lap, she appeared almost demure—if he didn't know better.

The candle shone from the windowsill where she had placed it. He took the only remaining seat in the room—at the desk. How he wanted to think that her choice of chairs was a sign that she had accepted him as master, but he knew better.

"Although I have no proof, I know you've contrived to cheat the crown of its rightful profits," Nick began.

Becky glanced briefly at the closed desk, then back at

her hands. The stark color of widow's black contrasted with her white skin, reminding him of the pearly luster inside a seashell.

"How have I cheated the crown?" she asked with the innocence of a child.

He felt irritated, more with himself than at her. "Don't pretend to be blameless. We both know you're not."

"I don't know what you're talking about."

He opened his mouth to argue, but he decided against it. He'd not show temper. She would only take that as a sign that she'd won the argument. He needed more time to think over how to proceed with this tricky wench.

"You do look tired. Perhaps we should discuss this in the morning." He noticed her eyes brighten with relief. She stood and rushed to the door.

"Before you leave, show me to the master's suite. I trust the maids have prepared it for my arrival." He picked up the candlestick from the windowsill. Damn, how he hated the manor's lack of furniture. He'd ask tomorrow where the original furnishings were stored. The barn, most likely. Damn foolish way to run an estate.

Becky stood on the stairway, her face puzzled. "Why can't you sleep in Baby Harry's room?"

Nick's impatience grew. "Because it's not fitting for Sir Nicholas Sinclair to sleep on the nanny's cot. The master should sleep in the master's quarters."

"B-but I—I don't..."

From the expression on her face, he guessed the dilemma. "You've taken over the master's suite for yourself?" He smiled. "Say no more. I understand."

"You do?"

"Aye." He held the candlestick higher. "Show me to your chamber, mistress."

Becky gasped. "My chamber?"

He smiled, nodding.

She gave him a skeptical look, then flew up the stairs.

Nick followed. When he arrived on the third floor, he saw the candle flicker as Becky ducked inside a chamber down the hall. When he came upon the open door and glanced inside the room, he almost laughed.

The halo of light coming from the taper Becky held lit the cobwebs hanging from the exposed ceiling beams. The room was bare except for a thin mattress on the floor. Surely this was some sort of joke.

"This bedchamber is available, Sinclair." She couldn't quite keep her mouth straight.

"Available for what? Pigs?" He kicked the mattress. Clouds of dust puffed into the circle of light. "Stuffed with corncobs, eh?" He shot her a sharp look. "I asked to be shown your bedchamber, mistress."

"Nay!"

Ignoring her, he strode from the room. She followed him, her shorter steps clattering along the floorboards. The first chamber was locked. He tried the next door and pushed it open.

"Aha!" The room was taken up with a large bed. Although sparse of furniture, the air of femininity reminded him of Becky. A vase of pink gillyflowers adorned the windowsill and the lacy sleeping cap he had remembered her wearing was peeking out from the pillows. The mullioned windows were ajar, and fresh air ruffled the billowing lacy curtains.

"Too dainty for my tastes, but for tonight, it'll do."

"You cannot sleep here, and you know it." Becky hovered at the doorway, her teeth clenched. "Where am I to sleep?"

"Let it not be said of Sir Nicholas Sinclair that he threw poor Mistress Becky from her bed." He gave her a licentious glance. "The bed's large enough for both of us." Her eyes widened, and he could hardly keep a straight face.

"If you don't care for my reputation, think of Aphra, Peter and Baby Harry."

"Then show me to my suite." He bounced on the bed. "Although this chamber is very pleasant, it would never accommodate the master's quarters. There are no dressing rooms, no private study with crystal decanters, tobacco humidors, divans for my guests." He waved his hand in the air, then he noticed the double doors within one side of the wall.

"Aha! What have we here?" He fumbled in his pocket for the keys. After several minutes, he fished through all the metal rods, but none of them opened the lock to the adjoining rooms.

He turned to Becky, who was watching him from the doorway. "Hand it over, and don't annoy me with your silly excuses." His voice revealed the frustration he felt.

"That, sir, is the general's chamber. If you don't mind, with all the other rooms in this house, I'd rather you do not disturb my late husband's suite."

"I do mind." He glared at her. "Give me the key."

"Nay." Becky sat on the edge of the bed, her breasts lifting and lowering with her ragged breathing. "You'll incite all the more the ghost of my departed husband."

In the candle's glow, her face paled as though genuinely afraid. Damn, her theatrical talents rivaled any he'd seen at Drury Lane Theater. "Don't try to fool me with the general's ghost." He lifted a brow. "We both know why Ol' Winky chose tonight to rattle his bones. You thought that little trick would frighten off the manor's prospective buyers, didn't you? Well, the Prescotts will not be so easily frightened, especially when you admit to them that it was all a trick."

She glared at him. "You wouldn't speak that way if you knew of my late husband's easily aroused temper."

"Hmm, you must have kept him close to apoplexy at all times."

She made a face. "I've lost the key to his chamber."

"Very well, I'll break the door down."

Nick tested the wood panel with his fingertips. Solid mahogany. He winced inwardly at the thought of what damage that wood could do to his shoulder.

By the startled expression on her face, he guessed she didn't know that anything less than a battering ram wouldn't nick the wood. "Of course, if I break down the door, there'll be nothing to save you if I should sleepwalk tonight." He gave her a lazy smile.

"Wait!"

Nick watched her dash to the mantel and stick her hand inside an urn. He saw Becky's face appear in the looking glass above the fireplace, her mouth pursed into earnest concern. If he thought about it for very long, he'd feel ashamed of himself for acting like a bully. But she needed to learn who was master, and the lesson was long overdue.

"Here," she said, crossing the room to him. "When you've opened the door, I'd like the key back. You'll find the chamber has another entrance that leads to the hall."

"Thank you, Mistress Becky." He gave her an elegant bow.

She aped a face at him.

Chuckling, he placed the key in the latch. With a half turn, the lock clicked open. He glanced over his shoulder and tossed the key to her. She caught it in midair.

"And may I have the use of one of my own candlesticks?"

"Of course."

He thought he saw her mouth twitch when she placed the lit taper into the ceramic holder and gave it to him.

"Good night," he said, before he opened the doors. If she answered, it was so soft he didn't hear.

The doors creaked open. Nick stepped inside the cavernous room. The faint candlelight barely brightened the darkness. Lifting the taper higher, he stared at the four bare walls broken only by two windows. Bootsteps thundered as he tromped across the bare floor to the door on the other side of the room. It opened easily, but it led to the main hallway. "Damn!" He slammed it shut. Lifting the candle higher, he noticed another door, smaller— what he guessed might be the dressing room.

He threw it open. Mold and dust from past generations rushed back at him. Choking and sputtering, Nick slammed the door.

Where were the beds, the nightstands, the paintings? Damn, but there wasn't even a table fit to hold the candlestick.

Nick tore back to the double doors that separated him from wringing Becky's neck. He grabbed hold of the knobs, but the mahogany remained steadfast. Damn, she'd locked them.

He overcame the urge to kick the door. Instead, with what remained of his dignity, Nick strode back through Ol' Winky's chamber to the hall. Frustrated as he was, it would bode no good to break into Becky's bedchamber.

Tomorrow was another day. Tomorrow, he'd show her who was the master of Thornwood Hall. Tomorrow, he'd see respect in her eyes when she looked at him. Tomorrow.

But now, he needed to find a place to lay his weary body and rest his throbbing leg. The cot in Baby Harry's chamber.

A few minutes later, he paused at the oriel window in the hall. The eastern sky was beginning to flush with a tinge of rose. Below, on a fence post inside the yard, stood a black rooster. It stretched its neck toward the horizon. The bird's red comb and wattle shook as it crowed, "Cock o' doodle doo."

* * *

Becky heard the rooster's song to the dawn as she lay, listening for Nick's bootsteps to trudge back along the hall. She remained waiting, praying he wouldn't come back.

No, he wouldn't be back. He was much too proud to break the door down. A tremor coursed over her. If he'd wanted to ravish her, he'd had the perfect opportunity, earlier. No, he wanted to show her he was the master, yet even if he demanded her to obey, he'd not force himself on her. For some strange reason, she knew she could trust him.

But she couldn't trust him not to report her crimes to the king, if he found out. *When* he found out, was more likely.

Becky tucked her legs under her, deciding what to do next. She must find out how the Willoughbys' guests reacted to Ol' Winky's ghost. Guilt weighed her down as she thought about her deception, but she brushed it aside. Too much was at stake to think of that now.

Already, Nick had used Willoughby's help to find a prospective buyer. She chewed her lip. If she had suffered any compunction before, all trace of guilt from inventing Ol' Winky's ghost was gone. She had to use every trick she could think of to stop Sinclair from selling the manor. Then, when he realized it was useless to try to sell a haunted estate, he'd be well back to sea and she could manage the property for him. That is, once she convinced him that she was the most astute overseer, even though she was a woman.

She smiled as she thought of the challenge. First, she'd change clothes, then visit Hazel. On the way, she'd see Molly and her lazy son. Nelda's babe was due soon, and Becky refused to permit that lazy oaf, Ben Twaddle, to pretend illness from keeping him from work any longer than necessary.

First things first. She'd deal with Sinclair when she had to. He certainly wasn't going anywhere. But now, she had work to do, and she'd start by spreading more tales of Ol' Winky's ghost.

An hour later, Becky had finished her ablutions and dressed in the best morning gown that she owned, the blossom pink dimity. After checking her reflection in the mirror, she swirled her hair in a roll atop her head, then placed the matching bonnet over her hair. Despite the fact that the pink gown matched her rosy cheeks, she remembered that Nick had said the color flattered her. As if she cared what he thought!

She tiptoed down the creaky stairs. The scullery maids' chatter along with the smell of baking bread floated up the stairway to greet her. She paused in front of the hall stand and grabbed her sword and belt. Beside it hung Sinclair's polished saber. A jolt of apprehension tightened within her. Aye, she could pretend he wasn't the most pressing problem, but truth be, he *was* the only problem. With a sniff, she rushed outside.

Nick stood at the buttery door and watched Becky hike her skirts and run through the tall, dew-covered grass toward the horse barn. So she'd decided against sleep, too? What urgency prompted her going out this early? He scratched his day's growth of beard as his gaze followed her along the path to the stable.

More than likely, she was off to check on her latest devilry. Ol' Winky's ghost, he mused. And which of her lackeys had she dressed in the general's uniform? He grinned at her audacity and hope that such a ruse might work. Damn, he admired her pluck. Too bad her hard work would come to naught.

Nick reached the horse barn in time to see Becky place her foot in the stirrup of the sorrel mare she always rode. "Where are you off to so early, mistress?"

Her violet eyes widened in surprise. "You?"

"Were you expecting Ol' Winky's ghost?" He grinned at the sharp look she gave him. His gaze drifted over the mare. "Handsome animal. Do you plan to buy her?"

Becky's brows flew together. "Whatever do you mean?"

"The mare. Have you forgotten? Today I become the legal owner of Thornwood Hall, and all of its property, or what little there's left, I might add." He grabbed the horse's bridle. "Which is what I'd like to talk to you about. Now!"

"May I remind you, sir, that *I'm* not part of your property." She glared at him. "I have a full day's appointments ahead of me, so if you don't mind—" she pulled on the rein "—I must be off."

He held the horse's bridle firmly in his hand. "Of course, dear lady. But you'll accomplish your errands on foot." He smiled lazily. "Dismount from my property, or I'll remove you myself."

Becky's cheeks flushed like pink roses and her delicate mouth opened in astonishment. "Surely you jest."

"I'm a reasonable man. I'll give you to the count of three to dismount." He glanced up at her stunned expression.

"One." He waited for some sign that she prepared to dismount. "Two." Her eyes darted from him to the barn door. Her lips pressed into an obstinate line. He knew she was planning to charge past him and make a break through the door. When he said the word *three*, he grabbed her by the waist and pulled her off the saddle into his embrace.

The mare whinnied. Becky shrieked. He knew she'd have kicked him if she hadn't feared striking the horse. He tightened his fingers around her wrists and pulled her arms to her side.

Becky's breath came in quick bursts as she struggled, grappling for control as though her life depended on it. He pulled her to him. Her wide eyes sparkled with outrage, but her body betrayed the message in those eyes. She knew she couldn't fight him physically, yet he saw no fear in her eyes.

Their gazes fixed with each other's, and for a brief span of time, the world faded around him, leaving only the two of them. He felt drawn to those innocent eyes, too naive to know how to hide the sensual desire he saw in their depths. He thought of the solid mahogany locked doors between her bedchamber and that of her late husband's. Had she ever experienced what was between a man and a woman? He thought not.

That would explain her coltish jitters when he drew her out into the moonlit garden more than a week ago. Perhaps she felt this thing between them then, as he did.

She lowered her gaze. Thick fans of black lashes shaded those incredible eyes, the changing color reminding him of dusk when the blue of the summer sky whispers its surrender to the violet night. God, he felt his soul being entangled by the unknowing spell this woman cast over him.

She shivered, and he was all too aware of her softly curved body trembling against him, and his reaction to her. Her breasts rose and fell against his open shirt, and he knew if he didn't release her soon, he'd never be able to.

She lifted her head, exposing the pulse beating at the delicate hollow of her throat. "When you look at me like that, I—I..." Her quavering voice was low and husky.

He recognized the longing in her gaze, and he knew she felt it, too. For a brief moment, he thought that maybe she wanted him as he wanted her. He lifted his hand, grazing her warm cheeks with his callused fingers. Bending his head, he cupped her chin and gazed deeply into her eyes. *Aye, I don't want to feel the way you make me feel. Damn, I want none of this!*

But his body betrayed his common sense. "I want you," he whispered as he moved against her. She gasped, yet she didn't turn away. Maybe she was stilled by the abrupt desire in his voice. Or maybe she didn't know what to do.

He pushed back the warning from his mind. "Slip your hand around my neck," he said hoarsely into her hair.

Becky gazed up into his face, and for a moment, he thought she'd refuse. But when her trembling hand slid to his shoulder, then to his collar, he thought his heart would burst.

He pulled her gently to face him, then lowered his mouth to within a hairbreadth of her lips. Fighting temptation, he waited for a sign from her as his heart hammered against her softness.

As though she finally understood, she pulled his head toward her slightly parted lips. He felt her eyelashes feather his cheek when her eyes closed. She kissed him with such openness and incredible sweetness that he felt imprisoned by the innocent offering. He groaned while he traced the outline of her lips with his tongue. She repeated the darting dance, and the exquisite sensations that riveted him nearly took his breath away.

Never had he experienced such a wrench of desire from such unpracticed sensuality. Instead of the designed lovemaking he'd experienced from the women he'd bedded, nothing had prepared him for his reaction as Becky unwittingly fed his hunger with her innocent awakening to him.

Afraid to startle her, he suppressed the urge to plunge his tongue into her mouth. Her hands pressed against his shoulders, their gentle pressure branding him beneath the fabric separating her exquisite touch.

Becky's tongue stroked his mouth, joining his. She

eased her hips against him as the primitive rhythm built between them.

"I—I don't know what you want of me," she whispered, her warm breath feathering his face. She pressed her cheek against his palm in a gesture of sweet vulnerability. He was reminded of a pink rose unfurling in his hand.

"Becky, I—I..." Words failed him as he buried his head in her hair. *Damn, what did he want from her?* He didn't want just a tumble in the hay. He could find that with a willing maid at the Seven Swans. No, he wanted more from Becky, but what?

He knew what she needed. She deserved a husband, who'd remain by her side, overseeing the harvests, repairing the estate she loved with such passion. She needed her own babies to care for, and a man who'd be there for their child's first steps.

He could never be that man. He came from a different world, nourished a different dream. She was land, he was sea.

Her lips found his again, and he took her mouth with such fierceness, she stumbled back, her eyes wide with surprise.

"I—I shouldn't have," he muttered hoarsely. "You don't know what your touch does to me," he added, hoping to erase the bewilderment from her face.

Anguish strained her features, as reasoning returned. She stepped back as though she thought to strike him.

He almost hoped she would. He deserved it. Glancing away to the open barn door, Nick took in the morning sunlight spreading across the fields. He gazed back toward her. "Let me help you back on the mare. You said you had errands to do."

She jerked away from his touch. "I've changed my mind." She grabbed her bonnet from the hay-strewn floor and marched out the door, her back ramrod straight.

He rubbed his unshaved chin, and thought about the throbbing effect she had left on him. He shook his head. Damn, but she still held the control, he thought with a wry smile.

He strode to the last stall where his horse stood. "Come, Rex. I think we both need a good run. Let's ride out and have a talk with the crofters."

Chapter Nine

Nick squeezed the knotted muscles behind his neck and watched his horse drink from the river. Resting beneath the shady umbrella of oak that stood along the bank, Nick wondered if Becky came to the river to find comfort from the sultry August heat.

The sun baked the lush green earth without mercy. If he were at sea, the wind would give comfort from such swelter. But water always provided him comfort from most everything.

If he were at sea, he'd be away from the violet-eyed minx, who drove him to such distraction. She taunted him by her very presence. And she was totally unaware of him, *in that sense*, except to show how much she despised him.

He picked up a rock and hurled it across the great span of river, watching the stone disappear between the crotch of a tree. If only his sense were as good as his aim. But when she was near, he wanted to feel the ebony silk of her hair between his fingers, to hear the music in her voice when she said his name. How he wanted to taste those sweet lips again, smell the scent of pink gillyflowers on her skin.

Damn. What good had it done to leave her when all he did was think of her?

Without another thought, he removed his shirt and untied his breeches. No one was about on this remote stretch of land. He might as well enjoy the one pleasure on the estate—the river. Besides, the cold water would do him good, too, he thought wryly. It had been over an hour since he'd last seen Becky, but his body still responded as though it had only been minutes ago.

Moments later, Nick was undressed. Naked, enjoying the simple freedom, he pushed the discarded garments in a pile with his foot and dived into the river. He swam, each thrust of his arms powering him farther along the stream amid a rush of bubbles. The water wrapped his skin like cool silk. He lifted his head above water, shaking the hair from his eyes.

How he wished Becky were with him now. He could almost imagine the glistening droplets streaming from her black hair down her naked back as she dipped and darted in the water. Her creamy shoulders, bathed in sunlight, would break the silver surface. He could imagine her smile, eyes sparkling with invitation, like an ancient siren luring sailors to their destruction. Before she would disappear, she'd rise just enough to show the swell of her breasts, then she'd dip beneath the bubbles as the alluring vision faded from his mind.

Damn, he needed a woman, that was the simple truth of it. Yet the women at the Seven Swans didn't hold an appeal—not after meeting... He forced the thought from his mind. Becky was becoming a fever in his brain, and he didn't know how to stop it.

Ducks quacked along the bend. A fish jumped. If he stretched his imagination, the sound of lapping water against the shore might remind him of sea waves slapping the ship's hull on a quiet morn. He wriggled his toes with a boyish sense of freedom. The sun beat down on his neck and shoulders, warm and soothing, when only minutes before, he had felt blistered and out of sorts.

The river. Water had always calmed him, even as a child. He floated on his back, the wind ruffling the hair on his body.

What simple luxury. He spread his arms wide, then dipped beneath the surface again. The sun shimmered in wavy patches along the bottom. He closed his eyes as he swam, forcing visions of the lovely Becky Forester from his thoughts.

Water. Glorious water.

Becky's hands arched across her brows as her gaze strained against the sun. Aye, it was Sinclair's huge stallion grazing along the shore. But where was he?

Her gaze drifted along the grassy riverbank. A westerly breeze tossed the leafy branches along the forest edge in playful mirrored patterns along the river's surface. But Sinclair was nowhere in sight.

She gently touched her heels to the mare's sides, then rode along the ridge that overlooked the river. As she urged the horse closer, her view was obstructed by the thick stand of trees the crofters called Fair Oaks. Slipping from her mare, Becky crept to the spot where Sinclair's horse grazed.

In the far bend of the river, she spied Sinclair. He was swimming, and from what she could see of him—which was all of him—he was naked as a... Her hand flew to her mouth.

She gulped. Naked as a babe didn't seem appropriate. This naked man was a *man*. No mistaking that.

She couldn't remove her gaze. Never had she seen a man completely naked before. Of course, she'd seen the general undressed on the day he died, when she'd helped the women lay him out in his finest Sabbath clothing for his meeting with the Almighty. But his body had looked nothing like...

She continued to stare. Nick's skin was sun-bronzed; most likely he'd swum like this many times before. Muscles along his forearms, back and legs were well formed from lifting and heaving. A mat of black curly hair covered his legs. His arms, limned with fine black hair, brought back the memory of when he'd held her.

A warm, fluttery feeling deepened inside her. How she'd wanted to kiss him. Yearned with it as she'd never known before.

If only she'd brought the telescope with her. The thought brought an embarrassed chuckle. Dear God, what was she thinking? She didn't even know herself anymore.

He might come out of the water at any moment. She must leave before he saw her. Just then, Nick slipped to his left side. Mesmerized, she watched his sun-browned back and hips skim along the water, his muscular legs kicking while his arms pulled himself along. She gasped. What a beautiful man.

Powerful, yet graceful. His hand brushed back his wet hair, revealing the thick sideburns curving low on his firm jaw.

Becky forced her glance away. Stepping carefully from view, she feared a sudden movement might alert him to her trespass. Her arms and legs trembled when she scrambled back on the path and mounted her horse. The leather saddle, warmed with the sun, felt hot through her skirts as she dug her heels into her mare's sides and made her escape.

Across the fields Becky rode, the wind whipping her hair about her face in a tingling way she'd never felt before. The fragrance of blossoms almost overpowered her senses. It was as if she'd never before inhaled their magic. The mare's hooves beneath her drummed a syncopated rhythm she'd never before heard.

Thornwood Hall, familiar yet strange, loomed ahead. Somehow, Becky felt certain her world would never again be as it had before Sir Nicholas Sinclair came into her life.

How long Nick swam, he didn't know, but when he finally felt refreshingly exhausted, he lifted himself onto the bank, the warm wind bracing against his wet skin. From behind a tall copse of alders, a covey of ducks burst into the sky, the explosion of rustling wings breaking the still morning. Nick dressed hurriedly, wondering what had frightened the birds. Almost immediately, he heard a resounding whacking noise. After pulling on his boots, he carefully made his way toward the sound.

Barely reaching the bend in the river, he saw Peter striking the boat's hull with an oar. Between each angry thrust, the boy shoved his long dark hair from his face. The sharp pounding riveted the summer stillness, each crack hammering the memory of Peter's dark scowl when he'd called Nick a lying bastard.

For an instant, Nick actually considered leaving before the boy saw him. It would be so much easier if he would. But no good came from avoiding the lad. Besides, for his sake, Nick needed to at least try to explain why it had been necessary to hide his real identity.

Nick braced himself for the rebuff that was sure to follow. "Peter," Nick called out. "Put down that oar!"

Peter froze, then straightened his shoulders. "Get away from me!" Red angry spots of color darkened his cheeks. He lifted the oar and with all his might, brought it down on the side of the boat. The oar snapped in two.

"Give me that," Nick yelled, trying to wrest what remained of the pole from the boy's grip.

Peter swung around, his fingers wrapped so tightly his knuckles were white. The lad tried to kick, but Nick evaded each attempt. Finally, Nick yanked the oar from the boy's fists.

"I hate you!" Peter cried. Balling his fists, he pounded Nick's chest like a drum.

Nick spread his legs, his feet firmly in place as the boy hammered away his frustrations.

"I thought you were my friend," Peter yelled finally, fighting back tears. He fought with everything in his young body.

Nick ignored the painful blows. In a way, he had them coming. But nothing could fortify himself from Peter's pain and his own frustration. "Go ahead, lad. Take your vexation out on me, not the boat. I'm the one you're angry with."

"You made a fool out of me. My whole family." Peter's hair hung limply around his face. "I hate you. I hate you," he repeated, fury blazing in his brown eyes. "You're no hero. Why couldn't you've died at sea, you bastard?"

A charge of regret washed through Nick. "I know, lad," he whispered. "Don't think I haven't wished that, too."

Peter paused, arching back. Uncertain, he swayed slightly, as though exhausted. Nick held a hand on the lad's shoulder, looking at him, man to man.

"Now that some of the fire has left you, Peter, let's talk this over."

The boy wiped his sleeve across his face. "I ain't got nothin' to talk to you about," he snapped back.

Nick took a deep breath. His duplicity as Ben Twaddle was as much of a deception as Ol' Winky's ghost. Damn, why did he get involved with these people? He glanced back at the young boy whose spirit reminded him so much of Becky's. Stubbornness and foolish pride must be a family trait.

Peter stared, his chin high with the brave show of courage.

"I'm sorry, Peter, that I let you think I was Ben Twaddle. What I thought was best at the time, I see now was a mistake."

The brown eyes glared defiantly. "I knew who you were all the time." Peter sniffed, then rubbed his nose with his fist.

Nick met the boy's gaze. "I'm sorry."

"I don't care if you're sorry." The lad tossed out the words like stones aimed at an assailant. "You're still a bastard—"

"Haven't you ever done something that you were sorry for? Or you wanted to take back and do differently?"

Peter remained silent, his face turned away.

In the lengthening silence, Nick watched Peter's thin brows twist with unresolved contempt. His smooth skin drew back into a frown—skin that had never felt a razor's nick when shaving.

Peter was too young to understand regret and he was as blind to logic as Becky. Nick could talk all day and neither of them would understand if they didn't want to.

"Saying I'm sorry is all I can do, Peter. I can't make you believe me." Nick turned and followed the path along the shore. Only when he was almost out of sight did Peter glance up to see Nick trample through the high grass around the bend in the river.

A short while later, Becky slid from her horse and strode toward her sister Betty's headstone. She dropped the clump of daisies beside the marker and blinked back the threat of tears.

"Oh, Betty. I miss you so." Her fingers toyed with the white petals while a flood of memories rushed over her. Shared laughter, uncontrolled giggles, whispered secrets.

"How beautiful you were on your wedding day, Betty. I remember when you told me that someday, I'd fall in love and then I'd know what true happiness was. If only you were here, now... I so need to talk to you."

Becky gazed at the cold stone, not feeling any of her usual peace and sense of connection with her family.

She felt dizzy, almost flighty. She couldn't keep her mind from Nick and the invading image of his magnificent nakedness, and how it made her feel. "Oh Betty, is this what you meant when you told me that I was too young to know this thing between men and women? I have no one to tell me," she whispered, "and I so want to understand."

Becky closed her eyes, willing her sister's image to mind, but her only vision was of the gleaming, sun-bronzed figure of Nick—powerful, proud and masculine—swimming in the water like a proud male swan.

Somehow, she knew this yearning was what Betty had meant. She glanced back at her sister's grave and smiled. For the moment, she felt as though Betty had shared another secret with her, and the thought comforted her.

The leaves of the trees rustled and Becky felt the familiar closeness once again. Glancing in her lap, Becky noticed with surprise that she'd plucked all of the petals from the remaining daisies. She got to her feet, shaking her skirts, the white petals swirling on the summer breeze.

Less than an hour later, Becky and Aphra knelt upon the striped rag carpet—Mum's rug—as the family affectionately called the handsome keepsake their mother, as a young girl, had woven for her marriage. As long as Becky could remember, the rug had lain beside their parents' bed in their croft. Such happy times when she and her sisters had gathered, giggling and confiding hopes and secrets. Always, Mum had been there.

Although Aphra hadn't uttered a word since their parents' death, Becky knew that having Mum's rug beside Aphra's bed would provide a special comfort. Becky's throat tightened with memories. She drew the brush through Aphra's mane, watching the sun-burnished highlights sparkle through the long curls. Aphra's locks were so like their eldest sister, Betty's hair—thick, lustrous and vibrant.

So many memories. Like treasured keepsakes, they lingered at the corners of her mind, waiting to spring, whenever she least expected them. Becky pressed her lips together, counting the even brush strokes. But try as she might, she couldn't get rid of the thoughts of Nick's hands caressing her, or the taste of his kisses when she responded so boldly.

She squeezed her eyes shut.

Aphra tugged on her sleeve. Becky opened her eyes and met Aphra's huge brown eyes, so like Peter's and their mother's.

Becky hugged her, then kissed the top of her shiny head.

"You've been patient long enough, dear Aphra." She let her go. "Run along and don't forget to take your doll with you."

Aphra grabbed the doll and hugged it under her arm. With a hasty curtsy, she threw open the door and almost ran into Sally.

"Tush, child!" Sally said, catching her breath as she came inside. "That child never walks if she can run."

Becky's smile was bittersweet. "She's growing up so quickly, Sally. How I wish…" She swallowed back the thought and peered at her cousin. "Did you want something?"

Sally's face straightened. "Aye. Sinclair has called everyone into the Great Hall. He ordered me to come and get you."

"He's meeting everyone in the Great Hall?" Becky asked, staring in disbelief. The Great Hall was the largest chamber in the manor, and for that reason, Becky had barricaded it from use, along with most of the third floor. No grand occasion warranted the expense to heat the rooms. Besides, she'd sold off the tapestries, paintings and furnishings for a tidy profit. "Are you certain Sinclair said the Great Hall?"

Sally nodded. "There's no mistake. Besides, he made quite a fuss when he said it." Her fingers played nervously at the lace at her collar. "Mercy! How he ranted on about the lack of furnishings. Not even a table and stool, he said."

Becky's mouth twitched. "If it's tables and stools the master wants, why not hold his lecture in the scullery?"

Sally frowned. "Becky, I'm worried. Sinclair is in a terrible mood. I'm afraid he may throw us all out."

Becky put her arm around her cousin. "Let's just see what the master has to say, first." She forced a grin. "Come, Sally. Let's not keep the lord and master waiting."

Chapter Ten

A few minutes later, when Becky and Sally entered the Great Hall, a hush fell among the family and friends gathered there, as though they had been waiting for them. All eyes were upon Becky as she glanced about the room. The household staff was present, at least forty men and women who were as dear to her as family. She knew from their expressions that they hoped she could provide some miracle. She gave them a confident smile, then took her place beside Sally and Keane in the back of the room. Keane gave her a sharp glance, his narrow face unreadable.

Sinclair glanced up from his place at the front of the chamber, his eyes on her. Becky met his gaze directly; she'd be damned if she'd show him any sign of weakness. A hint of a smile tugged at his mouth. It was as though he expected as much.

Sinclair began his speech, the forceful words echoing within the immense hall. "... Responsibility will provide the needed shape and substance..."

Responsibility? she mused. *Already, he'd managed to find a prospective buyer, a man named Prescott, who'd take the responsibility of Thornwood Hall from his hands. Who was Sinclair fooling?*

"... Discipline the servants to run a tight ship..."

Does Sinclair believe that discipline can gain productivity over labor done from sheer love of the land?

"... Improve the herds and flocks..."

What does a seafaring man know of beasts and fowl?

"... Repair the second- and third-floor chambers..."

Pox and calamity! How will he pay for fixing the upper chambers? Does Sinclair think he can harvest coin from the trees like apples?

"... I'll take responsibility to find you homes..."

Becky's breath caught in her throat. His gaze met hers, but the gray eyes gave no hint of his plan for her.

"I've asked Willoughby to help me find suitable employment for every able body who's willing to work," Nick replied.

"Suitable?" Becky called out. "Suitable to whom?"

The muscle twitched above Nick's temple. "Presently, Willoughby is preparing a list of townfolks who've offered to help," Sinclair went on, ignoring her.

Becky made her way through the crowd to stand a few feet from him. "And what is to become of those who are too young or too old to find suitable arrangements, Sir Nicholas?"

Nick swallowed. "I'll speak to you privately about your special needs, Mistress Becky."

Sinclair turned back to the others. "I want everyone to be assured that no one will be thrown out into paupers' row."

"And how soon will these changes take place?" Becky asked. Several other voices repeated her question.

"As soon as homes and positions are made available, which may be as early as this week."

A low murmur circled the room.

"I'll be speaking privately to each of you in the days to come, but for now, I wanted to lift your burden of worry." Sinclair stood with his hands behind his back, his back ramrod stiff. "I'm aware of the rumor that states I'm only interested in selling the property." His mouth twitched. "But my first concern is improving the manor's production."

Becky's eyes narrowed. *Aye, so he'll get a better price.* But she kept the thought to herself.

"I'll begin with improving the buildings." He avoided Becky's direction. "For a start, I noticed the brew house was in disrepair. Keane, gather a crew tomorrow to make bricks. By fall, we'll have finished the new building, then we'll put good use to the rich harvest of hops growing in the west lot. We'll produce our own beer, then sell whatever surplus you don't drink."

Loud cheers echoed within the room. Becky glared at the men. In the past, she'd bartered the hops in return for the small ration of brew she allowed the crofters to drink. But if Sinclair relished playing his role of lord of the bounty, there wasn't much she could do about it. But she didn't have to stay around to watch the spectacle.

Becky turned to slip from the room, but Nick noticed her. "Mistress Becky, I'll speak privately to you now." He dismissed the crowd, who broke into excited chattering among themselves.

She waited solemnly by the door as the familiar faces of friends and family passed her as they rushed out.

A few moments later, Becky was alone with him. She felt dwarfed by the room and the man.

Wait until you discover how much it will cost to heat those floors of rooms, she wanted to say. But why should she care? She wouldn't be living here.

"I wanted you to know," he began carefully, "that I've asked Willoughby to find you a proper family. One who will view it as good fortune to employ you and take in your siblings."

Becky wondered if he had rehearsed that little speech. No, she decided, Sir Nicholas spoke as smooth as honey.

He'd wielded vast experience handling his shipboard crews, no doubt. For a brief moment, she could almost visualize Sinclair aboard ship in a stormy sea, his hand clasped on the rail, his men's faces transfixed, waiting for their captain's next order.

She blinked away the image. "I've already decided what I'd like to do...."

Sinclair spread his feet, his arms resting casually behind him. "And what would that be?"

Becky stood as tall as she could. "I'd hoped you'd hire me as your new estate overseer." His eyebrows rose in surprise.

"I've years of experience observing Keane, and I'm quite certain I can be of better service to you than he has been managing Thornwood Hall."

"Your industry is admirable, mistress, but your argument is weak. Anyone could manage the estate better than Keane, wouldn't you agree?"

"But you haven't heard my offer—"

"There's no need." He gave her a silencing look.

Frustration warred within her. Becky glared at him, her mouth a tight line.

"You and your family may remain here until a suitable home is found for you," Nick said gently. "Enjoy my hospitality and—"

"Hospitality?" Becky interrupted, her words sharp. "We'll work for our keep, Sir Nicholas. I'll not be beholden to anyone for anything."

Nick shrugged. "As you wish." He strode to the door, then glanced back at her. "Tomorrow morning, I'd like you to ride with me when I meet the crofters. I wish to reassure them, as well."

"Most of the crofters are old and not well. They've toiled from sunup to sundown, every day of their lives. I doubt if a newly built brew house will reassure them of a tidy future."

She turned to leave, then whirled around to face him. "I wish you'd allow me to present my offer, Sir Nicholas. If I could manage Thornwood Hall for you, I could also find you a buyer. Then you could leave for sea immediately."

Nick's gray eyes glittered with something she didn't quite understand. She heard his deep, intake of breath as he silently watched her. The silence between them was more clamorous to her state of mind than the roar of a cannon. Finally, he said, "I'll keep it in mind."

She knew he only said that to be rid of her. But she wasn't through yet. As long as she had a breath in her body, she'd oppose his every effort to wrench her from the estate.

Becky bolted from the room, her footfalls clattering along the long empty hall.

The next morning, Nick was leaning against the horse stall, talking with Peter, when Becky entered the stable. She noticed the easy exchange between her brother and Sinclair. Becky felt relieved to see that Peter had managed to make peace with Sinclair, and knowing her brother's stubborn streak, she knew Sinclair had performed a near miracle.

"Good morning," she said cheerily to no one in particular, but her attention was focused on Nick when she marched toward her mare, saddled and waiting.

"And a fine morning it is," Nick replied easily.

Yesterday—the last time she'd saddled her mare—Nick had kissed her. She wondered if Nick remembered that, too. His lazy smile as he watched her lead the animal past him on the way out toward the paddock told her he had. She averted her gaze, and with Peter's assistance, she mounted quickly.

The mare broke into a lively canter around the paddock while she waited for Nick to mount his stallion. Before long, they were riding along the hedgerow path toward the crofters' land.

They rode side by side, racing across the fields, only to slow down when they came to the stream.

Becky urged her mare carefully through the water, her thoughts on the upcoming meeting. Nick had promised to be fair, but that wasn't what was worrying her. She glanced at the man who so drove her to distraction. What if the crofters—her poor relatives—were taken in by his honey-coated promises? Didn't Sally say only this morning that the kitchen maids were all aflutter over the handsome new owner?

She bit her lip. But the crofters were loyal. Not only were most of them related by blood, but they were her friends. Besides, the men wouldn't be so taken in by him. The thought of her unbending great-uncles and male cousins brought a respite to her tense nerves. They'd see through Nick's sweetened words for what they are—a ruse to gain the crofters' labor in order to restore the manor into a more salable estate. Aye, beneath that silken smile lurked a devil whose only interest was his own. And she had best not forget it.

By the time they reached the apple and cherry orchards, Becky felt more confident. Certainly the crofters wouldn't say anything that would give Nick an inkling of Becky's deception with the tax collector. In fact, the mood of these loyal folks might turn ugly if they saw through Nick's scheme. But a word from her, and the crowd wouldn't touch a hair on his head.

More than likely, Nick would enjoy seeing her squirm in fear that one of the crofters might snitch—especially if Nick baited them with the right price. Her gaze drifted over the low rise where Molly Twaddle's stone cottage nestled beside the stream. Her son, Ben, might be so tempted, Becky thought uneasily. But Ben knew nothing of the crofters' aid in return for not paying rents. For now, she was safe.

When Becky and Nick rode to the rail in front of Molly's croft, the old woman stood in the yard, spreading wet laundry to dry among the thornberry branches. Her white-capped head lifted when they dismounted and came toward her.

After Becky made the introductions, Nick took Molly's hand and bowed elegantly.

"Mistress Becky tells me your son had a recent accident," Nick purred. "How sad. Will the lad be abed for long?"

Becky smoldered with irritation. The very idea! Sinclair knew very well that Ben Twaddle was gaining as much sympathy as he could get away with from his latest attempt to get out of work. She turned away in disgust.

Molly cleared her throat, her mouth a firm line.

Becky could hardly keep from chuckling. She exchanged a knowing glance with Nick. Obviously, these people wouldn't talk to him unless she gave her consent.

Nick began again. "Mistress Becky tells me what a fine lad your son is, and I was hoping to offer him a position."

Molly's brows lifted and she glared suspiciously at Becky.

"I remember meeting your lad when I first arrived. Ben impressed me as a man who knew fine horseflesh." Nick waited, assessing Molly's surprise. But she refused to speak.

Nick glanced from Molly to Becky. "When Ben is feeling better, have him report to me. I'd like to offer him the position of gentleman of the horse. He and his family will be provided room and board in the manor house, with a tidy sum for spending."

Molly's jaw dropped. "Me Ben? A gentleman...?" Her blue eyes widened. After a few awkward moments, she spoke. "The doctor says Ben'll be up an' about in a few days, *Your Grace.*" She bobbed a short curtsy.

Becky rolled her eyes. Poor Molly wouldn't know that one calls only a duke *Your Grace.* She shook her head.

"Ben's family...there's Nelda and the babe. An' me, o'course," Molly added excitedly.

Becky glared at Molly. Sinclair was tricking her. Didn't the poor woman understand that? How would Nick pay Ben wages, and where in the manor would they stay? Then she remembered Nick's lecture this morning. Of course! He was restoring the second and third floors to move the crofters there in exchange for their cooperation.

"If Nelda wishes," Nick said, "she'll be mistress of the nursery. She can have whomever she chooses to help her."

Molly bowed her head and patted her white cap. "Ben and Nelda will be most pleased, Sir Nicholas, but what of me?" She gazed up at him with her watery blue eyes. "I'll be left to the wolves without me son to take care of me."

Becky sighed, folding her arms in front of her. "Your sister Clara and the other crofters will care for you, Molly."

Molly shot her a sharp glance, then gazed up at Nick.

He took her gnarled hand again. "I was hoping you'd accept my offer of a special position, Mistress Molly. You may live at the manor close to your grandchild, and be taken care of in your old age. Besides, you'll be doing me a very special favor."

Becky tapped her foot, waiting.

"You'll be known as Molly about the house. Your position will be equal to the clerk of the cheque." Nick smiled at Molly's beaming face.

"Clerk of the cheque?" Becky stared incredulously at

him. "Ah, Sir Nicholas, may I have a private word with you?"

"Later, mistress. First I'll hear what Molly has to say."

Molly's jaw dropped open. "I'd be delighted, Your Grace."

Becky cleared her throat, but Molly refused to look at her.

"Well, dear lady, if there's anything you need before you move, let me know." Nick's words sounded almost sincere. "When you're ready, I'll see to it that you'll be comfortably situated in your new home." He patted Molly's hand. "I must be off to speak to the others. I only wanted to introduce myself. I'm certain you've heard the gossip about the monster who's been awarded Thornwood Hall." He ignored Becky's groan. "I hope, dear lady, that I've restored some peace to your mind."

"Thankee, Your Grace." Molly dropped into a curtsy as though she had an audience with the king.

"I'll stop in to see you later," Becky said, putting on her riding gloves. It was obvious Molly had no sense when it came to men. Molly's older sister, Clara, wasn't as gullible. She could hardly wait for Clara to mince Nick's sweet words and spoon them back to him laced with vinegar.

Becky stepped outside into the sunlight when she heard sheep bleating, amid the deep grumbles from the small crowd of men and animals coming toward them. A skitter of apprehension shot through her when she realized these men might turn on Nick when they realized who he was. She'd forgotten that the shepherds would bring their herds to drink along the river on sweltering mornings as today.

Nick was already striding toward the throng. She lifted her skirts and dashed after him. By the time she reached the crowd, Nick was introducing himself and shaking hands with the men.

She recognized her great-great-uncle, several distant cousins and two of her father's brothers among the shepherds.

"A handsome herd," Nick remarked to no one in particular. "You must have reaped a handsome profit from the shearing this spring," he stated confidently.

No one uttered a word. The cautious faces turned toward Becky. She felt her face flush when Nick stared at her.

"It was a better year than most," she offered, careful not to give herself away. If she hoped to persuade Nick that she would be a responsible overseer, she couldn't give him proof that the herds weren't productive. Yet she dared not reveal more profit than the ledgers showed. "Wouldn't you say so, Uncle Fred?" She directed the question to her great-great-uncle.

Fred scratched his white whiskers and leaned on his staff. "Aye, better 'n most."

"And the new crop of lambkins was numerous?" Nick asked, smiling lazily, seeming to be enjoying himself.

Again, the shepherds waited for Becky to answer.

"Aye, better than most," she said, nodding her head.

This time, the men nodded. "Aye, better 'n most," they repeated in unison.

"Good show, lads." Nick brushed his hat brim in salute. "If you have problems or need anything, come and we'll deal with them together." He dug into his pocket to produce a handful of coins. "Have a dram or two at the Seven Swans. I believe in rewarding good men for their good deeds."

The shepherds circled around him, smiling and friendly as they took the coins from Nick's extended palm. "We'll toast yer fine health," someone said. Several of the men thanked him more than once. Fred chewed on the coin's edge with the few teeth he had left, but it was obvious that all of the men had been as easily swayed as Molly had been.

By the time Becky and Nick had returned to their horses, she was so frustrated she could hardly speak. When they mounted and rode out beyond earshot, she turned to him.

"Is this what you're planning to do? Flatter the women and buy drinks for the men? You must think they're foolish peasants who can't see through such trickery."

Nick held her gaze. "Is it trickery to appreciate the hard work of the crofters, Mistress Becky?" He lifted a dark brow. "I'd think it would please you greatly that I care about these people you so love."

"Ha! You only want their cooperation so they'll not fuss when you throw me out and bring in the new owner."

"That's not true. And I've told you before that neither you nor any of your family will be thrown out. I've given you my word."

"What is to become of me? Are you going to allow me to be your overseer, or am I to have one of your fancy titles...." She paused. "Maybe, Lady of the Roasting Pit...or Lady of the Needles and Pins." She glared at him.

"I'll deal with one matter at a time. But I can assure you, mistress, you won't be offered a position at Thornwood Hall."

Her stomach tightened. *But that was exactly what she had wanted—to be the manor's overseer.* She swallowed. If only she'd hold her tongue when her temper threatened to boil over.

She took a calming breath. "Tell me honestly, you care not a bean for Thornwood Hall. You only care about improving the manor so you'll gain a higher profit when you sell it."

"And what about you, mistress? Tell me honestly that it's not the money that you're skimming from the profits that you truly care about."

"You can't prove that."

"Not yet, dear Becky, but I soon will." He smiled, but it did nothing to warm the challenge in his gray eyes. "Too bad you can't be made to see that perhaps we both might gain from this unfortunate circumstance the king has put us in."

"What do you mean?"

"It's quite simple. I want to go to sea as soon as my ship is built. You want me gone. But until I offer the king a reason for the estate's past failures, I must remain here."

He leaned against the tree trunk. "If you convince the crofters to work with me, the manor might show a bountiful harvest. That should prove to the king that the estate is profitable enough to pay taxes. Then your crofter friends will be taken care of inside the manor instead of their drafty huts, and I might sell the estate to Willoughby's friend." The gray eyes darkened. "That is, if you admit to the Prescotts that Ol' Winky's ghost is a fraud."

She sniffed a dismissal. "What reason will you give King Charles for the estate's past failures?"

"What do you suggest I tell him?" He smiled, waiting for what he considered her confession.

"One year we had the terrible drought. A raging flood the next. The following year, the herds died mysteriously, and—"

"What happened to all of the manor's furnishings?"

Becky swallowed uneasily and averted her glance. "Robbery."

Nick huffed. "Aye, and I know who did the dirty deed."

"You can't prove it."

"Maybe I won't try, that is, if you don't fight me about the crofters moving to the manor so I can rent their lands to Willoughby, who's offered for it."

Becky shifted uneasily. "I'll think about it."

"I suggest you do, mistress. It's a very handsome offer. Because it won't take much to convince the king that you've been understating the estate's profits. That's a serious offense. Prison, most likely. But the right word from me, and your problems will be over."

Becky refused to look at him. She didn't know if it was a trick, or not. Instead of answering, she kicked her heels into her mare's sides. Only when she'd ridden for several minutes did she realize that Nick hadn't followed her.

Sally glanced up from weeding when Becky ran into the garden. "Mercy, what happened to you?"

"I've just had the most awful time with Sir Nicholas, who else?" Becky lashed out the words, confusion and frustration raging within her. She took a deep breath in a futile effort to control herself.

"What has he done?" Sally came beside her. "Come, sit down on the bench, Becky, here in the shade."

Becky refused to be fussed over. "Sir Nicholas thinks he can bestow fancy titles on the crofters, flattering words and a few coins, and they'll be eating out of his hand."

"Surely the crofters aren't so easily swayed, Becky."

"Oh, but they are. You should have seen Molly!" Becky shook her head. "Sinclair can be very charming when he wants to be."

"Aye, and he's so handsome, too," Sally said dreamily.

"You know what Mother always said," Becky said with a snap.

"Handsome is as handsome does," Sally recited the well-worn phrase, but her expression said otherwise.

"Sally! How can you forget that he's waiting to trick me into letting my guard down so he'll have proof that I understated the manor's profits these past years. He practically threatened me with the crime. Then he said he'd fix it if I'd help sway the crofters to his way of thinking."

Sally's face brightened. "What did you say?"

Becky scowled. "My first concern is to convince him to hire me as overseer. Then when he leaves for sea, we can get about our lives as before."

Sally smiled, the faraway look in her eye. "It's been rather nice having him about."

Becky jumped to her feet. "Sally, haven't you heard a thing I've said?" She instantly regretted her words. She was out of sorts with herself and what she needed to do was to busy herself in work, thus forcing away the image of the man whose silver-gray eyes and crooked smile kept her tottering on edge.

"I'll find Aphra. She can help me give Baby Harry his bath."

"Aphra isn't inside. She's playing with her doll in the woods beside the meadow. I'm surprised you didn't see her."

A thread of worry skittered over Becky. "How long has Aphra been gone?"

Sally tilted her head. "An hour, perhaps. You know how she loses track of time when she plays with her doll. I wouldn't worry about her."

Becky hesitated, then turned back toward the garden gate. "I'll just have a look in on Aphra. As you said, I should have seen her if she was playing along the woods."

"Do you want me to come with you?" Sally's voice held an edge of concern.

"No, dear. I'll ride out myself. When I see her, I'll

come right back. I don't want her to think I'm overly protective.''

Sally smiled. "Aphra's at that age when she wants to have her independence. Remember, Becky?"

Becky only grinned. She dashed to her mare, pulled herself up on the saddle and took off toward the meadow.

Chapter Eleven

Beyond the gentle slope of the hillside, Nick rode in silent appreciation of the beauty of the sun-dappled meadow. Golden oats ripened against the azure sky and the verdant green orchards hung heavy with fruit. No wonder Becky loved this place.

The thought gave him pause. Was he beginning to see the land with fresh interest because of the lovely Becky, or was he merely enjoying the improvement, however slight, of the estate? In the short time he'd been here, he'd insisted upon the hedgerows being straightened, the uneven fields leveled for new cropping and several new gates built. The rush of pride was as gratifying as if his crew had carried out his orders at sea.

Nay, his pleasure was only to leave Thornwood Hall in better condition than he'd found it. There was nothing personal in whatever small pleasure that gave him.

Nick rode along the fence path, lulled by the steady rhythm of his horse's hooves. When he'd reached the knoll near the cemetery, a flash of yellow, darting between the gravestones, caught his eye. He shifted in the saddle, then urged his mount in that direction.

Moments later, he saw Becky's sister, Aphra, dressed in her yellow frock, bending over a fresh mound of earth in the grass. Dismounting, Nick tied the horse to a tree, then hurried as fast as his stiff leg would permit him. As he approached, Aphra lifted her tearstained face to him.

"What's the matter, Aphra? You look as though your heart is breaking?" No sooner had he spoken when he remembered the child couldn't answer his question. Embarrassed at his thoughtlessness, he knelt on one knee, determined to help.

Grass stains soiled her yellow gown and white apron. The fingernails of her dirty hands were torn and bleeding. At her feet was a pile of loose dirt covering a linen-wrapped bundle. Nick realized that she'd buried something in the makeshift grave.

Maybe a pet had died, and she'd buried it in the family cemetery. A wedge of sadness clenched at him. He bent down and met her brown-eyed gaze, wet with tears. "There, there, Aphra. Would you like me to help you dig a proper grave?"

She pouted, as though unsure whether to trust him or not. Nick wondered what Becky had told Aphra about why he was here at Thornwood Hall. Did the little girl think he was an evil monster who was taking away the only home she knew?

"I wish I could say something to make your tears go away, but I know I can't. If you'd like, I'll get a shovel and dig a proper grave. We can get the wagon and you can pick a suitable headstone from Keane's rock pile." He cupped her chin and smiled. "Would you like that, Aphra?"

Her wet face beamed with approval. She nodded quickly.

Nick felt relieved. "Very well, little one. First, let me see what you've buried, then we'll be off."

Her mouth pressed into a brave line as she stepped back. Nick stood, then gently brushed the layer of earth covering the blanket-wrapped bundle. Lifting an end of the spread, he recognized the doll that Aphra always carried. Its wooden head had come loose from its cloth body.

Nick met her stare. Big tears pooled in Aphra's eyes; her chin quivered. A sudden paternal longing to protect this child wrenched inside him. Dear God, grief was hard enough to bear, but for a child, it must be devastating. He remembered that Becky said in the past year since their parents died, the shock had claimed Aphra's ability to speak. And from what the doctor said, there was little hope of recovery.

Words weren't needed between them. Somehow, Nick sensed that this child understood that he, too, knew the meaning of loss. He felt the bond between them.

"Dear Aphra, your doll is broken, but she's not dead. I can attach her head to the body and make her good as new."

Aphra's face darkened with disbelief.

"Aye, truly I can." He bent down beside her. "I'll carve a notch in the neck," he said, pulling his knife from his boot. "Watch while I chisel a new notch around the neck, like so…" Within a few minutes, Nick had cut a groove to secure the cloth body with only a few deft motions of the blade.

"Now, I'll fasten the body to the notch and attach it thus." He strode to his saddlebags and pulled out the wire he remembered using to open Becky's desk, more than a fortnight ago. Brushing back the memory, he twisted the strand around the doll's neck, attaching the torso, then fastened the body securely. When he'd finished, he held the doll up for Aphra's inspection.

Aphra's face beamed, her smile reminding him of Becky's. He felt almost as happy as Aphra. "Come, let me give you a ride back to the manor. Your sister will be wondering where you are."

Aphra reached up and hugged him.

"There, there, my girl." He held her, gazing at the

gaping hole in the grass that she had dug with her bare fingers. A wave of compassion swept him. If only he could repair her deep sadness as easily as he repaired her broken toy. But he knew that nothing could fill the emptiness of grief.

He wiped the tears from her cheeks. Her somber brown eyes, so like Peter's, shone with gratitude.

"I was about your age when my father died. My mother died a few years later, then I went away to sea." He swallowed back the lump in his throat. "And recently, I lost some friends who were as close to me as brothers…"

Aphra studied him, her wide eyes pensive.

"We didn't live in a manor house, but a ship," Nick went on. "At sea, we had chores to do, just as you have at Thornwood Hall. Each man was part of the crew, a family, you might say."

Aphra patted his sun-browned arm with her soft white hand. The gesture brought a tightness to his throat. He drew back stiffly. "Would you like to hear more stories about life at sea?"

She nodded enthusiastically.

"Very well then. I'll tell you some while we ride back to the manor." Aphra cradled her doll under her arm as she took his hand.

I promise you, Aphra, Nick said to himself, *that whatever happens, I'll see to it that you're well provided for.*

From the alders beside the meadow gate, Becky watched with amazement as Nick's strong arms lifted Aphra on the saddle, then her sister leaned comfortably against his chest while they rode off toward the house. In fact, if she hadn't seen her shy, withdrawn little sister respond so willingly to a stranger, Becky wouldn't have believed it.

Relieved to have found Aphra safe with Nick, Becky had thought to interrupt them. But when she saw how

Nick fixed Aphra's beloved doll, and heard the bits and pieces of his comforting words carried on the wind, Becky thought better of it. His tone had been so gentle and caring that Becky was reminded of her own heartfelt talks with her beloved Da.

Regardless of the threat Nick brought to their way of life, Becky knew he had a gentle side. And she was very grateful...for Aphra's sake, anyway.

Becky strode to the shade of the larch tree where her mare waited, her thoughts on the man who drove her to such distraction. Although Nick never spoke of the loss of his crew, she could sense that beneath his ready smile was a man who knew grief. He was a man who kept his pain, mental or physical, to himself.

Although he said nothing, the pain from his wounds must still bother him. Although Nick still limped, the injuries must keep him in constant pain.

She gazed over her shoulder at the tiny fresh mound of soil amid the watch of the silent gray stones. If only Nick's comforting words to Aphra might help heal him, too.

As they neared the house, Aphra sucked her thumb and hugged her doll, leaning contentedly against Nick's chest. He couldn't help but grin, remembering how distrustful Aphra had been when Becky first introduced him. Maybe Aphra's suspicion of strangers was a way of protecting herself from future loss.

A clatter of wheels jolted Nick's attention to the path ahead. Keane drove the horse and rickety wagon directly in front of their path.

Nick reined in, giving the overseer's cart a wide berth. Keane's scowl was the only admission that he'd seen Nick and Aphra. The older man's gaze remained fixed ahead until he brought the rig to a stop in front of the work house, minutes later.

Wanting a few private words with Keane, Nick continued riding toward the garden where Sally was weeding. He dismounted, then carefully helped Aphra to the ground. Her sweet smile was his reward, before skipping off toward Sally, who waited for her.

Nick hurried to the work house where Keane was busy unloading turnips. When he stepped inside, sunlight slanted through the overhead openings where roof thatch had previously blown away. The ignored disrepair nettled Nick.

"I told you last week to get a crew together to lay new roof thatch," Nick said, pointing to the opening above their heads.

Keane muttered under his breath, refusing to look up.

"And the front lawn has grown hip-high. A disgrace," Nick continued. "See that the grass is scythed and raked before tomorrow afternoon when my guests will arrive."

Keane straightened and glared at him. "I'd think ye'd be more impressed with gettin' the crops to market than wastin' men's labors with somethin' that'll grow back in a few days."

"Use the raked grass for fodder," Nick shot back. "But it's bad for morale to let things deteriorate. Neat and tidy is how this estate will be run. It's a matter of pride, Keane."

"Humph!" Keane wiped his face with his sleeve.

"Tomorrow, I've invited Willoughby and his friends, the Prescotts, for dinner. See that the roof is repaired and the lawn scythed."

Keane snorted. "Ye think the Prescotts will buy a haunted manor?"

Nick wondered if Becky had told Keane that the Prescotts were interested in purchasing Thornwood Hall. Now he knew. "Haunted? You don't believe in ghosts, do you, Keane?"

Keane squinted one eye. "Ye wouldn't ask that if ye'd known the ol' general. Everyone feared 'is temper."

Nick remembered that Geer had said Keane believed that General Forester had been his natural father.

Keane's eyes glittered. "The general is churnin' in his grave, knowin' a king's man is sleepin' in his bed."

Nick chuckled. "But I heard that Royalists owned Thornwood Hall before Cromwell confiscated the estate to award it to General Forester. Ol' Winky didn't seem to mind sleeping in a bed formerly used by a king's man?" Nick enjoyed seeing Keane's face redden with unspoken rage.

"We'll see." Keane snarled the words.

Nick folded his arms and leaned against the wagon. "As I recall, you weren't at the Willoughbys' social. Yet you're a staunch believer for a man who didn't see Ol' Winky's ghost."

Keane shot him an offhand glance. "Not fittin' for me to attend the social. But I've seen Ol' Winky's ghost since."

"Ah, I see. Then it's not only Mistress Becky who told you about the ghost?"

Keane dropped the last sack of turnips and wiped his hands on his hips. "Aye, Mistress Becky believes. So do the good folk in the shire. They know the ghost 'as put a spell of bad luck on the estate. Ye'll not find a buyer for Thornwood Hall. Never!"

"Well then, what do you propose I do with the property?"

"Go back to sea and leave matters as they were."

"With you overseeing my property?"

"Aye."

"But the manor is a disgrace—the result of poor management. I think if I can't sell the estate, I should hire a proper overseer. Wouldn't you do the same if you were me?"

Keane balled his hands into angry fists. "I'm not ye," he shouted. "I've never had things given to me. Just taken away. Mistress Becky's the same as me. Yer not our kind," Keane shouted. "So don't ask me what I'd do."

Keane's angry yelling caused the horse to bolt and whinny. Tossing its head, the animal jarred the wagon. Several sacks toppled over, turnip globes rolling along the dirt floor.

"Damn you!" Keane grabbed the animal's bridle with one hand and punched the frightened horse in the muzzle.

Nick wheeled around and seized Keane by the collar. "That's the last time you'll mistreat an animal on this estate." Nick threw a punch. Keane attempted to duck, to no avail as Nick felt his hand connect with the man's eye. That should cause Keane an embarrassing black eye, Nick thought with smug satisfaction.

"That's what the horse felt. And, so help me, if I ever see you strike a helpless animal again, you'll get far worse than a black eye." Nick patted the horse's cheek while Keane glared at him from the floor.

"A strong hand is needed here at Thornwood Hall," Keane said, his hand cupping his eye.

"You're not strong, you're a bully," Nick replied, his voice dangerously low. "I won't tolerate that sort of thing. You're through. Tell Geer to pay you this month's wages. I want you off my property by tomorrow night."

Keane stared, his mouth open in disbelief. But he regained his composure in a few seconds. He steeled his jaw, hate glittering from his cold blue eyes.

Nick turned and strode out the door. He knew that Keane might plead his case to Becky, but he didn't care. He should have replaced Keane immediately. But another thought came to mind.

If Keane was the *ghost* of Ol' Winky, then on such short notice, Becky would be forced to ask Geer to take his place during tomorrow's arrival of the Prescotts and Willoughbys. Nick would have to make certain that Geer would be too busy to comply. He grinned at Becky's pluck. No doubt she was planning one last chance to scare his dinner guests with Ol' Winky's ghost, but Nick couldn't afford to let that happen.

A few hours later, Nick rode his horse across the stream toward the Willoughby estate. The sun on his face reminded him of the same simple pleasure aboard ship. It suddenly dawned on him that for these past few days, although he'd thought of the sea, the deep homesickness had lessened. Surprise and an uncertain feeling flittered through him.

Perhaps it wasn't so strange, after all. With the enormous responsibilities to prepare the manor for sale, and the burden of the crofters and servants, he had much on his mind. Regardless of what Becky thought, he wouldn't turn a deaf ear to the crofters. If only Willoughby and his wife, Hazel, had solutions to offer.

When a suitable home was found for Becky and her siblings, he'd return to London to wait for his ship to be built. He'd lodge with his partner, Michael Finn.

Nick pressed his horse into a gallop. Pray God, by tomorrow night, the Prescotts would make a handsome offer for Thornwood Hall and he'd put an end to the ghost of Ol' Winky. Hopefully, a home could be found for Becky, and she'd finally come to understand that her future happiness wasn't at Thornwood Hall.

Chickens cackled from their straw nests, but Becky ignored them as she stared at Keane's red, swollen eye. "Sir Nicholas did this to you?" She laid the basket of eggs down on the chaff-littered floor and leaned closer for a better view. Although the injury wasn't serious, she knew the assault to Keane's pride was much more grievous. Never had she seen her overseer so outraged.

"Sir Nicholas came at me like an animal. Tossed me off the land, he did. Gave me till tomorrow night to be gone."

Becky knew there was more to the story. If she knew what really happened, no doubt she'd take Nick's side. He was a fair man who wouldn't have thrown Keane out without good reason. Yet the thought gave her pause.

"Sir Nicholas is in charge, there's nothing I can do." She felt relieved not to have to jump into the growing confrontation between the two men. "Molly is in the kitchen," Becky added, returning to pick the eggs from the nests. "Ask her to put mullein leaves on your eye. The swelling will go down soon."

"Mullein leaves?" Keane waved his arms, and the chickens flew squawking into the air. "I'm almost blind! I need more than leaves to fix me eye."

Becky turned around, surprised. "You see well enough to ride as Ol' Winky tomorrow, don't you?"

"Aye, I'll ride. Nothin' will keep me from it." Keane growled the words.

Relieved, Becky picked up the egg basket and moved to the next row of cages. "I'm glad, because it's too late to change plans now." She held an egg to the lighted candle, then put it into the basket. "I'll tell Sir Nicholas that you'll need more time to pack your things. Then tomorrow morning, take Ol' Winky's uniform to Molly's old hut. It's vacant now that she's moved into the manor. Bring a horse. You can change there, then make your ride while I'm showing the Prescotts the gardens."

Becky pursed her lips. "Obviously, Sir Nicholas guessed that Ol' Winky will ride tomorrow when his dinner guests arrive." Her mouth quirked. "We don't want to disappoint him, eh, Keane?"

Keane came beside her, his eyes like chipped ice. "Is that all ye care? Are ye lettin' him get away with throwin' me out?"

She shrugged. "There's nothing I can do. Stay out of sight for the rest of the day. Especially out of Nick's sight."

"Nick, is it? Yer growin' soft on him, ain't ye?" Keane's words were a statement, not a question.

"Soft?" She blinked. "Whatever do you mean?"

"Smitten. I see the way ye look at each other when ye don't think anyone sees ye."

Becky felt her cheeks flame. "I'm not about to speak of my feelings to you, Keane. You've stepped beyond yourself." She went to move past him but he grabbed her arm, sending the egg basket crashing to the floor.

"Beyond meself, is it?" He yanked her closer. "Ol' Winky was me father, and the greatest general who rode with Cromwell. If he'd o' married me mum, this manor would be mine. An' so would ye, Becky Forester."

Becky blinked. "But Keane, that's not true—"

"Me mum told me who me father was, and she wouldn't lie. I'm the same man I'd be if I'd been born on the right side of the blanket. Then you'd look at me like you do Sir Nicholas." He moved closer. Outrage forced the veins to stand out in his neck.

She pushed away. "Keane. You don't understand. I could never..." She paused, knowing this wasn't the time to explain her feelings. How could Keane believe that she would ever marry him?

"After the general died, I thought that after a proper time to mourn, then we'd marry." Keane stepped closer. "But then that damn Sir Nicholas came and ruined everythin'."

Becky's hand pressed her cheek. "Keane, I want you to leave, and never speak of this again."

He grabbed her shoulder, spinning her to face him. "Maybe yer soft, but I've got what it takes to stop Sir Nicholas." Keane released his grip on her arm, then marched out the door.

Becky's knees buckled and she sank down in the straw, her heart pounding. She'd never seen Keane so angry. Dear God, what had she done to make him think that she'd consent to marry him?

As a child, Keane had been abandoned, then taken into Ol' Winky's household out of the generosity of the general, a man who had through no fault of his own been tagged as Keane's natural father. Yet, instead of feeling gratitude, Keane always resented him.

She had to warn Nick about Keane's threat. But if the ghost was to frighten Nick's guests tomorrow, Keane was the only man who could fit into the padded uniform and ride as Ol' Winky.

Guilt tagged her as she ran toward the stable. She must convince Nick to allow Keane more time before he left. Hopefully, Keane's threat was only blind anger for the moment. But she must warn Nick, just to be safe.

Chapter Twelve

Nick had barely taken a seat in the Willoughbys' to-bacco-smoke-filled parlor before the white-haired gentleman made his point.

"Hard times for a family these days," Willoughby said, shaking his great white mane of hair. "Most men have more mouths than they can feed. No one wants to take on more bairns, especially when they're too young to earn their way."

Nick sipped his drink and watched the older man take a long pull on the pipe's end, the white smoke curling from his mouth. "Are you saying that you couldn't find a suitable family who'd take in Mistress Becky and her family?"

Willoughby's sharp brown eyes studied him. "I didn't say that, Sir Nicholas. We've had a most generous offer from the vicar and his wife." A wreath of smoke circled above his grizzled white head. "Mistress Becky'll have a fine home and position as housekeeper. In good time, she'll meet a fine Christian man who'll offer for her, and she'll soon set about having her own home and family. You'll have done your duty by her nobly, Sir Nicholas."

Nick shifted in his seat. "And Becky's siblings?"

Willoughby grunted and shook his head. "Ye don't

seem to understand, Sir Nicholas. Children are harder to place. T'would be different if they were her own, but siblings are thought to be the woman's family's responsibility. Becky has uncles and second-cousin crofters. Her siblings belong with their parents' folk, not Becky's household.'' His gnarled hand reached out to stroke one of the hounds asleep by his feet.

"Before Becky's parents died, she promised to keep her siblings with her. I don't think she'll consider anything else," Nick said uneasily.

"Tush!" Willoughby shook his head in disgruntled reproach and puffed on his long pipe. "Ye know as well as I, Sir Nicholas, that females like Mistress Becky suffer the dangers of the imagination. They're given to fantasy, and it's a man's duty to protect them from such." He poured himself another glass of Canary. "Tush! It's your duty to make her understand, Sir Nicholas."

Easier said than done, but Nick kept the thought to himself. "What about Miss Sally?"

"Miss Sally is of marriageable age. Her virginity will be her dowry. She might find a man from the parish. If not, she's a strong lass. She'll make a good crofter's wife."

Willoughby leaned back in his chair and scowled. "What ails Mistress Becky is that she thinks too much." He narrowed his eyes. "A knowing woman is like a comet. She bodes mischief whenever she appears. Mark my words, Sir Nicholas, Mistress Becky needs her own hearth and her own children to take up those stray thoughts."

Nick drained his glass. "What homes have you found for the children?"

"We've been lucky, especially the youngest. How I remember my own youngsters at that age. Noisy nuisances. Outgrow their clothes almost as fast as it takes to dress 'em." Willoughby furrowed his thatched brows.

"Mrs. Waters lost her boy last year, and she's willing to take in Baby Harry. When Mistress Becky hears the news, she should be on her knees in thanks."

Nick knew nothing would be gained by arguing the point. "And what about the older boy, Peter, and little Aphra?"

"Peter's old enough to be on his own. You might encourage him to go to sea, like yourself, Sir Nicholas."

"Becky hoped the boy might get an education—"

"Such fancy!" He rolled his eyes. "Women are the weaker vessels. They can't be expected to know reason."

Nick winced. Although Willoughby meant well, his beliefs about education remained with his kind—a son followed in his father's trade.

"And little Aphra?" Nick asked, already fearing the worst.

Willoughby gazed over the plumes of smoke from his pipe. "I've asked at every Christian hearth in the shire, but I'm afraid the child will fare best at the foundling home in Surrey."

As though expecting the look of distaste on Nick's face, Willoughby quickly added, "The maid will be brought up in a wholesome place. She'll earn her keep taking care of the other orphans." He stared unblinking. "You're a man of the world, Sir Nicholas. You know what might happen to a lass with her handicap. Believe me, it's for the girl's best, and it's your duty to convince Mistress Becky to follow our suggestions."

For a moment, Nick wondered how he'd break the news to Becky. But damn, there must be a better way. If Becky thought Aphra, Peter and Baby Harry might be separated, she'd move the heavens to prevent it.

"What choice does Mistress Becky have?" Willoughby's white eyebrows rose questioningly. "Be firm. She'll agree once she's had time to think on it."

Nick stood up. "Thank you, Willoughby." He turned

toward the door. Nothing more could be said, so he might as well leave.

"One more thing," Willoughby said, relighting his pipe. He puffed furiously until the bowl finally brightened with embers. "I'd like to offer a fair sum for that black bull of yours."

"Tumbledown Dick?"

"Aye, that's the one. I've wanted that beast ever since the general bought it. Good bloodlines."

"But the animal is Mistress Becky's pet."

Willoughby scowled. "Tush! It's your bull now, Sir Nicholas."

"I'll let you know," Nick said as he turned to leave.

Willoughby rang the servant's bell. Almost immediately, a maidservant appeared to show Nick to the front door.

"I'll be looking forward to seeing you, your wife and the Prescotts at Thornwood Hall for dinner tomorrow," Nick said before bidding Willoughby farewell.

"We're honored to be your first guests, Sir Nicholas." The older man remained seated by the fire. "The Prescotts are eager to view Thornwood Hall. Fine sort, they are, too."

Nick hesitated. "I trust they weren't disturbed by the stories of Ol' Winky's ghost," he added lightly.

"Tush! Someone's idea of horseplay, I'd say, although it unsettled a few of my guests." He chuckled.

"Horseplay. Of course," Nick said easily. "I'm looking into who's behind the prank." He took his cape, gloves and hat from the maid, then hurried to the door. He suddenly felt the need for fresh air.

Riding back to Thornwood Hall, Nick clenched his jaw as he mulled over the options Willoughby had offered. Damn, he couldn't blame the old man—it was the times in which they lived. But how to make Becky understand?

Peter, so smart, so talented. He'd find it difficult, but

at least the lad was old enough to choose for himself. Nick had been only a year older when he'd left to make a life on the sea.

Baby Harry. Could another woman love and cherish that little tad like Becky and Sally? And how would Baby Harry understand when he was taken from the only loving home he'd ever known?

Nick closed his eyes. At least the child was young. He might forget and soon come to care for his new parents and new home.

But sweet, gentle Aphra. He felt his heart twist at the thought of placing the child in a foundling home. He could almost see her winsome smile fade in disillusionment at a world that takes away everything she loves.

Damn, how he wished he'd never heard of Thornwood Hall!

Becky bit her lip as she watched Nick lead his horse along the field of daisies. The breeze parted furrows in the white sea of flowers, and for the moment, she was reminded of a tall ship run aground on a white chalky reef.

What a silly idea, she mused. She was the one who should feel lost, not he. She yanked at a daisy and pulled idly at the white petals. Yet Nick was the stranger to the land, cast adrift amid the daisies dotting the tall grass like white caps on a green sea.

As though sensing her presence, he wheeled the stallion in her direction. He tipped his hat, not in the least surprised to find her waiting for him. "How lovely to see you," he said a few minutes later.

She felt as jittery as a filly. She brushed back the feeling. No doubt her anxiety was caused by the recent encounter with Keane.

"Did you come looking for me, or are you gathering

wildflowers?'' He smiled, but his eyes held a sadness, as though he'd been worried about something.

''I'd hoped to find you. I've a matter to discuss that can't wait,'' she added quickly.

The black stallion nickered impatiently. Nick shifted in the saddle, his gaze studying her. ''Ah, an important matter…'' With a sigh, he hesitated a moment before dismounting. ''I'll wager that Keane wasted no time whining to you about the black eye I gave him.'' He grabbed the reins and strode toward her.

''I'm not here to defend Keane. I'm here to warn you.''

A dark brow lifted. ''Warn me? Of Keane?'' His eyes lit with genuine amusement.

Becky squared her chin. ''It's not my business to intervene in your quarrels. In fact, I'm quite certain Keane deserved whatever he got.'' She couldn't help but notice that Nick displayed no sign of injury from any of Keane's blows. ''But you shouldn't ignore his threats.''

''I'm quite touched at your concern for my welfare.''

He was teasing, but she had to make him see that Keane wasn't a man to ignore. ''Keane acts first, then thinks afterward. He resents you, and I—''

''Don't you resent me?''

''Well—'' She couldn't think when he looked at her like that. ''It's not the same thing.''

''Really?'' He grinned rakishly. ''How is your resentment different?''

Her cheeks flamed with his deep perusal. She turned away, snatching the head of a wild daisy in her fingers. ''Keane might do something foolish. I, on the other hand, have no recourse but to obey the king's edict.''

''Ha!'' Nick burst out laughing.

''I wish you'd take me seriously.''

''Indeed, Mistress Becky, I've always taken you most seriously.''

"But you don't—" Her voice faded when she saw his eyes grow dark. Her insides melted when he looked at her like that. Or was she imagining it? Maybe it was the heat. Or the play of late-afternoon sunlight. Or maybe she should have worn her sunbonnet before running out to find him. Aye, too much sun must be what addled her senses.

Nick brushed her hand, causing her breath to catch. "Let's talk in the shade of that lovely old tree." He pointed to a giant sycamore, its deep leafy canopy beckoning invitingly.

She nodded, then fell into step beside him. Their footfalls wended silently amid the cushion of waving grass.

When they sat beneath the tree, she couldn't help but steal a glance at him. A breeze parted his dark hair becomingly about his face. The blue-black shading of beard heightened his strong jaw. The straight nose. The black, winglike brows. How magical to watch the trick of light change his eyes from granite-gray to steel with a tilt of his head. She could stare forever and never tire of looking at him.

Nick's voice deepened with feeling. "How serene it is here."

"Aye, this meadow is one of my favorite places."

"I'd like you to show me all of your favorite places." His voice was husky, and Becky felt her pulse quicken in response.

She urged herself to answer, but she didn't trust her voice.

"I'm glad you came out this afternoon. I'd been thinking of you." Nick glanced toward the rolling white meadow, the patches of golden wheat, the trees bordering the hedgerows beneath the perfect summer sky. "When I first saw you, you were riding across this field to save Tumbledown Dick from Keane." He gazed back at her, his smile warming something deep within her. "I thought you were magnificent."

So that was how he discovered that singing to Tumbledown Dick would cause the animal to move. She smiled. "You were acting as Ben Twaddle, as I remember."

"I had a feeling you knew who I really was," Nick admitted. His hand covered hers and she made no move to protest.

"I didn't find out who you were until Hazel Willoughby told us that Ben Twaddle had fallen on her property late one night, running from the devil." Becky chuckled. "When I rode out to find you bringing the bull to Keane, I knew for certain."

"And is that why you decided to employ me as the children's nanny?" His eyes twinkled. "Punishment?"

Their shared laughter was a refreshing change, and she longed for the fragile peace between them to continue.

"Ben Twaddle is quite taken by his position in the stable," Nick said. "He's asked for a proper uniform, befitting the gentleman of the horse."

"Molly about the house has taken to her new duties quite seriously, too." Becky grinned at the thought. "She and Cook have marked off each other's area of the kitchen to keep peace." She paused a moment, reflecting on the changes Nick had put into effect these past few weeks.

"I didn't agree at first, but now I see the sense in moving the crofters inside the manor and giving them specific titles with their chores. Molly's work gives her little time to fret, and Ben has taken over the livery with the pride of a new hen with a brood of chicks. Even Nelda walks with a purposeful gait when she tends the children."

"I'm glad you agree."

"My brother Peter told me that you helped him fix up

Da's old boat." Becky felt gratitude welling inside her. "Thank you for your kindness to him." She glanced away at the daisies poking from the tall grass.

"Peter's a good lad." A shadow skittered across Nick's face, his humor suddenly vanished at what Willoughby had suggested. But the news would break Becky's heart, and he couldn't tell her. Not just yet. "Would it break your heart if Peter didn't go to university, Becky?"

She drew back. "Aye, of course it would." She stared, wondering why he'd ask such a question. Then she realized that she'd removed her hand from his. Feeling unsettled, she plucked at the daisies, gathering the flowers into her lap. In the growing silence, she braided several of the stems together.

"I also wanted to thank you for repairing Aphra's doll." Becky hoped to recapture the gentle ease that had developed between them. "That doll is her only plaything." She cast on several more flower heads to her chain. "It's her constant companion since…our sister and parents died."

"I showed Aphra the new kittens in the stable," Nick said. "At first she was reluctant to play with them, but when she saw the kits didn't have their eyes open yet, she seemed to want to protect them."

"Aye, several times I've found her watching them. I'm surprised, she's always been timid around animals."

He smiled, and their conversation about the youngsters reminded her of two married people talking with loving pride about their children. The idea made her breath catch.

"I think Aphra preferred her doll to pets because…" Becky hesitated, choosing the right words.

"Because she's afraid to lose someone close to her," Nick finished for her. His eyes held a faraway look of sadness.

Becky remembered the afternoon when she'd found Aphra with Nick at the cemetery. Suddenly a sense of overwhelming gratitude rushed her. "My thoughts exactly."

He leaned back, watching her silently for a few minutes. "What are you making?" He stared at the chain of daisies twisted in her lap.

Becky held up the braided daisy wreath that she'd fashioned, as she'd done so many times with her family in the past. "Didn't the girls from your village make daisy chains?"

He shook his head. "I left home when I wasn't much older than Peter. But if they had, I'm sure I'd have remembered." He pressed one of the yellow centers between his fingers.

"Mum used to say that if we made a wish upon the daisies as we braided them into crowns, then our wishes would come true...." Her words faded, but she finished the memory to herself: *If your true love kisses you while you're wearing the crown of your secret wishes.*

She blushed, thinking how foolish her thoughts. She felt like a love-struck milkmaid.

Nick rolled on his stomach and gathered a handful of daisies. "And what would you wish for, Becky Forester?"

The space between them held an air of expectancy as her eyes met his. It would be so easy to relax with him. She took one of the daisies he offered and joined it to the others. "I'd wish for Aphra to regain her voice."

His clear gray eyes darkened. He handed her another flower.

She held it a moment, then joined it into her bouquet. "I wish Sally would marry a good man, someone who would appreciate all of her wonderful qualities."

He gave her a third flower. Becky plucked it from his fingers and hastily twisted the stem with the others. "I wish Peter to grow to be a strong, noble man like his father.''

Nick grinned, handing her another blossom. She continued to wish upon each daisy until finally Nick paused, refusing to release the next flower.

''You've covered wishes for your siblings, the crofters, your friends, neighbors and the manor. What about yourself?''

She tilted her head and smiled in that impish way that he loved. Then she jerked another daisy from his fingers.

''Very well, but first I'll make a wish for you.'' Becky wove the stem into place, her fingers weaving the ends into a circle. ''I wish for you, Sir Nicholas Sinclair, the fighting ship of your dreams.'' Her violet eyes sparkled.

''Thank you, but these are your wishes, not mine.'' Nick couldn't help but think how utterly charming she was when she was playful. He swallowed back the lump in his throat as he gave her another flower. ''What is *your* heart's desire?'' he asked huskily.

She took the daisy and braided the blossom into the circle. ''It's a secret,'' she said when she'd finished. But despite her coy smile, Nick knew that her wish was to own Thornwood Hall again.

Everything between them always came back to that, didn't it? he thought irritably. Damn, why had he spoiled the mood by pressing her to make a wish? What had he hoped she'd wish for?

He had no right to know of her dreams. But rights had nothing to do with it. He wanted to know everything about her.

Lifting the wreath from her lap, Nick placed it upon her head. The simple crown of daisies graced her shiny tresses like pearls upon black satin.

''You're so beautiful.'' His hands moved along her cheeks, cradling her face to his. Her cheeks flushed pink beneath his fingertips, and he pulled her into his arms.

When his mouth found hers, her sweet lips allowed him entry. White heat rushed at him as he took her kisses as he wanted to take her body.

Her arms circled his neck, and she drew closer, his hands molding the length of her as she surrendered against him on the fragrant tangle of daisies.

Chapter Thirteen

This must be what was between a man and a woman, Becky sensed. This overwhelmingly incredible sensation when Nick's lips took hers in sheer mastery. She kissed him in return, unafraid, willing and trusting.

Nick shifted her on top of him, and Becky felt his hard warmth beneath the thin fabric of her skirts. The sensation seared through to her skin. When his mouth trailed kisses along her throat, and she felt his fingers untie the ribbons at the valley between her breasts, she was filled with such sudden desire it almost took her breath away.

In a faraway part of her mind, she heard a meadowlark call to its mate, then her mare's soft whinny. Otherwise, she could have easily imagined that she and Nick were in their own little world, away from...

The horse whinnied again, this time louder. Nick shifted her to the side and craned his head through the grass. "Damn, it's Twaddle."

"Ben?" Becky blushed, straightening her gown as she regained her dignity. "What does he—?"

"He doesn't see us," Nick whispered huskily. "Stay here. I'll find out what he wants." He got to his feet, brushing the bits of grass from his shirt and breeches.

Becky watched as Nick meandered through the field

of white. The minutes felt like hours as she waited. Just when she decided that she could no longer stand the suspense, she saw Nick return.

"Twaddle says that my friend Michael Finn just arrived." Nick's face was serious as he reached down to help her to her feet. "Come, I'll walk you back to your mare."

Becky's face was still burning from his kisses as she stood beside him. His shirt was open at the neck, and as she leaned against him, her fingers slipped inside the fabric and touched his black-curled chest.

His gray eyes were dark with desire. "I've never known anyone like you, Becky," he whispered in her ear, then the words faded as he traced a heart against her ear with his moist tongue. "It grieves me to leave, but if we don't, that big lug of an Irishman will come bounding along looking for me."

Nick slipped his arm around her waist as they ambled toward the meadow gate where her mare waited. The wind rushed her senses, lifting her hair from her face as she leaned against his muscled chest. She squeezed her eyes shut, wanting to keep the memory of his kiss within her heart. He'd be gone soon, and although she didn't believe in the magic of wishes, she knew she wanted to. She had been so practical all of her life; if only she could wish upon a daisy and have the dream come true.

But when she reached the gate where the mare she had raised from a foal was tethered, she remembered that the animal, as well as everything of material value, no longer belonged to her.

For a fleeting moment, she'd dared to make a wish that somehow Nick might love her enough to want to be with her, but now she had been called back to reality. Wishes were impractical in her world, yet there was no denying the reality of need thrumming in her veins.

When Nick and Becky arrived at the manor, Ben

Twaddle was waiting by the rail, ready to take their mounts. Nick felt a tremor of foreboding the moment he heard that Michael Finn had arrived. Only the most pressing emergency would bring Finn from London, where he'd been overseeing the building of their ship.

Nick escorted Becky inside the withdrawing room where Finn's long frame perched uncomfortably on a stool across from Sally, who was settled on the sofa.

"Finn, this is a surprise," Nick said cheerfully, giving no hint to his thoughts.

Finn rose to his feet, and one look at his forlorn, dark blue eyes and Nick sensed something terrible had happened.

While the introductions were made and during the necessary small talk that followed, Nick's mind whirled with questions. He'd known his friend too many years not to recognize that below Finn's easy Irish charm lurked a troubled man.

Nick sat on the arm of the sofa beside Becky, while Finn continued. "Waiting for ye has been delightful, Captain, thanks to my charming companion." Finn smiled broadly at Sally, who blushed prettily at his compliment.

"Mr. Finn has been entertaining me with the latest happenings at court," Sally said, toying self-consciously with her fan. "Your colorful turn of description makes me long to see the sights of London myself, Mr. Finn."

"Perhaps someday I can have the pleasure of showin' ye, Mistress Sally." Finn smiled.

"And what business brings you to our shire, Mr. Finn?" Becky asked. Despite her guileless demeanor, Nick knew she was as curious at Finn's unexpected arrival as he was.

"A private matter, mistress." Finn's blue eyes met Nick's anxious gaze.

"I hope your business leaves you enough time to truly

sample our little bit of England," Sally said to Finn, as though she didn't notice the men's exchange.

"Thank ye, but from what little I've already seen of the finest English beauty—"

"I should warn you, Mistress Sally," Nick interrupted, hoping to alert Finn not to give away any information until they'd spoken privately. "To say my Irish friend has a way with words is like saying the ocean is wet, eh, Finn?"

Finn's smile softened his rugged features.

Becky made no move to excuse herself and leave the men alone. Nick knew her curiosity was flying at high mast and nothing short of a cattle prod would extract her from the room.

"Come, Finn, I'll show you around the manor," Nick offered.

"A fine idea," Becky remarked. "And who better to show Mr. Finn the estate than I." She winked at Nick as she scurried past to take Finn's arm.

Nick sighed. "How kind of you to offer, Mistress Becky, but Finn and I wouldn't wish to impinge upon your time with the children." His accentuation of the last word caused her smile to vanish.

Finn cleared his throat. "I regret the loss of yer delightful company, ladies, but I have an urgent matter I wish to discuss with Sir Nicholas."

Becky curtsied gracefully. "Of course, Mr. Finn. I hope you both have a pleasant evening." She gave Nick a look that clearly indicated she expected his full confidence later.

After the women left, Nick motioned Finn to take a seat. Closing the door, Nick crossed the room to the leaded panes and shut them, just in case a curious ear, pruning the hedges outside the window, might overhear them.

Nick splashed amber liquid inside two glasses, then

handed one to his friend. "Tell me, Finn. What's wrong?"

Finn stared at the brandy, then gulped it in one swallow. His gaze followed Nick as he sank back in the middle of the sofa. "I thought it would be easier if I came directly instead of sendin' a messenger. Besides..." Finn put the empty glass on the floor, then cradled his blond head in his hands.

Nick sipped the brandy, waiting. He'd known Finn since Nick's first voyage as cabin boy. Yet he'd never seen Finn so distraught. "Can't be that bad, old chap."

"Truth be, I—I didn't know how to put the events into a letter." The silence of the room grew deafening.

"Damn it, Finn. Tell me straight out."

Finn clenched and unclenched his fists. "After ye told me that the king's mistress had agreed to help ye arrange a mortgage on Thornwood Hall, I went to see her. Ye had already left for Thornwood Hall. Barbara Villiers made the arrangements with a moneylender, whom she said was discreet."

Nick remembered the king's sultry mistress, and the greed in her eyes when she was assured of a generous percentage for her help. "Go on, Finn."

"When Barbara gave me the moneylender's address on Bow Street, I set out immediately." Finn paused, taking a deep breath. "The moneylender gave me the sum, but by the time I left his chamber, it was too late to make it to the shipbuilder's office that night. So I took a room at the Oak and Ivy, plannin' to order our new ship the first thing in the mornin'."

Nick drained his drink, then poured each of them another.

"Oh, Christ, Nick. I don't know how to tell ye the rest."

Nick took a deep breath. "You didn't invite a tavern wench to your room, did you, Finn?" It was the oldest trick in the book, and Nick knew Finn's weakness for a pretty face.

Finn shook his head. "Nay, although there were plenty willing lasses working the tap that night. I ordered a bowl of stew and a mug of ale. When I went to pay for me supper, me purse was gone."

"Gone?"

"Aye. The money was nicked by some common thief. I don't even know when it'd happened." His gaze dropped to his dusty leather boots. "Christ, Nick, I feel so damned stupid."

"Did you call a constable?"

"The tavern keeper called him. The owner accused me of makin' up the story of robbery to get out of paying for me meal." Finn's mouth twisted with anguish. "I told the constable what happened, but what could he do?" Finn shook his head. "If I hadn't given the pub owner my silver money clip to pay for my meal, I'd still be there."

Nick frowned. "Then where did you go?"

"I was afraid to go back to Whitehall. I thought if I spoke to Barbara, the king might find out that ye'd taken a mortgage against Thornwood Hall."

Nick rubbed his chin. "The first payment on that note will be due next month." He let out an audible sigh.

"Lad, if I had any personal funds, I'd give them to ye, but I haven't a shillin'."

Nick pressed his hand on Finn's shoulder. "We'll think of something," he managed, yet for the moment, he only felt shock. He leaned back and tented his fingers in his lap. "So what did you do next, Finn?"

"I remembered Rose, one of the ladies-in-waitin' to Barbara Villiers. The next day I went to the palace and gave Rose a note for Barbara, asking for an audience."

Nick leaned forward. "What did Barbara suggest you do?"

''That was the strange part. The next day, Rose came to me room with her answer. Barbara had refused to see me.'' Finn raked his fingers through his long dark hair. ''She offered no explanation. Later, I wondered if Barbara had deliberately sent me to that moneylender with orders to rob me.''

Everyone knew about the king's many mistresses, yet Barbara had always been the monarch's favorite. Recently, however, Nick knew the king was infatuated with the younger Frances Stuart, and court gossips had said he was in a frenzy as Frances continued to refuse him.

Barbara was a shrewd woman. She knew the time would come when she'd be discarded as easily as the court's rotten pineapples. Nick wouldn't blame her to do whatever was necessary to amply provide for herself when that day came. ''It was Barbara who'd suggested the moneylender. I think she's one possibility that we shouldn't overlook.''

''What can we do about it?'' Finn's brow creased with worry.

''First, we need to know more.'' Nick swirled the remaining amber liquid in his glass. Had avarice been Barbara's only motive or was it more? Nick decided not to tell Finn that Barbara had invited Nick into her bed. When he'd refused, she'd barely contained her fury.

Finn leaned forward, his head in his hands. ''I must have been robbed soon after leavin' the moneylender's office. Drury Lane was crowded with carriages and patrons going to the theater. I thought I'd make better time on foot.'' He took a deep gasp, shaking his head. ''Damn, I feel like such a gull.''

''No use beating yourself over the head, Finn. If Barbara and the moneylender were in this together, there's not much you could have done.'' He forced a smile. ''We'll think of something.''

Finn lifted his head and stared at him. ''But how? We

can't speak to the king. I met with the boatbuilder, but he won't talk to us without money. He's nearly bankrupt from the Royal Navy not paying their war debt.''

Finn peered around the room, as though seeing it for the first time. "Are there paintings or furniture that ye can sell?''

Nick's mouth tilted. "I'm afraid that's already been thought of.'' He ignored Finn's curious expression. "But there's hay soon to be cut, and harvest crops are ripening. There might be a profit after the harvesters are paid, but not enough for a ship.''

Finn's brow lifted. "Have ye found out why the manor has failed to make a profit these last years?''

"Aye, but I'm not ready to present my report to the king.'' Nick rose and went to the window. "I'd like you to remain here for a few days, Finn. By the look of you, you could use the rest.'' Nick glanced back at him. "I've invited some guests for dinner tomorrow. I'm hoping they'll make me an offer for the estate. Perhaps your Irish charm can help me convince them.''

"By God, Nick. Ye're not angry with me?''

Nick shook his head. "Of course not, my friend. How could I be? After all, you saved my life, although at the time, I wasn't too happy about it.''

Finn shifted on the stool. "And does that black-haired beauty have anythin' to do with yer change of heart, lad?'' His eyes twinkled with good-natured teasing.

"Becky is quite a woman.'' The lengthy pause that followed told Finn not to press the matter.

Nick glanced out the window again. "If Barbara and the moneylender were behind the robbery, more than likely the robber followed you from the moneylender's office. Did the moneylender see where you stashed the money he gave you?''

Finn thought for a moment. "He left me alone in his office after he counted out the sum. I placed the guineas into a leather money bag, then tied it to me inside vest pocket. Later, when I went to fetch it, the strings of the bag had been cut."

Just as Nick thought. "Although the man left the room, he must have watched you to see where you hid the money on your person. No doubt the accomplice was waiting with him. And they knew you'd be thrown into the jostling theater crowd where the deed wouldn't be noticed."

Nick opened the window, and the early evening air rushed into the room. Outside, Becky and Sally came into view, followed by Baby Harry and Aphra, holding her kitten. "Finn, let's join the women for a walk before dinner. In the meantime, put the problem out of your mind. With luck, the Prescotts, who'll be visiting tomorrow, might offer me a handsome sum for Thornwood Hall. Then you can be off for London with a tidy purse."

Finn moved beside Nick, his eyes bright with unspoken thankfulness. He extended his hand.

Nick shook it, then patted Finn on the back reassuringly. Words weren't needed between friends.

Moments later, Finn watched Becky and Sally toss a ball to the children. "Tell me, Captain. Is that pretty, fair-haired lass, Sally, spoken for?"

Nick couldn't help but grin. "She's Becky's cousin, and a sweeter lass you'll not find this side of the equator."

"I could tell that ye've already set yer sights on the lovely Becky," Finn added. "Ye've a way of lookin' at her that I've never seen with yer other female companions." He lifted a brow, obviously curious.

"I've a responsibility to the manor's occupants, Finn. I'm not about to chase skirts where my duty is concerned."

"Ah, then it's duty that makes ye soft in the eye when ye look at her." Finn was obviously enjoying himself.

"Becky needs a husband who'll help her bring up two brothers and a sister, not some man whose heart is with the sea." A flash of guilt washed over him as he thought of how he had kissed her in the meadow. Good Lord, he'd have done more than that if Twaddle hadn't interrupted them.

Finn leaned back and studied him. "She must be a spirited young lass to have shouldered such responsibility."

"Aye, she's that and more." Nick grinned. "You'll see what I mean tomorrow."

"Tomorrow?"

"Aye. Do you believe in ghosts?"

"Ghosts?" Finn's face blanched. "I believe in leprechauns, but ghosts? Is the manor haunted?"

Nick took Finn's reaction for a yes. "Becky will want you to think it's haunted. But with your help, maybe we can catch the ghost and put an end to the rumors."

Finn turned back to Nick. "Dear God, what have ye gotten yerself into?"

Nick glanced back to the window. "Whatever it is, Finn—" his gaze was fixed on the laughing Becky "—I think I'm in over my head."

That night after dinner, Becky strode toward the study, hoping to find Nick alone. A shaft of candlelight glimmered beneath the door. She pressed her ear to the wood and listened. Hearing only silence, she rapped softly.

"It's open," Nick said, his head bent over the open ledgers in front of him.

"I wished to have a few words with you." He sat at her desk, and she remembered how she'd been prepared to hate him for taking over her study, but instead, Nick looked as though the role suited him, despite his reluctance.

Nick wants to sell the estate and return to sea as fast

as possible. She should want that, too, but since a few hours ago, when she'd found such happiness in his arms, she knew in her heart that she didn't want him to leave.

Finally Nick looked up and smiled. "I know why you're here."

Becky took a seat across from him. "I expect you do."

A hint of a smile played at Nick's mouth. "You want to know why Finn came to see me."

"Of course I want to know." There was no use fooling him.

"Bad news, I'm afraid." The glow from the flickering taper softened his otherwise serious features. "Thank you, Becky, for your concern, but there's nothing that can be done." He placed the quill back in the holder and closed the ledger.

"Can you tell me what the trouble is, Nick?"

His gray eyes glittered in the candlelight. "I'm in desperate need of money."

"Why?"

Nick's mouth twisted. "When I was recuperating at Whitehall Palace, I borrowed money against Thornwood Hall to finance my new ship. Finn took care of the arrangements while I left to come here. Today, Finn told me that he'd been robbed of the money. The first note payment is due on the mortgage, and we have no money for a ship." He looked at her, his gray eyes melancholy. "My only hope is to sell the estate as quickly as possible to Prescott, without waiting for a prime price."

"I see." Her knees felt weak. A cold shiver washed over her. Nick was desperate for someone to buy the estate, but she was equally desperate to prevent it. If she could only manage to scare the Prescotts away with the ghost of Ol' Winky, then it might buy her some time.

Time for what? Perhaps he'd grow tired of trying to sell a haunted estate and let her manage the property for him. She drew in a breath. "I'm sorry that you have such worry," she replied, feeling sincerely unhappy for him. How she'd changed in the time he'd come here. Gone was the woman who despised the war hero, the enemy who came to usurp everything that she'd worked for. But could she truly carry out her plan to be rid of him?

She got to her feet and hurried toward the door. "I must meet with Molly and Cook about tomorrow's dinner preparations. If you'll excuse me."

He rose from the chair. "Becky..."

She hovered at the door.

He moved around the desk and strode toward her. "I know that you're planning to scare the Prescotts tomorrow with Ol' Winky's ghost." His mouth felt dry, the words tight in his throat. "But I'm begging you not to do it." There, he'd said it. "Please, Becky. I must sell Thornwood Hall. Don't do anything to stop me."

He watched Becky's violet eyes darken, her hand rose to the blue ribbons gathered above her breasts. The ribbons his impatient fingers had untied only hours before.

He took her small hand in his and felt her tremble. "Please, help me, Becky."

Nick watched the warring emotions cloud her lovely face. Finally, she drew her hand from his, then disappeared into the hall's darkness.

The following day, Becky and Sally watched nervously as they stood on the lawn while the black-lacquered Willoughby coach and six rolled up the new stone driveway that the crofters had only finished laying the day before.

A few minutes later, a second coach, as magnificently polished as the first, rumbled into view.

The Prescott family, Becky mused—the couple with their two daughters and two sons from Hampshire— Nick's prospective buyers.

At the edge of the driveway, Nick stood, tugging at the ruffles at his cuffs. Becky's heart fluttered each time she saw him, so grand, dressed in his uniform. But she enjoyed seeing him in the loose, linen shirt he was accustomed to wearing. His hair was unpowdered, pulled back in a queue behind his neck.

A flicker of movement near the garden caught Becky's eye. She glanced behind the yew hedge to see Geer peeking out at her. She peered back at Nick, who strolled toward the Willoughbys' coach as the footman helped Hazel from the vehicle.

Hoping not to be seen, Becky hurried toward Geer.

"Mistress Becky, it's Keane."

"Keane? What's the matter with him?"

"He's drunk as a 'chuck." Geer's long face paled. "I've ne'er seen 'im like this." His white brows rose.

"Keep your voice down, Geer." Becky watched through the branches as Nick conversed with the Willoughbys while the second coach rolled to a stop.

"I must return before Nick notices I'm gone. We don't want him any more suspicious than he already is." The last time she'd seen Nick, she remembered how miserable she felt when he'd asked—no, begged—that she give up her plan to scare the Prescotts.

"Oh, Geer. Are you certain that Keane can't ride?"

"Aye, mistress. He can barely stand."

She paced back and forth.

Geer's face lit up. "I'll tell Nick that I'm sick, then I'll ride in Keane's place."

Becky paused. "Nick asked you specifically to show the property to the Prescotts. I'm sure he had his reasons." She tenderly gazed into the old man's face. "With all the padding we've sewn into Ol' Winky's jacket, the uniform is too small for you, Geer. But thank you, dear friend."

"But what can we do?"

"I'll do it." Becky grinned when she saw Geer's white brows fly together and his mouth drop open.

"Mistress Becky! Nick will notice yer gone. Ye'll be the first one he'd think of who'd dare do such a trick."

"Nick will have to prove it." She smiled confidently. "I'll make the ride, and Nick won't suspect me, especially if I greet the guests first, then stroll the gardens with Mrs. Prescott and her daughters."

Geer scratched his white head. "How'd you do that?"

She smiled. "I'll have Sally change into my hat and gown, after I've made my first appearance. Then when Sir Nicholas sees me strolling the gardens, he'll never suspect that the lady in the pink-striped gown isn't me." She felt buoyed by the idea. "I'll sneak along the pathway to Molly's hut, change into Ol' Winky's uniform, then make my ride before anyone knows I'm gone."

Geer shook his grizzled white head. "I don't know—"

"By the time I return," Becky interrupted, "Sally will be waiting in my room, ready to exchange dresses. Afterward, we'll join the women in the garden and Nick won't be able to prove a thing." She felt exhilarated by her plan.

Geer shook his head. "Aye, but what if yer caught?"

"I won't be caught. No one will see me. You'll be with Nick and the others on the opposite side of the estate. Besides, no one knows the hidden shortcuts along the back fields as I do." She patted his arm reassuringly. "Have faith in me, Geer."

Geer rubbed his chin. "I wonder why Keane started drinking?"

Becky said nothing, but she had an idea. Hopefully, once Keane was sober, she could persuade him to leave peacefully.

Becky glanced to where Nick and the guests strolled along the front expanse of green. Beside the Willoughbys, a middle-aged couple sauntered ahead of their two young sons and two older daughters.

"I must be getting back." She gave Geer an encouraging wink.

A few minutes after Nick introduced Becky to the Prescotts, and he had listened to her polite conversation with the Willoughbys, Nick excused himself. Becky watched as Nick called Geer to his side, then both men trekked off to the barn.

More than likely, Nick was giving Geer last-minute instructions on the more prosperous fields to show the Prescotts.

Becky took Sally's arm and held her back from the others as Hazel Willoughby, Elizabeth Prescott and her two marriageable-aged daughters sauntered toward the gardens. It took Becky only a few minutes to whisper the new plan to Sally.

Moments later, Nick and Geer came out of the barn. Becky's heart beat faster as she watched Nick join the other men outside the stables.

Pox and calamity! If only they'd hurry. Her earlier eagerness was fading. But she couldn't give up now. Becky took a fortifying breath and smiled pleasantly at the women.

"Have you seen any evidence that the manor is haunted, Mistress Becky?" the younger Prescott daughter asked.

"Hush, Elinor," Mrs. Prescott said with a start. She turned a flustered face toward Becky. "I'm so sorry for my daughter's—" She hesitated, embarrassment clearly in her face.

"Of course Elinor is curious," Becky said. "And you both have a right to be." Becky heard Sally's sharp intake of breath. Becky carefully avoided looking at her cousin.

"Aye, the rumors are true, Elinor." Becky gazed off in the distance. "We've often seen his ghost ride the fields, vengeful against Royalists."

Mrs. Prescott's features pinched with fear. She exchanged glances with her daughters. Elinor's eyes grew wider.

"I imagine you'll get used to the specter," Becky said, her face serious. "Besides, I've never known the general to do harm to women and children."

"Do harm? Why, you don't think…?" The question hung in the deathly pause that followed. Mrs. Prescott almost swooned.

"Why, I'd forgotten!" Becky drew a breath. "Your husband rode with the king's army, I believe Sir Nicholas Sinclair said." Becky had trouble keeping a straight face as the fright grew in the three wide-eyed Prescott faces.

Mrs. Prescott shifted uneasily. "Where is my husband, Mistress Becky?"

Becky glanced across the gardens to the horsemen trotting from the stables. Nick and Geer flanked Willoughby and Mr. Prescott and his two sons. "They're off to view the back pasture." Becky smiled reassuringly. "I'm certain we'll be safe until they return," she added mischievously.

Just then, Nelda stepped from the scullery yard. Aphra tagged along with Baby Harry.

Sally whirled around. "If you'll excuse me, I must check with Nelda about the children's dinner." She winked at Becky before she turned and strode toward Nelda and the children.

Becky returned her glance, aware that it was almost time for her to rush back to her room, where Sally would be waiting to change into Becky's pink-striped gown and matching bonnet.

Taking the lead, Becky said, "If you'd like to come inside, ladies, I'll show you to your rooms so you may refresh yourselves before dinner."

Mrs. Prescott glanced around, her hand to her throat. "Has the ghost ever appeared inside the manor?"

Becky shrugged, hiding her amusement. "Not to my knowledge, but there's always a first time, my dear."

Chapter Fourteen

It had taken Becky less than an hour to sneak away from her guests, who had taken to their rooms for a much needed rest after anxiously listening to the stories of Ol' Winky's rides along the dales. Bless Sally for her help, Becky thought, or she could never have gotten away from them so easily.

After Becky had left her pink taffeta gown and straw hat in Sally's room, she quickly changed into the breeches and shirt that her cousin had left for her. A few minutes later, Becky arrived at the barn, where Geer had left her mare saddled.

Without a moment's hesitation, Becky rode along the path hidden by hedgerows, across the fields to the west meadow, where Molly's vacant cottage nestled among the other empty huts. Before she urged her mare into the clearing, she glanced around, but there were no signs of Nick or his guests. No doubt Geer had steered them to the far fields of ripening wheat and oats. If only her luck would hold.

Becky quickly dismounted and strode to the shed behind the cottage. Inside was Keane's bay gelding, black silk covering the animal's back and sides. The red and white stripes of Ol' Winky's banner hung over its saddle, plainly visible. Becky checked the saddle and bridle, and finally satisfied, she went inside the cottage.

Ol' Winky's uniform, helmet and armor were neatly placed on the table. The small room smelled of ale, and she wondered where Keane was. No doubt, Geer found an out-of-the-way place for Keane to sleep off his drunken state.

The important thing was, Keane was out of sight. Good, Becky decided. She wasn't up to facing Keane deep in his cups. She had a job to do and as her parents had always told her, if something important needed doing, best do it yourself.

She forced thoughts of Nick from her mind. With all good intentions, he was showing the estate to its best advantage to the Prescotts, and she was doing her best to undermine him.

She had only to scare Mr. Prescott. Prescott's wife and daughters were already dreadfully unsettled by the stories of Ol' Winky's ghost, and another sighting of Ol' Winky would be the final blow to Nick's hope to sell Thornwood Hall.

By the time Becky had changed into the Roundhead uniform, attached the general's sword to the red bandolier around her chest and buckled the awkward metal pieces of armor to her back and shoulders, she sank back on the stool to rest. In the late August heat, the woolen shirt, leather tunic and the weight of the heavy breastplates almost took her breath away.

She staggered to her feet and finished the costume by placing Ol' Winky's metal helmet over her head. The visor snapped over her face, but she quickly lifted it back out of the way.

Adjusting the metal armor plates across her chest, Becky gasped from the extra weight. Straightening her shoulders, she noticed the extra length of leather breeches dangling by her shins. Quickly, she tucked the extra fabric inside the general's boots before she staggered to the door.

Becky peeked outside to be sure no one was about before stepping into the sunlight. Certain she was alone, she hurried for the shed where Keane's horse waited.

Already, beads of perspiration dotted her hairline. Her sword clanked against the metal armor plates as she mounted the charger. Inhaling a deep gulp of air, she felt better.

She pressed the horse into a gallop toward the manor, the banners of silk fluttering in the breeze. When she came to a stile by the fence, the horse jumped the obstacle with agility and grace. The successful leap caused Becky to feel a bit more optimistic. But when her horse hit the ground, the thud forced the shield on her helmet to slam down over her eyes.

Pox and calamity! She forgot to stuff something inside the crown of the too-large helmet. Now, with the face shield clamped shut, she couldn't see except for the few feet in front of the horse.

She had no choice but to go back to Keane's hut and find something to stuff inside the helmet. She didn't dare take a chance and attempt the ride without better vision.

Becky wheeled the horse around and cantered back toward the cottage. It took her longer this time because of her limited visibility. When she recognized the familiar bushes and trees in front of Molly's hut, she thought to dismount. But before she did, Becky heard hoofbeats approach, then a familiar voice rang out.

"Off your horse, Keane."

Her heart pounded with dread. Becky didn't have to see Nick to know she'd been caught. She was glad the visor covered the shame on her face. She could hear him dismounting on her left, about twenty paces away. Dear God, what was she to do?

She shifted back in her saddle, then pulled the sword

from its sheath and waved it over her head. "Death to all Royalists," she yelled in a forced low voice. Wheeling around to the right, she took a chance to escape.

The horse beneath her sensed her fear. She rode low, sword in hand, praying the beast would carry her to safety.

A few minutes later, she tore at the visor, desperate to rip it from her face. But try as she might, she couldn't unsnap it. However, she could view the ground through the mouthpiece. She guided the horse along the path, certain she was heading in the direction of the manor.

"Halt, or I swear…"

Becky couldn't believe that Nick had caught up with her so quickly. She kicked her heels into her mount. The horse sensed her desperation and responded in kind. Becky and the horse were one as the grass beneath her raced past. She trusted this horse—she had no other choice—for she couldn't see past the horse's nose.

Suddenly, she felt her mount vault through the air. Remembering the last time, she held on, leaning close to his mane, confident in his power. The horse regained his footing with grace and speed. Thank God.

Would Nick be so lucky?

"Damn you, Keane. I've given you fair warning!"

Nick's threat sounded directly behind her. Becky felt so relieved that Nick's horse had successfully made the jump that she almost cried out.

She tried lifting her visor, to no avail. For a moment, she sensed her horse had slowed down, and she wasn't certain in what direction they were heading.

To the right was the river. She was traveling in the opposite direction from the manor house. Up ahead was the woods. Dear God, she had to turn off before—

A sharp thrust in the middle of her shoulders took her breath away, and her horse bolted left as she felt herself windmill through the air, then hit the ground with a thud.

"Damn your stubborn—" Nick stopped and pulled the metal helmet from the fallen rider. Becky's silky black hair spilled down around her shoulders. "Becky! Dear God—"

Nick was down on his knees, his fingers shaking as he loosened the buckles across her chest. "Oh God, no!" His hands trembled as he laid her down upon the grass. "Becky, do you hear me?"

She moaned, her face twisted in pain. Thank God she was still alive. This was his fault. He drove her to this, damn him.

Nick cradled her head against his chest. "Don't die, Becky."

For an instant, the urgent screams of his crewmen filled his mind. The brilliant orange sky ignited with the mortar attack. He could see their terrified faces, amid the flames of the burning ship in the water. He closed his eyes, moaning, clutching Becky to him.

"Please God, take me instead. Please God, I beg of you."

Becky shifted slightly, her eyes still closed.

His face pressed to hers, his eyes shut, he prayed for a miracle. When he'd finished, he noticed the tears on her cheek were his own.

"Becky, my darling. Can you hear me?" He rubbed his fingers through her hair, feeling for a welt along her scalp. He found none and was instantly relieved. Thank God she'd worn that silly old helmet. It had probably saved her life.

Becky blinked, then stared at him. "Nick?"

"Aye, Becky, it's me, my love. Where do you hurt?"

Her eyelids fluttered shut. "Everywhere," she whispered.

He whispered a prayer of thanksgiving. "Don't move. I'll send for Geer with the wagon."

"Nay," she said, trying to sit up.

"Becky, that's an order. You've had a shock."

"The horse…is he all right?" She glanced around, then smiled with relief when she saw the animal grazing near the bank.

"Aye, he's fine, which is more than I can say for you." He should be angry with her, but how could he? He wanted to hold her, to kiss her, to keep her safe with him forever.

"Please, Nick. I'll be fine in a minute. Let me catch my breath." She wrapped her arms around his neck. "Help me to my feet."

"Nay, you can't—"

She glared at him. "Don't use that word with me, Sinclair." She tightened her grip around his neck and smiled at him. "Help me to my feet."

He gave her a hand, then slid both arms around her waist. "You *feel* just fine," he said with a grin.

She gave him a feigned scolding look. Taking a deep breath, she leaned against him. "Nick…I'm so sorry." She gazed into the dark smoky depths of his eyes. "If only you could understand how important it is for me to keep Thornwood Hall for the children." She felt her chin quiver. "If only you'd let me manage the estate while you're at sea."

"Becky, I must sell. I need the money. I have no choice."

Her heart sank. She couldn't look at him. "Are you going to tell the Prescotts about…Ol' Winky's ghost?"

"Nay." Nick hesitated. "You're going to tell them, Becky. And you'll tell them why you did it."

Becky glanced up at him. She picked at the few grass strands remaining on her sleeve. "My reputation will be ruined."

"Maybe the Prescotts will hire you to take care of their girls?"

"They'll think of me as a liar and a charlatan. They'll

be right." She bit her lip and for the first time he could remember, the sparkle of tears were in her eyes.

"Becky, I don't want to do it, but—"

"But you must. Otherwise, how else will you sell the property." Her chin held firm. "Come, I'll tell the Prescotts. I want to make it clear that it was my idea, solely, and no one else is to blame. Are we agreed?"

He sighed. "I don't think that's necessary."

"Nick, please. I need your promise that Sally or Geer or any of the others won't suffer for this."

Nick glanced away. "As you wish."

She sighed. "Will you help me back to the manor?"

"Of course." He strode toward the horse and gathered the reins as he brought the animal to her. Damn, when did she slip inside his soul, captivating him until she became part of his very being? Before he helped Becky on the horse, he cupped her chin, staring into her lovely eyes. He stroked her cheeks, her chin, and his heart wept. How he'd liked to tell her that all would be well, but he couldn't. He had no choice but to carry on with what he had to do. He prayed, in time, she'd understand.

No one was around to witness her humiliating return, thank God. Becky took Nick's hand while he assisted her from the horse. Every bone in her body ached as she limped to the scullery door. He said nothing as he left with the horses.

Good! He had been very clear, therefore there was nothing else he need say. She was ruined. He cared nothing to help her.

She tried to accept her fate, but she just couldn't give up. There must be something she could do. She'd take the entire blame for the idea to spread the stories of General Forester's ghost, but she'd be damned if she'd make a spectacle in front of the Willoughbys and the Prescotts.

Becky tried not to limp as she walked past the kitchen

maids busily preparing dinner. Her right hip throbbed, but her biggest ache came from the crushed expression on Nick's face. She wondered if a body could die from embarrassment.

She moved slowly up the back stairs and went directly to Sally's room. She rapped softly. Footsteps clacked across the floorboards toward the door.

Sally gasped. "Becky! What happened?"

"It's a long story," Becky answered, each joint in her body crying out in pain. "I'm all right, but Nick found me dressed as Ol' Winky. He's going to expose me when the men return."

Sally's mouth dropped open and her hand flew to her cheek. "Becky, I'm so sorry." She hugged her, and Becky didn't push back the tears stinging her eyes.

"I'm sorry, too." Becky swiped at her eyes. "Oh, Sally, I'm afraid I've failed all of you." She sniffed, unbuttoning her shirt.

"Becky, I won't hear such nonsense. You did all you could. I'm so proud of you." Sally helped her out of her clothes and into the pink-and-white-striped gown that Becky had first worn.

"I don't know how we'll manage, Sally," Becky said, wiping a tear from the fabric. "But somehow we'll manage to stay together. I can't imagine my life without all of you."

Sally hugged her, and for the first time in a long while, Becky wasn't ashamed to let the tears fall.

"Sir Nicholas," Mrs. Prescott said, nervously pacing back and forth along the front lawn. "You don't think something has happened to my husband, do you?"

Nick glanced across the fields where he expected Geer to appear with Finn, Willoughby, Prescott and his sons at any time. "Geer has probably shown them the best angling spot on the property, or the bounty of pheasants along the cornfields and the hedgerows." He smiled reassuringly.

"It's getting quite late." She looked around to where her two daughters sat watching Peter apply another coat of paint to the boat's hull. "I hope Mistress Becky's headache improves. I wonder if she'll be well enough to accompany us at dinner."

Nick wondered that, too. "Pray, let us hope so."

Mrs. Prescott glanced back at the horizon. "I wonder…" She cleared her throat. "Sir Nicholas, have you ever…not that I believe in ghosts, mind you. But have you ever seen—"

"Here come the men now," Nick interrupted, relieved that he didn't have to explain about Becky's chicanery. He removed his handkerchief and wiped his face. Damn, it was hot this afternoon. He wished he could escape his host duties and spend a quiet hour at the river.

Mrs. Prescott walked to the edge of the gardens to await her husband. Nick excused himself to look in on Becky. When he came to the foot of the stairs, he saw Molly coming from the hallway.

"Mistress Becky will be right down," Molly said, her cheeks red from the heat. "She asked me to tell ye that she's feelin' most fine and will be joinin' ye shortly."

"Becky took a nasty spill. She should stay in bed," Nick explained. "Send Ben for the doctor. In fact, I insist upon it."

Molly raised her white brows. "Aye, Yer Grace. But Mistress Becky won't be pleased."

"Damn what Becky wants. Just do it."

Nick's brows tightened with frustration. When was Becky going to learn to follow his orders? A sound of footfalls on the stairs and the swish of fabric, and he turned his head. Above him, like a beautiful goddess, Becky stood before him. She had changed back into the pink-and-white-striped taffeta gown, her black hair piled atop her head in thick coils. She glided down the stairs in one fluid motion.

His breath caught in his throat. He'd never seen her look lovelier. He smiled and took her hand as she went to him. For the time being, he didn't want to remember anything but this moment. He wrapped her hand around his arm and led her to the edge of the garden where the women waited. The blossom-scented warm summer air drifted along the verge.

Geer led the riders along the path toward the house, where the women waited with Nick. The Prescotts' sons joked with each other while their father and Willoughby chatted behind. Ben Twaddle, in a makeshift uniform, looked quite handsome as he waited with the grooms to return the mounts to the stables.

While they waited for the men to join them, Nick gazed down into Becky's violet eyes, and he felt a rush of desire such as he'd never known was possible. If only he could make the world and their problems go away, if only...

"Dinner is served," Geer said, looking most respectable with his ramrod deportment and wig worn straight atop his head.

Nick turned toward the manor, and with Becky's hand on his arm, began to lead the procession inside. Before they crossed the threshold, a clamoring yell echoed across the front lawn.

Nick and the guests turned toward the din. A tall, straggly soldier on a sorrel mare bounced across the grass, waving a sword in one hand, gripping the saddle horn with the other.

"Good Lord, it's Keane," Willoughby yelled.

Keane's hat slipped from his head, bouncing off his back. He held on to the saddle for dear life, as he bounded up and down to the horse's lumbering gait.

Mrs. Prescott cried out when her two sons chased

Keane. Sally almost fainted beside Finn, who laughed merrily at the sight. Willoughby only stared, his hands tucked inside his waistcoat lapels. Hazel Willoughby's jaw fell. The Prescott girls covered their mouths, their eyes wide as saucers.

"Down with the Royalists!" Keane roared, lunging a thrust. His horse suddenly veered dangerously close to the guests, who then turned and scattered toward the safety of the house.

"Keane, get down from that horse before you hurt yourself," Nick yelled, running after him.

Keane jerked back in the saddle when he recognized Nick's voice. His right hand waved his sword, but the motion threw him off balance, tossing him to the ground.

Becky stared, aghast, as she watched Nick help Keane to his feet. She closed her eyes, as the embarrassment of such comic disaster came crashing around her. They were a laughingstock, and it was all her fault.

"It was Keane all along," Willoughby said, shaking his head. "Well, I'll be..."

Hazel glanced at Becky. "Oh, dear Becky. How awful for you."

Becky stood, waiting for Nick's announcement. At least she would take the punishment that was due her. She was tired of the lies. She had done her best, but she had been wrong. She had told lies, and ruined the general's good reputation to suit her ends. She was relieved finally that everyone knew.

Keane shook his head, groggily. "Here's the ghost of Ol' Winky, everyone," Nick said, holding Keane by the shoulders.

"Do you admit you did this of your own free will, without anyone else's knowledge?" Nick asked the tall, wiry man. Keane's shoulders slumped, his knees bowed, and he still looked as though he was feeling the effects of too much drink.

Keane's glassy stare focused on Nick. His face blanched before he spoke. "Aye, I did it alone."

Nick smiled, then let go of him. Keane staggered a few feet before he balanced himself. "Geer, take him back to his hut where he can sleep it off. I don't see any harm done. No need to call the bailiff."

Becky couldn't quite believe what she'd heard. She paused, while Nick strode toward her. "Shall we go in to dinner, Mistress Becky? We've kept our guests waiting long enough."

Relief along with intense admiration filled her heart as he escorted her inside. He wasn't going to expose her? But why?

She bit back the question as he brought her to her chair and pulled it back for her. His smoky gaze met hers. Why? she asked with her eyes.

"Keane and I made a deal," Nick whispered. "I told him that I wouldn't file charges if Keane confessed that he acted alone."

"But why would you spare me?" she whispered.

"I think you know." He held her hand longer than necessary.

She sank in her chair and watched him return to the other end of the table. Within a few minutes, the guests were seated, and amid the light banter of the evening, she saw no one but Sir Nicholas Sinclair. Amid the borrowed silver candlesticks from Hazel Willoughby, and the china and silver and lace tablecloths that Nick has also borrowed from Hazel to surprise Becky, she felt almost giddy with relief.

Crystal vases of roses, at each end of the table, sent their intoxicating fragrance drifting on the air. The Prescotts chatted with Nick and the Willoughbys, while Sally and Finn gazed longingly into each other's eyes.

Mary, Becky's mother's second cousin, helped Aphra serve the poached cod and braised hen. For the moment,

Becky felt more than relief. Nick could have cast her out, yet he didn't.

He proved to her that she could trust him. Regardless of the consequences, Nick would protect her...because he loved her. A glorious sense of joy filled her heart. She loved this man, this incredible man who sat at the end of the table from her. He was her opposite, as different as summer was to winter. But she was hopelessly in love with him.

Mr. Prescott raised his glass, commanded a toast to Nick. Becky raised her glass, aware only of Nick's appreciative gaze lingering over her.

Candlelight flickered as the family members rushed back and forth, serving and removing each course. Becky couldn't remember what was served or what she tasted, her thoughts only on Nick. As he gazed at her across the table, she couldn't think to do anything but stare back at him. She felt like a love-struck maid. How could she allow herself to love the man who was negotiating to sell her very home from her?

How could she, indeed? But it had happened, and she didn't know what she was going to do about it, either.

Chapter Fifteen

Long after the Willoughbys and the Prescotts had left and the household had settled in for the night, Becky lay awake, fighting the traitorous feelings of Nick's embrace, his kisses and the startling realization that what they shared was far more than desire. What he had done today proved that she could trust him. He had the perfect opportunity to expose her ruse, using her late husband's reputation as a means to keep Thornwood Hall. Yet he loved her, despite her faults. He truly loved her.

Tears stung her eyes and her throat tightened. What was she going to do? Nick was a good man, a courageous man, but he was wrong about what was best for her. She'd promised to keep her brothers and Aphra together, and even her love for Nick wouldn't allow her to break her word to her parents. Besides, she'd always been practical. To do otherwise, regardless of how pleasurable—wasn't her nature.

But neither was uncertainty. If only she could come up with a plan that might solve their problems. If only…

Then an idea struck like a thunderbolt. She'd find the strength, she always had. She'd do what had to be done. Becky tossed aside the covers and slid from the feather bed. Wiping her eyes, she lit the candle. She had to speak to Nick, and he couldn't refuse her.

A few minutes later, she had dressed and was scurrying down the stairs before she had a chance to change her mind. Although it was long past midnight, she sensed that Nick might still be up, mulling over Prescott's offer. The slant of candlelight beneath the study's door confirmed her belief.

Her hands shook as she held the candle and knocked on the door. Dear God, she wasn't making a mistake.

"Come in," Nick said offhandedly. She stepped softly into the room. He glanced up from the pile of invoices. His roguish smile told her that he wasn't entirely surprised by her late visit. She took the only other chair in the chamber.

Nick had changed from his dinner jacket into a wheat-colored shirt, open at the neck. The garment's full cut set his powerful shoulders to splendid advantage. The tight-fitting leather breeches emphasized his long, muscular legs. Her pulse quickened and she fought to keep her wits about her.

"I was expecting you." Nick shot her a knowing look. "Have a goblet of wine. I had Molly order a special keg from the cellar for the occasion. It's an especially fine vine."

She nodded, then watched him splash the deep red liquid into a glass. The wine might steady her nerves.

"Why were you expecting me?" Becky ventured. She forced her hand not to tremble when she took the goblet from him.

His mouth quirked as he poured a glass for himself, then leaned back in the chair. "You want to know if I accepted the Prescotts' offer for Thornwood Hall."

She met his gray stare. "I admit I'm curious." She rubbed her fingers over the glass rim.

"They've made an offer," he confirmed. "I told them

I'd consider it and let them know my answer in a few days."

"I see." After a lengthening pause, she moistened her lips. "I've come to make you an offer, as well."

Nick felt a twinge of disappointment. In the past, Becky came armed with one wily plan after another in order to outwit him. Somehow he'd hoped they had moved away from such games. But exactly where were they now? He pushed the thought from his mind.

He took a sip of wine. Damn, already his body was reacting to her; he silently cursed himself. "What do you have in mind?"

"I'm offering you my savings, free and clear, if you don't sell Thornwood Hall."

Nick frowned. "Where did you get the money?"

"It's not a great sum, but I thought that you might consider buying an older ship, and rebuild the vessel into a seaworthy craft. That's what my da did whenever he needed something. He taught us to be frugal. It's a lesson all Royalists might stand to learn," she said smugly.

Nick barely hid his amusement. "Are you so eager to be rid of me that you'd pay me to sail to war in an old, leaky ship?"

"That's not what I said, and you know it." She couldn't help but smile at him.

"Where did you get the money?" he repeated.

Her chin lifted a notch. "What difference does it make?"

He sighed. "It's the money you've stolen from the profits of Thornwood Hall, isn't it?" Nick spoke the question as a fact.

She flinched, her mouth a firm line.

"Never mind. You don't need to admit it. Guilt is written all across your lovely face."

She set her jaw in that familiar way he found so adorable. Nick sighed again, then crossed his arms. "If I don't sell the estate, where does that leave you?"

"I'll remain here with my family and manage the estate for you, sending your share of the profits to your bank, of course."

It seemed like an eternity before he spoke. "Why didn't you offer this money before? I'd think this plan would have been far easier on you than resurrecting the ghost of Ol' Winky?"

Her brows furrowed. "My savings isn't nearly enough to buy Thornwood Hall, or a new ship." She cast her gaze to the small bag of coin in her hands. "Besides," she whispered, "I didn't trust you then as I do now."

Nick knew she meant that he could have exposed her as a thief. Or did she sense that he was in love with her and could never do anything to cause her harm?

"We're a lot alike, Becky." He smiled when he saw the surprise light her eyes. The wine was relaxing her, and he enjoyed the thought that she trusted him.

"We've both been cast adrift, and now we're facing an unknown future, Becky. I want to return to my life at sea, and you want to return to your life on land." He took another sip of wine. "But I'm afraid it's not that simple for either of us."

Her brow rose. "Why not? You haven't even counted my money. I say you're giving up your dream without even a fight."

Nick almost laughed aloud. Damn, if he didn't love her spirit. "Although I admire your optimism, there's no way we can come up with enough capital to pay off the moneylender and repair a ship, if we were lucky enough to find a suitable rig."

"You don't know until you try," Becky said, enthusiasm bringing high color to her cheeks. She saw that for the first time, he was seriously considering the possibility. She took another fortifying sip of wine.

"There's just one thing," she added, hoping her nerve wouldn't fail. Then she decided to just come out with it. "I want you to marry me."

Nick choked on his wine. "M-marry you?"

Becky straightened her shoulders. "It's the only guarantee I'd have that I'd keep the estate if you were lost at sea. Finn said the Dutch are winning the war. If you're going after De Ruyter, you may not come back. But as your widow, I'll inherit the estate."

"I see." His tone was cutting. "Practical as ever."

"Are you willing?"

He poured each of them another glass of wine while she opened the bag of coins in her lap and spilled the gold sovereigns on the desktop in front of him.

Nick's eyes widened in amazement. "My God!" His fingers slid over the shiny pieces. When he'd finished counting, he put the coins back into the bag. "It's not enough for a ship, but..." He paused. "I wonder if Finn could raise some money, too. With the money from the fruit and wheat harvest that's soon going to market, and if we find a used ship that's seaworthy..."

His eyes met her expectant gaze, and he felt a rush of hope.

"Then we have a deal?" She pursed her mouth into a bow. A very kissable bow, Nick thought. He watched the candlelight play against the delicate hollows of her throat, and he remembered the taste of honeyed sweetness of her skin. Her lashes shaded her eyes; he could only wonder at the thoughts within those violet depths. She lifted her gaze to his, waiting for his answer.

He reached across the desk and took her hand. It felt cold and small inside his palm. Then he realized that despite her confident air, she'd been worried that he might have refused her.

"I know what this money means to you, and I thank you." His voice was husky. He traced his finger along the calluses of her palm, and he wished he could promise her that she'd never have to work that hard again.

But he had nothing to promise her. She'd given him the money she had stolen for Peter's education, for Sally's dowry, Baby Harry's future and Aphra's lifelong care.

"I've offered my savings as much for myself as for you," she said, as though guessing his thoughts.

He refused to comment; he wouldn't take away her pride. But he knew that Becky had offered him everything—including herself.

He didn't want a business relationship with her, damn it. He wanted so much more. He wanted her as he had the first day they'd met, when she'd taken that old sword to him in the hay barn. Then, she believed that she could fight the world for what she wanted. He didn't want to be the one to break her spirit.

He studied her in the fluttering candlelight. Then he stood and came beside her. When he took her in his arms, she didn't refuse. As he cupped her chin, their eyes met, and her unspoken invitation to kiss her beckoned him. Her violet eyes darkened with passion. A welling knot of aching desire tightened Nick's chest when he realized she wanted him as much as he needed her. The temptation to slant his lips over hers in a fierce, stirring kiss almost overcame his better sense. But what if she accepted him only as a token to finalize their agreement?

Damn, that was not how he wanted her. Reluctantly, he pulled away, his fingers lingering a moment in her luxuriant hair. He felt her body tremble, and he knew she wondered why he didn't kiss her. A crooked smile was his only answer.

How incredibly beautiful you are, he thought as he drank in the sight of her.

When had he fallen in love with her? Damned if he knew. But he had, as surely as they stood here in each other's embrace. He hadn't meant to let that happen. Now, what the hell was he supposed to do?

"Then you accept my offer?" she whispered.

"I'll accept your money, but there's no need for us to marry. I'll sign the deed over to you. I've never wanted the estate, and if I can buy something that floats, then you might as well have Thornwood Hall, if that's what you want."

Nick watched her surprised expression turn to bewilderment, then her face clouded with something else....

Disappointment? Was she disappointed because he wouldn't marry her? The idea gave him pause.

He held her at arm's length. "Unless, of course," he teased, "you've set your heart on becoming my bride."

Her eyes snapped with renewed spirit, but he didn't miss the sudden pink flush to her cheeks.

"As you said yourself, I'm only being practical," she said. "As the widow of our country's hero, I couldn't be removed from the estate by King Charles if something were to happen to you." She took several steps toward the door, then whirled back at him. "Even with the estate's deed in my name, if we don't marry, I'm still the widow of a Roundhead general."

"Of course. I hadn't thought out your little plan as carefully as you have, I see."

She ignored his sarcasm. "Then you accept my offer?"

"Aye. I'll send a message to my London solicitor in the morning. You'll want to be married as soon as possible?"

"Aye, the sooner the better." Becky bobbed a small curtsy, turned and left the room.

After she had gone, Nick sat back in the chair. The only sound came from the low, sputtering wicks in the tallow candles. He steepled his fingers, his mind deep in thought.

Marriage. A sham of a marriage. But why did it matter to him if it solved their problems?

He grabbed the bag of coins from the desktop and turned the pouch over and over in his hands, studying the scarred leather. *Becky had sacrificed so much of herself for her small fortune. Imprisonment, if all the facts became known to the authorities.* And what did that make him if he took her ill-gotten gain for his own selfish purposes? All he was offering was the security of marriage?

Nick drained the remaining wine in his goblet, but not even the delicate blend of the vines could sweeten the bitter taste in his mouth.

Becky placed the candlestick on her bedroom windowsill, then propped herself against the mound of feather pillows in her bed. She stared outside the window for the longest time, trying to make sense of her jumbled feelings.

Watching the white summer moths cavort and dance outside the glass, Becky thought how foolishly the flying insects fought to draw themselves toward the flickering candle flame. With stubborn persistence, they'd perish if she opened the glass and allowed them entrance. With a sigh of regret, she couldn't help wonder if she were as foolish. Nicholas wanted her. She had seen the desire in his eyes only a little while ago. And she had wanted him, too.

But she wasn't foolish enough to think he could truly love her. His mistress was the sea, and she'd never be able to win him away from her, however she tried.

Dear God, but she wanted to. Becky wrapped her arms around her knees, staring at the millers bouncing off the leaded window. She wanted him, more than she ever thought possible. Alone, with the sputtering candle and the white fluttering against the predawn sky, her heart spoke what she had been too afraid to see before. She'd never be able to stop loving Nick, even if she tried.

How could she stand aside when Nick left her—and she wasn't foolish enough to believe a man could change. Hadn't her mother said that to try to change a husband was to make him an enemy?

Becky bit back the longing as she thought of the agony of her future without Nick. If only she had his child. An infant with thick dark hair to nestle to her breast. A baby to love and to raise—Nick's baby.

She brushed back the tears that she hadn't been aware she'd shed as an incredible sense of hope filled her. How she wanted a precious infant, conceived from their love.

The following Wednesday in the sewing room, Aphra held her arms above her head while Becky slipped the measuring ribbon around the girl's slim waist. Molly hummed while she cut out the cloth pattern. Sally sat upon the window seat, her blond head bent over the delicate silk heaped in her lap. Her hand rose and fell with each fine stitch that she sewed.

"Aphra, you'll look as pretty as the flowers you'll carry in the wedding," Becky said, winking at her sister.

Aphra smiled, her enthusiasm for a new gown evident by her unusual welcome assistance—a fact Becky felt was attributed to the child's trusting friendship for Nick. Becky still felt a lump in her throat when she remembered how Nick had repaired Aphra's doll when he found she had buried the toy in the family cemetery. How very happy her little sister has been since Becky and Nick had announced their marriage plans.

But how will Aphra adjust when Nick returns to war? A flash of concern jolted her, just as it did every time she thought of how things would change after Nick left.

"What's the matter, Becky?" Molly asked, her forehead creased with concern.

Becky shook her head. "Why, nothing, Molly. I was thinking how tall Aphra has grown this summer." Becky swallowed the lump in her throat while she gave her sister a hug.

Aphra grabbed the blue satin ribbons from the table and idly rubbed her fingers across the shiny material.

Sally lifted her head from her sewing. "How adorable she'll look in her new blue gown with her basket of flower petals. She's such a pretty child."

Aphra beamed with the compliment.

"It was a warm August afternoon, just like today, when you, your mum and your sister Betty were sewing her wedding dress. Remember, Becky?" Molly paused from her cutting. "We got to giggling, la, I thought my ribs would never stop hurting from laughing." Her smile faded. "To think that a week later—"

"Molly, why don't we take a brief rest." Becky interrupted, preventing Aphra from hearing the story Molly was ready to tell. For it had been only a few days after Betty's wedding when she became sick. Within days, Betty's wedding dress, freshly laid away, had been unpacked to bury her. Within days of her funeral, Ma and Da became two more victims of plague.

Molly realized immediately that Aphra was in the room. "La, you're right, Becky." Turning to Aphra, she said, "Let's see if the tub of sweet cream we put in the stream has cooled off yet." Molly trudged to the door with the child.

"Go ahead with Molly, dear. I've finished taking your measurements," Becky said. After Molly and Aphra had left, their footfalls fading down the hall, Sally stood, then shook out the material in her lap.

"If truth be told, I was thinking of your sister Betty, too." Her pale blue eyes brightened. "But nothing's going to ruin your wedding, Becky."

Becky dropped the sewing basket, the pins scattering to the floor. "Oh, how clumsy of me!"

"Every bride is nervous before her wedding day," Sally teased, stooping to help gather the pins.

A chill crept over Becky in spite of the warm afternoon. She brushed the morbid memory from her mind. For the time being, her problems were over. She was marrying the man she loved, and for what little time they had together, she refused to be sad.

The sound of Nick's familiar steps outside the door caused Becky to glance up. She smiled when he came into the room, but her happiness faded when she saw his serious frown.

"I'd like a word with Becky alone," he said, his voice grim. Sally rose, her worried expression mirroring Becky's thoughts.

When Sally left and closed the door, Becky noticed the folded yellow parchment in Nick's hand. Her stomach clenched with fear when she recognized His Royal Majesty's elaborate red seal. The only other time she'd seen the royal crest had been on the king's order informing her that Thornwood Hall had been awarded to Nick.

Nick took the seat beside her, his gray eyes worried. She braced herself for what was to come.

"The king offers us his best wishes for our wedding, and he's sent along a gift. A bottle of brew made by Dom Perignon. He's a French monk who supplies the French court. The wine's called champagne, and King Charles found it in great favor when he tasted it in Louis's court before the Restoration."

Becky's impatience grew. She knew something was troubling Nick, and it wasn't like him to evade a problem. "What else does the message say?" She hoped her voice didn't hint at the dread she felt.

Nick stood and paced to the window. "He wants my

answer to what troubles the management of Thornwood Hall.''

Becky's breath caught in her throat. She stared at him. "Do you think he's found out about my cheating him out of the tax revenues?"

Nick came beside her. "Of course not. And he won't find out," he added. Gazing down at her, he added, "The king is desperate for tax revenues. As soon as he hears the estate will be producing a profit this harvest, that will be the end of it."

"B-but, what excuse will you give for the losses these past six years?"

Nick grinned. "I'll tell him something." Despite his smile, his eyes were serious. "Don't worry, I'll protect you."

Her hands trembled. "I know you will, but I don't want you to lie or get into trouble because of me."

He took her hand. "Trust me, Becky. You're not the same woman you once were. You've given up your past bad habits. From now on, you and I are dedicated to return Thornwood Hall to its natural bounty, and the king will be pleased." He slipped his arm around her waist.

Despite his reassurance, Becky sensed something troubling him. "What else was in the king's message?"

He paused, then shook his head. "You know me well, my pet. Good news, actually." He sat down and read from the parchment.

"Sir Robert Holmes destroyed the Dutch East Indies fleet a few weeks ago," Nick read. Despite the victorious news, Becky sensed that Nick wished that he had been part of the victory.

"How glorious!" She moved beside him and placed her hand on his shoulder.

"Aye." Nick rolled up the message and shoved it inside his jacket pocket. "This doesn't mean we've won the war."

She bit back her thoughts. "Will you leave for White-hall after the harvest is over?"

Nick sighed. "It's best if I leave as soon as I can. This week, I thought. I don't want the king to send his agent to come snooping. Otherwise, the monarch may not be convinced I've set the estate on a healthy comeback." He grimaced. "If so, I might as well forget any hope of going back to war."

A sudden ache flashed through her, as it always did whenever he spoke of leaving. But she reminded herself of her marriage bargain. "Of course," Becky replied brightly. She wished her voice sounded more confident. "When will you be leaving?"

"As soon as we're married. This Saturday."

She gasped. "This Saturday!" They had spoken of a short betrothal time, but a week! "I'll never have the children's clothing ready in time—"

"The crofters will help." He smiled, his gaze fell to her lips, and she felt the excitement of a bride on her wedding night. "Saturday it will be."

Nick moved to the window, watching the deepening red of the evening's sunset. His brows tightened into a V. Becky knew he was thinking of his lost crew, the war and how much he missed his men. Whatever sad thoughts went through his mind, he always kept them to himself.

She thought of the afternoon they'd shared in the field of wildflowers, the circle of daisies she'd woven. Each flower a wish for the future. Now, her only wish was for Nick to want to remain with her at Thornwood Hall. Just as they were today. But she knew the days of their being together were drawing to a close.

Not wanting him to know her thoughts, Becky said, "I was thinking, unless we begin the work immediately, it will be impossible to have a wedding in so little time!"

Nick's smile lifted the tension in his face. "I never

thought I'd hear you admit to anything that was impossible, pet.''

Our future happiness is impossible, she thought, but she forced a smile. ''I'll ask Hazel to help me. I wouldn't be surprised if she offers me the use of her latest gowns and Willoughby offers to lend us his coach.''

Nick smiled as though grateful for her lightened mood. ''Then it's settled. I'll send my answer back with the king's messenger, posthaste.''

Becky's smile faded as soon as Nick left the room. She blinked back the sting of tears as she gazed out the window. Outside, Aphra and Baby Harry tagged alongside Nelda, who carried her week-old infant while she went toward the fowl house.

Beyond the ripening golden fields, fat cattle grazed contentedly. Would Thornwood Hall be enough to make her happy after Nick left for sea? Becky knew the answer, already feeling the shadow of the coming loneliness.

If only Nick could forget the vengeance that fueled him to go to war. If only he loved her enough.

Recognizing the self-pity, she immediately rebelled against it. She refused to be a noddy who spent her life wishing *if only.* She'd made a bargain and she'd go through with it.

There was no other way.

The next few days were warmer than usual as the household scurried with the wedding plans. Becky wiped a trickle of moisture from her brow. It was so hot! Even the children had been coaxed into taking an early-afternoon nap.

Sitting in the upstairs chamber where a cool breeze blew in the window, she put the finishing stitches to the hem of her wedding gown. Could it be possible? Two more days and Nick would be her husband.

Her needle paused, poking through the white silk. A

husband in name only. Dear God, how she loved him, but he would never have her in the biblical sense. He was leaving for Whitehall as soon as their vows were exchanged, and she'd spend her wedding night as she'd spend the rest of her life—alone and wanting.

Becky placed the sewing aside and went to the open window. From the herb garden, the scent of flowering mint drifted on the warm air. She chuckled, remembering her mother's warning not to inhale its smell, which was thought to induce lust.

She needed no herbal to fire her simmering desire. What she needed was a potion with the opposite effect, she realized with amusement. Her gaze drifted to the steamy green hills beyond the barn. Where was Nick? she wondered. She hadn't seen him since breakfast, when he led a harvesting crew to the orchards.

God knew she truly loved Nick, and maybe it was time Nick knew it, too. Without another thought, Becky left the room and drifted down the stairs. Outside, the air felt stifling under the baking sun. But all she knew was that somehow, she had made her decision, and nothing would stop her.

She saddled her mare and a short while later, found herself riding along the shaded path toward the river.

She sensed he'd be there. The one place on his estate that truly made him happy. But as her gaze searched both banks of the river, a weight of disappointment engulfed her when she realized she'd been wrong. Nick was nowhere in sight.

She dismounted and tied her mare to a limb, then kicked off her shoes. A breeze brushed her damp hair, refreshing and cooling. Beneath her bare feet, the grassy clumps felt rough and harsh. Though she'd never thought of water as a restorative pleasure, like those who trekked to Bath and Tunbridge Wells to take the waters, this brief

escape provided her with a delicious, rare sense of freedom.

She hiked her skirts and dipped a foot into the river.
An immediate sense of delight enveloped her. She
stepped out onto the chalky bottom, the sun's warmth
illuminating the shallow depths.

A long, dark shadow shimmered in front of her and
she whipped around to see Nick standing beside her,
wearing only leather breeches. His hair-roughened chest
reminded her of that afternoon when she'd seen him
swimming gloriously naked in the river. Her breath
caught as tiny threads of desire slammed through her with
the memory.

He said nothing, his eyes said it all. She knew he
wanted to gather her in his arms, but he wouldn't touch
her. Because if he did, he wouldn't stop. The warning
message burned poignantly from his gaze.

Chapter Sixteen

"I—I came to—to cool off." Becky's pulse beat faster as their gazes held. "I—I see you thought the same." Frantically, she fought to keep her wits about her. She could barely think, barely imagine what she'd say to him for the blood thrumming in her ears. What if he turned her away? What if he didn't want her? What if he refused to give her a baby?

She swallowed back the unbidden thoughts and forced herself to look away. Her fingers flew to her throat in an unconscious gesture. Aware of her trembling hands... No, it was her entire body that shook with nervousness. She took a step back into the river. The hem of her skirts dipped into the water, slapping the back of her calf. The sensation sent shivers along her leg. She took a deep breath, certain her heart would burst with its wild beating.

The smell of newly-mowed hay from the recent harvest drifted from Nick's skin. She was reminded of their moonlight stroll in the moonlit garden.

"Do you remember when you asked me if I loved my first husband?"

His gaze never left her face. He didn't answer, but she spoke anyway. "I said that I believed I had. But I didn't tell you that I'd felt there was more between a man and a woman than I'd known. I've discovered something greater, Nick.''

He stepped toward her, his hands holding her, waiting.

Becky forced her mind blank, for if she thought of what she was saying, she'd lose her nerve. "I discovered that I wanted you to be the man to teach me the secrets of the night.''

"Becky…'' he said huskily. Standing before her, half-naked, somehow she knew that he wouldn't send her away. He wanted her as much as she wanted him.

Somewhere in the distance, a bird called melodiously to its mate. It sounded so far away as to be in another world. This was their world. For now, it would be just the two of them.

Her long hair brushed her arms and she shivered. He lifted her tresses from her shoulders, and she held her breath as he bent his head toward hers. His warm fingers traced the outline of her face, slowly and deliberately.

"Aye,'' she replied, unable to speak the words as her senses flooded with desire. She closed her eyes as he muttered her name, his warm, gentle fingers brushing back the loose ribbons at her neckline. A moment later, she felt the soft whisper of fabric brush her body as her gown billowed on the water's surface.

He lifted her dress and tossed it on the bank. Then he unfastened his breeches and slipped them off, leaving her only long enough to toss them ashore. Moments later, he was beside her, warm and ready.

She gasped, more surprised that the first rush of nervousness was gone. He moved her gently down into the rushing river, her hair cascading behind her on the water's surface.

Wearing nothing but sunlight, she felt no urge to cover herself. All she knew was that Nick was here with her, and that he wanted her. For now, that was enough.

He cradled her head as Becky arched backward as his

lips joined hers in melting softness. Her eyelids fluttered shut as his lips began to move on hers. Sliding his tongue along the sensitive sweetness of her mouth, she opened for him, eager, wanting. His tongue began the dance that shattered all of her barriers and left her senses reeling for more.

"Nick...please," she begged, her voice husky. "I want you as my husband, in every sense of the word."

She heard his answering murmur while his fingers traced the small circles at her breasts. "My darling Becky, are you sure?"

She could hardly speak. She nodded, then his lips nuzzled softly at the sensitive spot below her ear, then trailed ever so slowly down until his teeth and tongue sent shivers of ecstasy at the sensitive tips of her breasts.

Nick was seized with raw hunger as he lifted her from the water. Her arms circled his neck as he carried her on shore to the grassy nook along the river. He put her down upon a bed of forest ferns, then lay beside her.

Dear God, how he wanted her. Tomorrow, he'd regret this day, but for now, he needed to show her the pleasure that came from his loving her. He needed to see her beautiful face caught in the rapture of their love. He needed to hear her cry of ecstasy when they become one.

Slowly, Nick released his hand from her swollen white mounds and slid his fingers over her rib cage, moving in small circles around her flat belly.

He heard her soft moan of delight as he flicked his tongue along the trail his hand blazed over her satin skin. He shifted his face to the sensitive crevice, until Becky writhed against him in feverish pleasure.

She was everything he had ever hoped for in a woman and more.

Becky instinctively matched his movements, and her passion set him afire. He gasped with surprise as she tightened on him, drawing hard on him until she arched with surprise and swayed in wild abandon. Delighted by her raw passion, he pressed gently between her thighs.

She welcomed him urgently. His mouth closed on her nipple, suckling, while his hand guided her until she moaned with delight as his fingers prepared her for his entry.

Nick was bending over her, and another tremor of love and yearning quaked through her. His rippling muscles in his arms and shoulders were magnificent—he was magnificent, she thought, while shivers of delight and excitement raced through her.

His fingers deep inside, tenderly pleasuring her as desire deepened to her soul. His face was masked with passion and she felt his pulse throb beneath her fingertips at his neck.

Suddenly he lifted her to receive him, she felt his heat—hard and throbbing. She gave, willingly, trusting and eager as he entered her.

Wrapping his arms about her, he shifted forward, then withdrew, repeating the ancient rhythm as he drove into her. He had been fully aroused, but he held himself back, waiting for her throes of passion to come first. He almost lost control when she tortured him with her innocent, sweet touching.

As she moved with him, stabs of aching desire began to build within her. A welcome heat spread promise. When she was about to cry out for relief, an eruption of excruciating pleasure took her by surprise. She cried out with delight, moaning his name.

Wave after wave, they finally came together as one.

Lying together afterward, clinging, she felt tears of happiness well in her eyes. She pressed her cheek to his, listening to the strong beating of his heart with hers.

"Nick?" Her voice was a velvet whisper. He shifted her on top of him. Her black hair came cascading down around them. Pulling the strands away from her face, he smiled up at her. "What is it, my pet?"

"Have you ever thought to have a son of your own?"

His smile faded. His black winglike brows lifted. "Did you plan this?"

At first she didn't understand. "Well, I—I mean, I only thought that since we'll be married—"

Nick shifted her to the side, swung his feet around and sat up. He slipped into his breeches, knotting them at the waist while he moved toward the spot of sunlight where her clothing lay in a heap. "Get dressed," he said, tossing the garments at her.

"Why are you upset?" She brushed the hair from her face.

"I'm not upset." His voice gentled. "What happened just now was a mistake, Becky. I shouldn't have let it happen."

Becky's cheeks burned while she hurried to dress. "How can you say such a thing? I love you and you know that I do." She strode over the rough ground to where she'd removed her shoes. Wiping the mutinous tears that threatened the corners of her eyes, Becky fought to hold in her heartbreak. "Do you really believe I'm so devious that I'd trick you into making me pregnant just to keep you here?"

"Becky, I..." Nick wheeled around, wishing he could take the words back, but it was too late. She had already mounted her mare and was racing back along the path.

Damn, he'd hurt her. Of course he'd love to have a son...with her, but he couldn't be that man for her. He pounded his fist. Then why did he so want to be that man?

He lost track of the time as he lingered by the river, but the serenity he usually found was lost to him. Taking a deep breath, he called himself every kind of fool. For he knew in his heart that she possessed his soul for as long as he would live.

Sunlight. Laughter. Moonglow. She was that and more. Becky had ignited a fire within him that an ocean couldn't put out. But he'd made a mistake when he'd agreed to marriage in exchange for her savings. He'd been selfish, but he was seeing clearly now.

Thornwood Hall should be hers, and her siblings'. The king had been wrong to take it from her. And before Nick left for war, he'd see his solicitor in London and have the legal papers drawn. He'd see to it that Becky received a deed for Thornwood Hall, free and clear. And Nick would have his solicitor grant their marriage annulled on grounds of his desertion.

That way, Becky wouldn't need to fear her property would be taken from her. Yet, as a young woman with a thriving estate, she'd have her pick of husbands as soon as the annulment became final. With a good man at her side, helping her discipline the children and maintaining a strong arm with the new overseer—one Becky could choose. That was what Becky needed. And Nick would provide it for her.

But a baby! Dear God, she wanted his baby!

Nick made every attempt to avoid Becky until the day of their wedding. He and Finn had found an old cargo ship that could be outfitted with cannons, and Nick appeared consumed with the new project. Already, Finn had a crew starting work on her.

Becky refused to be sad. No one knew the real reason behind their marriage except Sally and Finn. Besides, in a few weeks when Nick left for sea, everyone would find out that their marriage was a sham. Thank God she still had her pride. That was all that mattered…for now.

The next two days were a blur of wedding excitement. Becky helped the crofter women braid wildflower gar-

lands and decorate the tiny parish church with colorful
bouquets. Cook had outdone himself—with Molly about
the house's assistance—to bake enough delicacies to bow
the dining boards for the wedding guests.

Too bad Nick wouldn't be here to enjoy the celebration, Becky mused. But he'd decided to leave for London
immediately after their wedding ceremony. And she'd
agreed, although what choice did she have? Soon, the
remodeling of Nick's ship would be completed and he
could return to his first love. Until then, Becky promised
herself to make the best of it.

On Saturday, she and Nick exchanged marriage vows
in front of their friends and family. When Nick kissed
his bride, the shouts and hoots were heard throughout the
valley.

Sally wiped tears from her eyes as she stood beside
Finn. Peter stood quietly beside Geer, and Becky thought
her brother looked almost grown-up in his new suit.

Becky swallowed back the lump in her throat as she
settled beside Nick inside the coach that took them back
to Thornwood Hall. Nick would remain only until Geer
and Ben returned from the church and changed into their
traveling suits, for both men were driving Nick to Whitehall Palace.

When the coach rumbled down the road, Nick took her
hand, and gazed at his bride. Becky didn't pull away, but
the blush of roses at her cheeks told him she was affected
by his touch.

His throat tightened with unspoken words. What a
breathtakingly beautiful bride she was. He'd planned to
only speak to her out of politeness once they climbed
into the coach. But when he saw her, for one heart-
stopping moment, all of his well-made plans flew out the
window.

He pulled his gaze toward the coach window. Fertile
green and gold pastures of Thornwood Hall couldn't keep

his mind from the vision of his magnificent bride. Her simple wedding gown, sewn with her own fingers. He'd remembered seeing the panels of fabric scattered over the tables when he'd gone to speak to her whenever he had the chance. He recognized the lace, for Aphra and Baby Harry had played with the remnants they'd found on the sewing room floor.

How the pristine white lace set off Becky's jet-black boundless curls, and the single string of pearls that Hazel Willoughby let Becky borrow matched Becky's flawless skin.

Dear God, would he always be haunted by his bride?

But she wasn't to be his bride. God, give him the courage to keep his decision to end their marriage. For once he was gone to sea for good, Becky would realize they had no real future, and she'd come to understand that he was right, after all.

By nightfall, a gray mist had settled over all the countryside. A most fitting mood, Becky thought dismally, as she watched the last wedding guests depart. She withdrew into her own room as soon as she said good-night to the children.

The house was unusually quiet as she closed the door of her bedchamber and drew a sigh. *Her wedding night.* She swallowed back the lump in her throat as she went to the window.

Nick had been gone more than nine hours. Somewhere out in the fog, Nick's coach jostled over the rutted paths toward London. Or had he retired to a room at an inn before darkness fell?

Becky pulled the window shut and took a seat by the fire. On the table was her wedding bouquet. She pulled a daisy from the spray, and held it to her cheek. Was Nick thinking of her? she wondered. Did he miss her as much as the wrench of their separation consumed her?

She brushed her fingers across her flat belly. If only her most fervent wish might come true.

"When is Nick coming home?" Peter asked as he held a fresh ceiling girder while Finn hammered the beam into place. Finn had taken over Keane's cottage ever since the overseer had been thrown out and taken a room at the Seven Swans Tavern.

"Any day, lad." Although Finn never thought that Nick would be gone as long as three weeks, there was no use worrying Peter. The boy was impatient enough, waiting for Nick's arrival.

"Now that Nick's married my sister, I don't see why he ever has to go back to sea."

Neither do I, Finn mused, but kept his opinions to himself. "A man has to do what he thinks best," he offered instead.

The clacking wheels of a coach rattled up the drive. "Nick's back!" Peter's call rang out as he scurried down the ladder and dashed toward the vehicle before Finn had a chance to put down his mallet.

The coach rocked and swayed along the rutted grassy path. Geer and Ben called out a greeting from the driver's seat. The dusty, mud-splattered vehicle sped past toward the manor. Minutes later, it jerked to a clamoring halt in front of the door.

"I was beginnin' to get worried," Finn said a few minutes later when Nick climbed from the coach. His gaze studied his friend's face. The unspoken question of whether Nick had spoken to Barbara Villiers about the stolen money was clearly on his mind.

"When I arrived in London, most of the city was in flames," Nick explained. "For the first week I was there, I helped as best I could. The king and his brother, James, fought the fire right alongside the rest of us." He wiped his brow. "Thank God, few were hurt, but most of the city is gone."

Finn shook his head. "Dear God."

Nick shrugged. "Already the king is planning the rebuilding of London. It's great to smell fresh air again."

"Give me a hand with the trunks," Geer called to Ben, "so we can return the coach to the Willoughbys before dark."

Peter gave Nick a manly handshake. "I say, you've grown another foot in the weeks I've been gone." Nick winked at Finn.

"The lad's a born carpenter," Finn added. "Did most of the work on the new cottage roof, hisself."

Peter stared at his feet, his fists inside his pockets.

Aphra, gripping Baby Harry's chubby fist, dashed down the front steps toward Nick. He scooped up both children and twirled them around. Baby Harry pounded his fists with glee.

Aphra pushed her face into Nick's chest, then peered shyly up at him. He'd had no idea he would miss the children as he had during his weeks in London. Nick studied the apple-cheeked little girl and boy in his arms. Despite himself, the youngsters had wormed their way into his heart. Baby Harry puffed his milky cheeks and smiled, his blue-violet eyes so like Becky's.

Would their child have Becky's blue-violet eyes? The thought struck Nick like a punch in the belly. He cursed himself for being every kind of fool.

He put both children down, then tousled Baby Harry's silky curls. The toddler skipped off to play with Aphra, and as he watched, Nick wondered if a boy as young as Baby Harry would remember him one day?

The upstairs window flew open and Sally stuck out her white-capped head. She waved, then closed the window and dashed downstairs. In less than a minute, she hopped down the front steps and came beside Finn.

"I've sent Molly to tell Becky that you've returned." Her face beamed with a serene happiness he'd never noticed before. "She's in the herb room, preparing a dram for Cook's earache."

Nick's pulse quickened with anticipation. Before he had a chance to be annoyed with himself, he recognized her footfalls on the stone path. Becky stepped from around the house and paused at the sight of him.

He could only stare. He'd thought he remembered how she looked with sunlight filling her hair, kissing each ebony strand with gleaming beauty. But as she stood there, her lovely face, expectant, she looked more beautiful than he'd dared remember.

"Becky, I—I..." How he wanted to tear across the lawn and lift her into his arms. Instead, he waited in respectful silence as she strode toward him, a vision of delicate grace.

"You had a safe journey?" Becky took his arm, and Nick noticed her fingers trembled slightly. He knew she was as affected by him as he was by her. The thought filled him with an agonized delight. Unable not to smile, he cupped her hand. *I want to take you in my arms and kiss your sweet lips, my darling.*

"It was a long journey, but uneventful." *I want to run my fingers through your hair, inhale your sweet fragrance that fills me with such desire.*

"The children missed you." Becky averted her gaze, and the simple gesture told him she'd missed him as well. *How will I find the strength to tell you that I'm leaving tomorrow, never to see you again?* A wrench of agony filled him, and he turned away from Becky to find Sally and Finn staring at them.

"Did you hear what Finn said?" Sally asked, her wide blue-eyed expression waiting for Nick's answer.

"Forgive me, Mistress Sally, I—I was...wool-gathering."

She grinned. "Finn has something to tell you. We've already told Mistress Becky, and she's given us her blessing." Finn's arm slipped around Sally's waist, his face shining with tenderness as he met her smile.

Nick glanced at Becky, then back to Finn and Sally. "Are you going to tell me or do I have to guess?"

"I've asked this lovely maid to marry me," Finn said proudly, "and Mistress Sally's done me the honor of accepting."

Nick saw the love beaming from their faces, and he felt a mix of surprise, happiness and a tiny thread of envy.

"I'm afraid this means I won't be sailin' with ye, Nick." Finn turned to Sally. "I've been a ship's carpenter for nigh on twenty years, and Mistress Becky said she'll hire me as the manor's carpenter. There's Keane's ol' cottage she's given me, and I'm eager to fix it up for the big family we want to have." His broad smile added to his rugged handsomeness.

"Your news makes me very happy." Nick embraced them both. Afterward, Sally and Becky excused themselves, as if knowing the men wanted to speak privately.

Nick and Finn meandered toward the bench beneath the mulberry tree. "So, you're giving up the sea?" Nick asked.

"It's the sea who's given me up, lad. I'm ten years older than you, Nick. I love the sea, I always will, but when I first saw Mistress Sally lookin' as bonny as an Irish yellow primrose, I knew I wanted to settle down. That is, if she'd have me."

Finn drew a long breath. "Lord, Nick. I thought I was kissed by the angels when I saw Mistress Sally for the first time."

"I'm happy for you, my friend. And I'll miss you."

Finn nodded, his smile fading. "Are ye sure, lad, that yer doin' the right thing in goin' back to sea? You've got a home here, and you can't tell me you don't love yer bride.'' Finn shook his head. ''Whenever you look at Mistress Becky—''

''I don't care to discuss it, Finn.''

Finn frowned, but he remained silent. Finally Nick spoke.

''I'm sorry, Finn. It's only that...'' He shifted to face him. ''I'm leaving for London in the morning. I haven't told Becky yet.'' Nick glanced out toward the golden fields of ripening wheat. The sky looked leaden. It would rain soon.

Finn turned to Nick, his face stern. ''The lads are dead, ye can't help them, Nick. But yer bride and her siblings need ye. How can ye turn away from them?''

Nick steeled himself from his own anger. ''Becky will have title to Thornwood Hall after I'm at sea. The marriage will be annulled, then she can have her pick of any man she wants.

''Becky has already chosen the man she wants.''

Nick snapped his head around. ''I can't be that man, Finn. She needs a man who's of the land.''

Finn scowled. ''I think it's the lady's decision, not yers.'' His brows furrowed together. ''Christ, if I thought like ye, I wouldn't have asked Sally to marry. Because I know she deserves someone wealthier, handsomer, younger. But I love her an' I'll make her the best husband I can be. If she wants me, then that's her decision.''

Nick sighed. ''I don't expect you to understand—''

''U-understand?'' Finn sputtered. ''What's to understand? Yer a fool if you leave a lass like Mistress Becky.''

Nick squeezed his eyes and rubbed his face with his hands. ''Are you through? Because if you are, I've got something important to tell you.''

Finn clenched his jaw. ''Go ahead.''

''I spoke to Barbara Villiers about the money that was

stolen from you. I told her that when you picked it up for me at the moneylender, you were robbed soon after.''

''What did she say?''

Nick shook his head. ''Barbara wouldn't admit to anything. But when I return to London, I'll pay a visit to the moneylender. It might do no good, but I'll get satisfaction from asking him about Barbara's involvement.''

Finn considered for a moment. ''So when are ye sailing?''

''I'll set sail in a few weeks. It will take me at least a week to sign on a crew, load cargo, then ready the ship.''

Something close to regret flickered across Finn's face. ''I wonder if a man ever gets the sea out o' his blood.''

''I hope I never have to find out,'' Nick answered uneasily.

Chapter Seventeen

Local folk usually didn't frequent the Seven Swans Tavern during the workday. That and the fact that Lily wasn't working today were the deciding factors that made Ben Twaddle agree to drop in long enough to collect his reward from Keane. If Nelda found out Ben had been anywhere near Lily, even a gold sovereign wouldn't be enough money to cool her temper.

Ben gathered his courage and trudged inside. Tobacco smoke, blue and thick, stung his eyes as he peered into the half-lit, nearly empty room. Several travelers hunched over their brews at a corner table. A lone man slumped against the wall, his hat brim covering his face. Keane. Ben headed toward him.

"I came as soon as I could. Ye bring the coin?" Ben asked uneasily, taking a seat across from him.

Keane pulled his hat back and scratched his unshaved chin. "Aye, but first, tell me yer news."

Ben glanced around before he spoke. "We arrived a short while ago. I asked Sir Nicholas when his ship will be ready, and he said she's near able, now."

Keane paused a moment, as though surprised. "Did he say when he'd be leavin' fer good?"

"Aye. I heard Sir Nicholas tell Finn that he needed to

talk to Mistress Becky, first. Then Sir Nicholas said he'll be gone before the end of this week.'' Ben wished he hadn't spoken so freely before Keane paid him. Maybe Keane planned to trick him out of the coin.

Keane took a long drink from his beer mug. His cold blue eyes brightened when he set the glass down. "Did Sinclair say if the king believed his reason for the estate's lack of profit all these years?"

Ben shifted nervously. He wouldn't answer any more questions until he was paid. A deal was a deal, after all. "Before I tell ye, I wanna see the coin ye promised."

Keane's eyes snapped. He grabbed Ben by the collar. "I'll pay ye when ye've told me enough."

Ben choked, gasping. Finally, Keane released his hold.

"Ye had no call to do that," Ben said, rubbing his Adam's apple. Damn, the man had a grip like a beast trap.

"What did Sinclair say after he spoke to the king?"

Damn, Sir Nicholas had said nothing when he'd returned from Whitehall, but if Ben told Keane that he didn't know, no doubt Keane wouldn't relinquish the money. Ben clutched his throat.

"Sir Nicholas was in a merry mood. He said the king believed everything he'd said."

"Are ye certain?" Keane leaned over the table, and Ben was afraid he might grab his throat again. For an instant, he wondered if Keane wanted the king to find out that Becky had been dipping into the estate's profits. "Aye, I'm certain," he lied.

Keane's brows lifted in surprise. "God's blood, she's gotten away with it." He leaned back, his gaze drifting out the smoky window. After an uncomfortably long pause, Keane shoved his hand in his pocket and clanked a shiny coin on the scarred table.

Delighted, Ben grabbed the coin, but Keane's hand clamped over Ben's fist. "Ye'll tell no one about seein' me, ye hear?'' Keane squeezed Ben's hand until he almost cried out. ''An' say nothin' about what I asked ye.''

The coin's edges pressed into Ben's palm. ''I—I promise,'' he managed.

''Ye better, Twaddle.'' Keane's thin lips lifted when he released Ben's hand. Ben grabbed the coin and stumbled to his feet.

How he'd love to wipe that smile from Keane's face. Instead, Ben bolted for the door. He was no match for him. Besides, there was bad feeling between Keane and Sir Nicholas. And he knew enough to stay out of another man's way. Especially when one was as spiteful as Keane.

Outside, Ben took a deep breath of the fresh September air. How happy Nelda would be when he showed her the gold coin.

Shirtless, Nick lingered by the shuttered upstairs window and listened to the children's laughter float from the garden below. He pushed the happy sound from his mind, to no avail.

If only he hadn't gotten caught up with these people! But how could he not? He'd fallen in love, and because of Becky's caring, he felt his soul restored. He could feel again, care and give again. But until he settled his unfinished business with the enemy who'd destroyed his crew, he didn't have the right to happiness.

He grabbed the homespun tunic and pulled it over his head. When he had finished dressing and turned to leave, Becky stepped into the room.

''Nick,'' she cried, surprise in her voice. She paused in midstep, a pile of clean clothing in her arms. ''I didn't know you were...'' The words faded as her gaze fell to the saddlebags packed beside the bed.

''Are you going somewhere?''

He swallowed down the answer as his heart twisted in

his chest. Damn, he had hoped to wait until later... "My ship is almost ready, so I'm leaving for London in the morning. I'll sleep in the livery tonight. There's perfectly good quarters going to waste now that Ben Twaddle moved into his new cottage with Nelda and the babe."

Becky threw down the pile of linens on the bed. "And when were you planning to tell me?"

He took in a deep breath and braced himself for the anger and hurt that he saw in the tears she was fighting not to shed.

"I would have told you later."

"How much later? So we'd have no time to discuss it?"

"There's nothing to discuss, Becky. We've been over this before. You always knew I was leaving."

"But why are you sleeping in the livery?" Her hands pressed against her hips.

"Because it's...easier."

"Easier? For whom?"

He sighed. "Does it matter?"

"Aye, it matters. If you choose to sleep in the livery, you do so because it's easier for you. Don't honey-coat your reasons to me, Nicholas Sinclair."

He wanted to touch her, to tell her what she meant to him, but he didn't dare. What good would it do? "You're a woman, you don't understand what I must do."

Her eyes answered him with glittering fury.

Damn, he hadn't said that well. "Becky, I—"

"Women don't understand about war?" she interrupted, her voice barely a whisper. "What do men know of waiting for their loved ones to return from the battles? Wondering if they're safe. Or whether they'll come home at all."

"What you say is true. I'm trying to spare you that."

Her eyes widened, angry and hurt. Her it's-too-late stare felt like a knife through him.

"Becky, you know I love you. But you need a husband by your side. Baby Harry and Aphra need a father. A real father who can be here when they need him."

Becky tipped her head and looked at him quizzically. "What are you saying? You are my husband—"

"That's the other matter I must tell you." He couldn't meet her eyes. "While I'm in London, I'll see my solicitor to deed the estate to you, free and clear. Also...I'm leaving instructions to have our marriage annulled."

"Annulled?" She backed away, as though he'd struck her.

He wanted to take her in his arms, kiss away the heartache from her eyes, hold her and never let her go. Instead, he folded his arms across his chest. "Then you'll be free to marry again."

"Marry again?"

"Aye. You're a young, passionate woman, Becky." He paused, unable to trust his voice.

"And you think it is *I* who don't understand!" She spit the words at him.

"I hoped you would—"

"I don't and I never will," she fired back. She searched his face, dismay and astonishment mixed with her anger.

"Finn is a man of the sea," she threw at him. "And..." The remainder of her unspoken words radiated clearly from her bright, violet eyes. *Love is enough for Finn, why not for you?*

"Finn was the ship's carpenter. I was her captain. I can't run from battle. I know my duty, and I do it."

"Then go! I'll not beg you to stay. I'll not beg any man." She tore from the room, her footfalls clattering down the hall.

Nick stood there, anguish ripping him in two. It was all his fault. It might be best if he just left in the morning, without saying goodbye. He had to leave while he still could.

Nick spent the evening with Geer and the crofters. As he left to feed his horse, Nick noticed the lantern in the livery hadn't been lit. Maybe Twaddle had been in too much of a hurry to get home to Nelda and forgotten to light it, Nick mused.

When Nick entered the livery, his horse, Rex, nickered excitedly from his stall. "What's the matter?" Nick stroked the animal's neck while he gave the horse some grain. When he finished, he strode past the other horses toward the small sleeping room in the back. The good rich animal smells charged with leather, grain and straw filled his nostrils. He realized suddenly how much he'd come to enjoy the simple pleasures of the land. He'd miss them.

He shook the foolish thought from his head. He was tired; he needed sleep. He'd be able to think clearly in the morning.

A darting motion suddenly took his attention. In the far corner of an empty stable, he heard a rustling in the straw. "Twaddle, is that you?" he called out.

Aphra jumped up from the empty stall, a wide smile on her face. Under one arm, she hugged her doll. A yellow kitten peeked its head from the crook of her elbow.

"So, you've come to show your doll the new litter of kittens?" Nick asked, delighted that the child had finally found the courage to make friends with the kittens.

Aphra's beaming smile told him he'd guessed correctly. Nick knelt to pet the fluffy yellow kit. He thought of Becky's wish that Aphra might one day regain her ability to speak. Yet the doctor had given very little hope, especially since it had been almost a year since Aphra had uttered a word.

He sighed, his fingers stroking the purring kitten. "It's

past your bedtime, Aphra. Becky wouldn't be pleased if she knew you weren't in your bed.''

Aphra's mouth pursed into a pout, revealing a dimple in her cheek, exactly like Becky's. Nick braced his shoulders. "Put the kitten back with its mother, Aphra, and go back to your bed.'' His voice held firm. "The kitten is too young to be away from its mother for very long.''

Aphra dashed out of the stall and placed the kitten in the wooden crate with the mother cat and the other kittens. He heard her footsteps fade as she ran from the shed.

Nick sighed, grateful for the sudden weariness he felt. He spread out the blanket upon the straw bedding, then blew out the lantern.

Thunder boomed in the distance. An immediate zigzag of lightning brightened the early dawn sky. Unable to sleep, Becky rose from her bed, slipped on a wrapper, then went to the window. Far off, lightning flashed again, and for a brief moment, it brightened the courtyard in daylight.

Were Nick's dreams filled with the wonder of their lovemaking, too? she wondered, staring out the window into the predawn darkness. Did he lie there, remembering how it felt to lie in her arms? Did he remember the ecstasy of their pairing as she did?

She had thought to go to him last night. He had shown her this thing between a man and a woman, but now that he had, he'd shown her a greater, deeper need. Now, she knew what she'd be missing.

She decided she wouldn't go to him. She wouldn't beg. He'd turned away from her bed, and she wouldn't allow him to show her that he was stronger than she.

Pride. She had her pride, and nothing would take that away.

Becky sighed, pulling the window shutters closed and

fastening them from the coming rain. The cool, damp air brushed her shoulders and she shuddered. Chilled, she dressed quickly, then went to check on the children. The storm was getting closer and Aphra and Baby Harry were frightened of lightning.

Picking up the candlestick, Becky left her chamber and tiptoed into Baby Harry's room. Nestled in his blanket, he slept peacefully, his thumb in his pink mouth, his sandy curls mussed with sleep.

Last night, after she had left Nick—after he had told her of his plans to leave so soon—she had taken consolation with Baby Harry. Her baby brother, so trusting and loving. When her parents had died, Baby Harry had brought her out of grief—rescued her from despair because the child had needed her.

Becky pressed her hand to the small lad's curls, then smiled softly. She wouldn't have Nick's baby; she wasn't foolish enough to hope that their one union would produce a child. But she wouldn't be ravaged by what fate had dealt her. She had so much, and if she was left with only memories, then she was richer than she was before Sir Nicholas Sinclair had come into her world.

Becky took the candlestick and passed by Peter's room as she moved to the end of the hall. She knew by his snoring that he was in a deep slumber. The pounding of iron anvils wouldn't wake up her brother.

As she approached Aphra's chamber, Becky noticed the door was ajar. Pushing it open, Becky held the candlestick higher and stepped inside. Her gaze swept the unmade bed, blankets tossed back in abandon.

A thread of worry washed over her. In the past, when storms had wakened Baby Harry and Aphra, Becky would often find the children flanked beside her, sound asleep. It wasn't like Aphra to roam around the dark manor at night.

Before she left the room, Becky noticed Aphra's doll

tucked beside the pillow. Her anxiety edged up a notch. Aphra never went anywhere without her doll.

Becky rushed downstairs, wondering if maybe the child had sought refuge in Molly's chamber. But a quick search found Molly alone, fast asleep.

More fearful than she cared to admit, Becky hurried through the halls toward the kitchen. If Aphra was nowhere to be found downstairs, Becky would wake everyone and have the grounds searched.

Fear, close to panic, charged through her by the time she reached the kitchen. Two scullery lads stretched toward the ceiling chandelier as they lit the tapers in the iron circle.

Cook stood beside the table, carving bacon in preparation for the milkers who'd be arriving soon.

"Have you seen Aphra?" Becky asked the large, beefy man.

Cook glanced up, his bald head shiny in the overhead candlelight. "Little Aphra?" he asked, surprised. "Nay, mistress. Not since last night when she asked the milkmaid for a saucer of milk for the kittens."

Remembering Aphra's attachment for the barn cat's litter, a well of hope rose in Becky. Maybe the storm had wakened Aphra and she was worried that the kittens might be afraid, too. So like her, Becky thought, as she dashed from the room.

Balancing the candlestick holder securely on the window ledge, Becky opened the heavy oaken door. A gust of wind tore at her skirts as she stepped outside into the early dawn rain.

"Aphra?" Becky called into the wind. Rain pelted down from the heavens. "Aphra?" she shouted, her heart pounding. A crash of thunder split the sky; a bolt of lightning flashed, and for the split second of light, Becky's gaze searched the yard. The mulberry tree trunk almost twisted in two; the wind howled like a wounded beast.

Dear God, protect Aphra. If something were to happen to her, she couldn't cry out like other children. Becky tightened her shawl as the raw wind played about her hair and riffled her skirts.

"Aphra!" The rain battered Becky's face. "Aphra!"

Chapter Eighteen

Her heart pounding with fear, Becky fought her way across the wind-torn grass, her boots slipping on the rain-soaked mud. Her voice could barely be heard over the driving wind, but she called Aphra's name, her ribs hurting with the effort.

Gaining her position from the brightness of each shattering branch of lightning, Becky stumbled across the distance toward the livery stable. Her boots sloshed in the mud as she darted along the path. If only she'd find Aphra, safe and warm with the kittens, waiting out the storm. Please, dear God!

When she reached the overhang of the livery roof, a high voice shrieked from the darkness. Was it only the wind? Becky listened, the rain beating against her.

Becky reached the livery door when the cry rang out again.

"Becky! Becky! Becky!"

Becky whirled around, the wind slapping her hair against her face. Running toward the sound, she dashed along the side of the building when suddenly Aphra collided into her.

"Becky!" Aphra shouted, collapsing against her skirts.

Becky hugged her for a wondrous moment, then pulled back to stare at her. "Aphra, are you all right?"

Rain and wind tore at the little girl's words, but Becky saw her nod and she knew her sister was safe.

A miracle had happened. Her little sister had regained her speech after a year of silence. Nothing else mattered. This was truly a miracle. Oblivious of the storm, Becky's tears mixed freely with the rain streaming down her cheeks. For a glorious moment, Becky drank in the shock and surprise as relief and happiness welled inside her. "Thank God, Aphra. Thank God."

Aphra tugged on Becky's arm. "Come!" She wrenched free from Becky's embrace and turned back toward the side door of the livery. Becky reached out to stop her, but the rain and wind made it impossible for the child to hear. With no other recourse, Becky followed after her.

"Becky, hurry! Nick's hurt," Aphra said, tugging on the heavy door. A bolt of lightning brightened the sky, and for an instant Becky saw the fresh tears brighten Aphra's eyes.

Panic forced Becky into action. She yanked open the door and followed Aphra along the darkened row of horse stalls. The animals tossed their heads, banging against the wooden sides, agitated whinnies piercing the air.

Aphra raced ahead. A few moments later, Becky found Nick, sprawled facedown on the hay. She heard a scream, then realized it had come from her.

"Nick, oh, my God!"

He didn't move. Becky touched his neck. When she felt his strong pulse, relief soared through her, but when she pulled her hand away, even in the darkness, she sensed the sticky wetness was blood. Fear gripped her heart when she saw the gash on the back of his head.

Her legs felt weak and she clenched her teeth to keep from crying out again.

"Aphra, run to the kitchen and tell Cook to bring help."

The child whirled around and made a beeline for the door. Becky took a parting look at her sister. "And tell Cook to hurry!

"Nick? Nick, can you hear me?" Becky crouched beside him and shifting him slightly, she managed to cushion his head in her lap. Her throat tightened with fear as she noticed the gash on the top of his head.

What could have happened? She bent over and kissed his brow, whispering his name. Her mind fought back the idea that he might not regain consciousness.

Where were the men? After what seemed like an eternity, Becky heard the shouts and a lantern's pale light brighten the walls of the stable. She cried out to the men as their footsteps grew louder along the dirt floor.

The lantern in Ben Twaddle's hand splashed grotesque zigzags along the hay piles and horse stalls as Aphra led Ben and Cook toward her. The horses nickered, their eyes wide.

"Mistress Becky…" Cook's round face paled. "La! What happened to 'im?"

Ben gasped, staring. Holding the lantern higher, his jaw dropped open.

Becky cradled Nick's head in her skirts. "Ben, don't just stand there. Give me the lantern. You and Cook help carry Nick into the house."

She clutched Aphra's hand while she hovered nervously as the men gently carried Nick toward the manor.

Becky's knees shook. Aphra scurried at her side, her small hand in Becky's.

"It was Keane," Aphra said, when they reached the kitchen. "I saw him hit Nick."

Becky paused to stare down at her. "Keane? Were Keane and Nick fighting?"

"Nay." Aphra frowned, shaking her head. Her fingers twisted a lock of hair.

Becky crouched down to Aphra's level. "This is important, dear. What did you see?"

Aphra's brown eyes widened. "I saw Keane hit Nick over the head from behind while he slept."

Becky heard Ben and Cook approach with Nick, and she paused. "We'll talk of this later, child," Becky whispered.

Becky took Aphra's hand and led the men up the stairs to the master suite. After Nick was settled into bed, Becky gave orders to wake every able man and meet in the courtyard. She'd give them their orders then.

The noise woke Sally, who met them on the stairs. "I've brought the herb chest, Becky. What else can I do?"

"Have Geer wake Finn, then have Geer ride for Dr. Rivers. Tell him there's no time to lose." As she watched Sally descend the stairs, Becky was reminded that she hadn't thought to tell her of Aphra's miraculous recovery. She took a breath, glancing back at Nick's still face against the white pillow.

No doubt, it had been Keane's heinous attack on Nick that shocked Aphra into crying for help. Because of Nick's gentleness with Aphra, a special bond had grown between them. When Nick was threatened, Aphra forgot her own fear in order to save him. Becky felt the tears build in her eyes. Whatever happened, she'd always be grateful to Nick.

Becky wrung out a linen cloth and began cleansing Nick's wound. "Tell me everything you saw, Aphra."

Aphra leaned on the side of the bed, her lip curled into a pout. "I don't want Molly to get angry with me."

Becky frowned in puzzlement. "Of course Molly won't be angry with you. Tell me what happened."

Aphra's eyes widened, tears hinting at the corners. "I only wanted to put the kitty back with its mother before Molly found out I'd taken it to my bed last night." Aphra pursed her mouth and rubbed her eye, sleepily. "Before Nick went to bed last night, he told me to put the kitty back, too." Her face darkened for a moment and her chin quivered. "But later, when Nick was asleep, I crept back and took the yellow kitten. I knew the kitten was lonely without me."

Becky hugged her sister. "No one will be angry with you, child. Now, tell me when you saw Keane."

"The thunder woke me up. I was frightened. But I was more afraid that Molly would find the kitten. She might forbid me to play with them anymore." She rubbed her eye again. "So I took the kitten back to its mother. I was playing with it when I heard the livery door open and someone come inside. I thought it might be Molly. I ducked down out of sight, but I peeked through the boards and I saw Keane sneak past."

Tears began to well in Aphra's large eyes. "I didn't know he'd do anything bad to Nick."

"Of course you didn't," Becky whispered, anger welling inside her. Nick had been right about Keane from the first. She should have fired him long ago.

"I peeked out to see Keane lift a wooden mallet and hit Nick with it." Aphra's lips trembled, her eyes wide. "I was so scared. Nick didn't move. I thought he was dead. I didn't know what to do."

Becky put her arms around her. "Where did Keane go?"

Aphra wiped her eyes with her fist. "I heard a horse gallop away."

A frightening thought occurred to Becky. "Do you think Keane saw you?"

"I dunno."

Becky tightened her arms protectively around her sister. "What did you do next?"

"I ran to Nick. I called to him, begging him to wake up." Aphra drew back and gazed helplessly at Becky. "He won't die, will he? He can't die, Becky. Please, don't let him die." She buried her head into Becky's shoulder.

Becky held her, crooning softly. The shock and fear for Nick's life had shattered Aphra's protective wall of silence. Nick would recover. He must.

Becky didn't know what to tell her. "Let's pray Nick will be well." She smiled bravely. "He's a great hero, after all," she added, forcing a smile. "What would the king say if we let something happen to our country's champion?"

Becky watched Aphra wipe her tears and force a watery smile.

"Because of you, dear Aphra, Nick has a better chance for recovery." She was warmed by Aphra's tiny smile.

She pressed the small cheek to hers. "We both love him very much, don't we, Aphra."

Her sister gave a weak little cry.

"I believe love can heal, darling," Becky said. "Let's hope that our love will be strong enough."

"You look tired, Aphra," Becky said a few minutes later when they returned to Nick's bedside.

"I'm not," the little girl insisted, and Becky couldn't help but smile.

"Very well, but I want you to lie down for a short nap as soon as you help me finish cleaning Nick's wounds."

Aphra smiled, grateful to be included. "Is he better?" she asked, craning her neck to see him.

Becky knew Aphra's leap of trust was still very fragile. She brushed a strand of light brown hair from the child's forehead. "We can't be certain until Dr. Rivers sees him." She winked at her sister. "But I think he's not as pale, don't you?"

Aphra stood on tiptoe and studied Nick's immobile face. She glanced up at Becky and nodded.

Dipping her hand in the basin of cold water, Becky moistened a fresh cloth and replaced the white linen from Nick's forehead.

Men's voices and trampling footfalls caused Becky to hesitate, then glance down at her sister.

"Aphra, tell the men that I'll see them in a minute." Becky smiled at her sister's eager grin. She bounded out of the room, proud to be able to speak to the men and show them her recovery.

Becky shut the door behind Aphra, then moved by Nick's side. She adjusted the wet linen covering his dark hair. Thank God the wounds had stopped bleeding. His skin felt damp and cool. She squeezed her eyes shut. *Please, don't let him die.*

Becky lost track of time as she sat beside Nick, waiting for any sign of movement. The sound of footfalls on the stairs alerted her that the men were congregating below. She opened the door to see Finn, Ben and Cook exclaiming over Aphra's recovery. The youngster lifted her gaze to Becky, then the circle of faces grew serious in the hush that followed as they waited for Becky's report.

"Nick is still unconscious," she said, her voice even despite her fear.

"May I see him?" Finn's angular face twisted with concern.

"Of course." She stepped aside as he brushed past. Finn held a fatherly concern for Nick that she respected and admired.

Ben leaned on one hip. "Take several men and ride to the magistrate," Becky said to him. "I want a warrant drawn up for Keane's arrest."

Ben's face paled. "Keane, mistress?"

"Aye. Aphra was in the livery when she witnessed Keane's attack on Nick," she explained. "Now, hurry."

Ben drew back, silent.

Becky whirled around to face Cook. "Assemble all available men from the house and the fields and bring them to the courtyard."

"Right away, Mistress Becky." Cook scrambled down the stairs, his loud boot steps clamoring on the wooden steps.

Becky took Aphra's hand. "Come, my dear. You've had very little sleep. I think a nap is in order." As she led her sister toward her bedchamber, Becky noticed that Ben hadn't left.

"Ben Twaddle, I gave you an order. Why are you still here?" Becky bit back her impatience when she saw his troubled face. "What is the matter, Ben?"

"Er, nothin', Mistress Becky. I'll leave right away."

Becky watched Ben start slowly down the stairs, then pause. Finally, he came back up the stairs. "Mistress Becky, there's somethin' I need to tell ye."

When Ben had finished his account of Keane's offer of a gold coin in exchange for information about Nick's whereabouts, Becky was all the more determined to see that Keane was arrested.

"Will you tell the magistrate what you told me, Ben? It means you'd have to testify at Keane's trial—if we catch him."

She studied the man whom she'd known as a youngster. Since Ben had married Nelda and she'd borne their son, he'd worked hard in the fields and given up seeing Lily at the Seven Swans Tavern. Although relieved for Molly's sake, Becky had still been skeptical about him. But she knew that Ben's confession to her just now had been an act of faith on his part.

"Ye can count on me, Mistress Becky." His Adam's apple bobbed when he swallowed self-consciously.

"It took courage to admit what you told me, Ben. I thank you." For the first time since she'd known the rascal, Becky saw something of Molly's goodness in the son. Becky felt she could trust him. That was what Nick would do.

Ben smiled shyly, then rushed down the stairs.

After Becky saw Aphra to bed, she hurried back to stand vigil beside Nick's bed. Finn waited with her, his face drawn. "The wounds aren't deep, but he hasn't come round yet." Finn's large fists squeezed against each other in angry frustration.

Tears threatened, but Becky refused to show any sign of weakness. She studied Nick's profile in the flickering candlelight. Tenderly, she brushed her fingers along the black roughness of his jaw, then rested her hand on his chest. The steady, strong heartbeat filled her with courage.

"If only there was something we could do."

"He's a strong lad," Finn said, but his worried frown betrayed his words.

Becky gave him an answering smile. "Aye, he's that."

All they could do is wait.

Over the next few hours, Becky hovered over Nick, waiting for any sign of movement. She recalled Sally and Molly coming in and out, bringing things, taking things. How many times had Molly asked her if she wanted something to eat?

"I'll be outside," Finn said finally. A few moments later, Becky heard the door hinges squeak shut, but it sounded as if the sound was far away. All she could think of was Nick. If only he'd move, show some sign of life.

Molly entered the chamber, fresh bed linens in her arms. "Dr. Rivers should be here soon, Becky." She moved to where Becky sat and gave her a hug. Words weren't needed between them.

Becky remembered the last time she and Molly had waited like this. A year ago. The simple gesture of Molly's hug had brought back the memory. Friends and family had kept the same vigil over Betty, then their mother and father.

Molly cast her a loving glance before she took the empty porcelain water pitcher and left the room.

Becky's lips felt dry. She stood and moved to the window. The storm had passed, but the sky was leaden, the early autumn air damp as her spirits.

When she returned to Nick's side, she pressed her cheek against his heartbeat and closed her eyes. If Nick hadn't been attacked last night, he'd be in London by now, she thought with irony.

Why was it that when things couldn't seem to get any worse, they often did?

Her gaze lingered on his familiar face, seeking comfort with his nearness. Try as she might, she couldn't understand him. Was Nick right? Were women unable to understand men and war?

Truly she couldn't understand such nobility. Sheer foolishness on his part, and most men would agree, she decided. But Nick wasn't most men. He was strong and loyal and he held an allegiance to the men who sailed under him that was noble.

Her fingers touched his firm, chiseled lips, so still. He moaned, his eyelids fluttered.

She jumped up. "Nick, Nick, can you hear me?" Expectation and relief pushed back her anxiety.

He opened his eyes, confused for the moment. "Becky?" His voice sounded surprisingly strong.

"Nick, I'm here." She offered her lips for his kiss. His fingers curled in her hair. He kissed her long and lingeringly and she was filled with an aching tenderness and relief.

He'd been given back to her. Maybe she had one more chance to convince him to give up his foolish idea to avenge his crewmen.

"Do you remember what happened?" she whispered.

He met her gaze and stroked his unshaved jaw. "I remember," he hesitated, as though it pained him to think. "It was night. Something woke me. I could sense someone was there, but before I had a chance to sit up, everything went black." Nick's fingertips felt the swollen knob on his head and winced.

"Aphra was hiding in the barn and saw Keane strike you." Becky told him what Ben Twaddle had revealed about Keane's curiosity about when Nick would be leaving for London.

Nick's eyes flickered with understanding. "He wanted to get back at me." He moved his head back and forth. "Damn him, but he did a good job of it." His mouth quirked.

"Keane won't get away with it. The men have left to search for him, and I've sent for the magistrate."

He said nothing, but she could see him considering her words. "How do you know Aphra saw Keane?" he asked finally.

Becky smiled. "When she saw what Keane did to you, she tried to help." Her eyes welled with tears. "The despair at the thought of losing you forced her to call out your name. When you still didn't respond, she dashed to find help."

In the flickering candlelight, she saw the amazement in his gray eyes. "Thank God some good came from what Keane did."

"Not what Keane did," she corrected. "In the short time you've been here, you've come to mean a great deal to Aphra." If she said any more, he might think she was deliberately making him feel guilty for leaving them, and he didn't deserve that.

"Aphra's sleeping, but when she wakes, she'll want to tell you all about it."

Nick cupped her chin and drew her face toward him. "I'm sorry for worrying you." He was so close she could feel his warm, moist breath on her face. She answered with a soft murmur.

He braced himself with the edge of the bed. "I think if you'll help me, I can sit up."

"You'll do no such thing!" Becky's voice rose as she gently pressed her hands against his shoulders. "Dr. Rivers will be here soon. Until he says so, you're not stirring from this bed."

Nick relaxed against the pillows, although reluctantly, she knew. He reached for her hand and smiled crookedly.

"Try to rest. I'll be back as soon as I tell Finn that you've regained consciousness."

"Aye, suddenly I feel rather sleepy." His eyelids lowered, the black lashes shading his thoughts.

Becky slipped her hand from his, then rose. She pulled the blanket over his shoulders. Before she left the room, she glanced back at him. He rested comfortably. His mind was alert and he had use of his faculties. She took in a deep sigh of relief.

When Nick heard Becky leave, he opened his eyes again. Dear God, Keane would roar with laughter if he knew what depths of hell he'd thrown Nick into. For instead of departing for the London docks, Nick was helpless on his back, teased and tormented by Becky's soft, alluring presence.

How she'd tried to hide the few gleaming teardrops on her lashes, but he'd caught sight of them, anyway. Even without her mentioning their love, he knew what torment he'd caused her. But when she gazed at him with such love, he felt wounded to his very soul. Better if she hated him.

Dear God, was he to be a prisoner, tortured by his decision to return to sea? He felt ravaged by guilt. How he loved her, but he didn't dare show her. It would be easier for her to bear if she thought he didn't love her enough. Otherwise...

He squeezed his eyes in a feeble attempt to rid his mind of her. Damn, she wasn't even in the room and he could still feel her warm breath stirring his skin and arousing his passion.

A soft rap at the door interrupted his thoughts. "Come in," he called. Finn peeked in, then stepped inside.

"Mistress Becky said that ye might be asleep."

"Nay," He'd only pretended so she would leave, but he didn't want to confess that to Finn.

"I'm glad you're here, Finn. I want you to help me up."

"Yer mad! I'll do no such thing." He made a face. "Are ye that eager to set yerself off to London, lad?"

Nick looked away. "The sooner I'm gone, the better."

"Why that lovely lady even bothers with ye, I don't know," he said.

Nick schooled his patience. "If you're going to lecture me, you can leave."

Finn took in a deep sigh. "Nay, I'll save me breath. An' if the doctor says ye can leave, I'll put ye in the Willoughby coach and take ye to the ship meself." He shook his head. "If yer that determined, maybe it would be better for Becky if ye were gone."

The stir outside the window caused Finn to glance up. "It's several riders. The doctor, I think." He looked back at Nick. "I'll wait downstairs with Becky and Sally, lad."

Nick stared at his friend, and memories of the years they'd shared aboard ship rushed through his mind.

"You're a good friend, Finn. The best I've ever had, and I want to tell you how much that's meant to me."

"Aye, now, lad. There'll be time to say farewell later."

"It's thanks I'm saying, not farewell," Nick said, smiling.

Finn squeezed his arm with a manly grip, but he couldn't hide the sentiment in his eyes.

When Finn opened the door, the doctor arrived at that very moment. Finn stepped back to let the man enter. Half Finn's height, Nick noticed, the doctor had narrow, pinched features and wire-rim spectacles perched atop a beaklike nose.

"Watch that he don't bite ye, Doc," Finn tossed out. "The man's a madman."

Chapter Nineteen

For the next several days, Becky did everything in her power to follow Dr. Rivers's orders: Keep Nick as quiet as possible; and feed him three goodly doses of the juice of henbane, hog's fennel, and plantain mixed in his ale. "An excellent cure for the toothache, as well," the doctor added for good measure.

Becky wasn't certain which remedy was the most difficult to carry out. Outside in the hall, she balanced the tray and entered the room to find Nick dressed and standing in front of the window.

"Wh-what do you think you're doing?" Becky set the tray on the bed and folded her arms in front of her.

"If that's another of your vile potions for me to drink, I think I'll jump out the window," he said, teasing.

She picked up the tankard and brought it to him. "That's not what I mean and you know it." She sniffed the brew, then feigned a dazzling smile. "It smells delicious!"

"I'll drink it only after you drink half," he urged, his gray eyes brimming with amusement.

"Very well." She took a gulp, and her mouth felt on fire. She shivered as she swallowed, determined to set a good example. But the lingering taste reminded her of

the smell of a rotted stump. Her tongue curled up in re-
vulsion and she couldn't help but gag.

Nick convulsed with laughter. Despite the obnoxious
taste left in her mouth, the sound of his rich laughter was
a balm to her soul. She couldn't be irritated at him for
going against the doctor's orders. She would have rebelled, as well, cooped up for several days.

"Now it's my turn," Nick said, forcing a straight face.
He took the tankard from her, opened the window shutter
and poured it out the window.

She laughed, and he joined her. The sheer joy of the
shared lighthearted moment made him feel more vital
than all of Dr. Rivers's medicines.

The sight of Becky, standing before the window, sunlight spilling over her, brought a lump to his throat. She
was the most beautiful woman. Her breasts moved freely
beneath the blue muslin day dress she wore as she drew
the curtains back and fastened the shutters open. He saw
her pulse beat fast in the delicate hollow of her throat.
Her eyes shone with laughter, and her ivory skin blushed
with pink roses in her cheeks.

"Perhaps I will sit down," Nick said, not wanting her
to see the physical effect she had on him. She took his
place at the window, her hands resting on the folded shutters.

"Listen to the meadowlark," Becky said brightly as
she peered out the sunny window.

"I remember hearing a meadowlark at the window
when I first awoke at Whitehall and I learned my ship
had been sunk." He sat on the edge of the bed, delighting
in watching her. "I thought the bird had been sent as a
lucky sign for my future."

"And was it?" Becky asked, coming to sit beside him
on the bed.

"Aye," he said. "I met you."

Sadness darkened the violet eyes and he felt a twist in

his gut. If only he had watched what he said. For the past few days, they had avoided speaking to each other, only when necessary. Why had he suddenly changed?

Because he needed to talk to her before he left. He had only been waiting until word came that Keane had been found and locked up in prison. Word had come that morning, although Becky hadn't mentioned it to him when she brought his morning tray.

Finn had told him. Although Becky hadn't said anything, she would have known that once Keane had been captured, nothing would keep Nick from returning to London.

Nick reached out and captured her hand. "Now that Keane has been found and his trial date is set, I'm leaving tomorrow morning." In the lengthening pause, he felt his words, like bricks, building a wall between them.

Becky's violet gaze drifted down to the squares of sunlight brightening the blue carpet.

"I beg you to understand, my love," he said after a few minutes. He entwined his fingers within hers. "I can't bear to hurt you."

"Sometimes we can't help it," she whispered, but her voice rang with censure.

"I can't help what I must do."

Becky lifted her head in that proud way that he'd treasure in the memories he'd have of her. "After everything, you still feel you must return to the sea?"

He pressed his fingers to his temple. "I love you, Becky. But unless I return to fight for my men, I'll never have any peace."

Her back stiffened. "You'll never have peace until you accept that you survived and your crew didn't." Her eyes bored into him. "It's humbling to realize that there's nothing you could have done. But it's a lesson we survivors must learn." Her hand pressed into his. "Why was I spared from the plague and my mother taken? Why Da and not his brother? We survivors must carry on, especially for those who were less fortunate, damn you!''

He raked his fingers through his hair in utter futility.

Becky drew in a loud breath. ''Women understand loss as well as men. We understand that it's an inevitable part of life.''

''I shouldn't have tried to explain. I should have just packed my things and left—''

''You never could have done that,'' Becky said, moving beside him. Her fingers toyed with a lock of his hair. ''You're not a coward, Sinclair. I know you better than that.''

''Sometimes I don't think I know myself.'' He gazed into her eyes, and for the first time since he awoke from the nightmare of the mortar blast that killed his crew, he forced himself to face his most inner dread. ''Deep inside, I'm afraid. I feel this niggling fear that maybe I might have done more that night to have saved my men.'' He swallowed the dry lump in the back of his throat. ''I'll never stop hating myself and feeling guilty for surviving if I don't face my demons again.''

''Your demons aren't at sea, Nick. They're here, inside your soul.'' She put his hand on his heart. ''And it won't help you or your crew if you let your demons drown you.''

Outside, he heard the wind pluck at the shutters, the wood creaking in a way that had become comfortingly familiar these past days in bed. Now, the sound hammered an irritating racket.

''Whatever you think you'll find at sea is here, with you today.'' Twin pink spots stained her cheeks. ''You must find the courage to live with your grief.'' She paced back and forth beside the bed. ''I thought I'd drown with my despair, but life changes and we must move on.''

She stood by the bedpost, her gaze fixed on him. ''But

my greatest anguish is knowing that you don't want me to be part of your life.''

"Of course I want you,'' he said, sitting up. "But I'm not free to be happy until I avenge the death of my crew.''

"Your crew is gone. They're in your past. They don't need you.'' Tears welled in her eyes. "But I do.'' Her hands trembled, and his heart clenched with turmoil.

"God knows I don't want to hurt you, Becky.'' He ached with the agony of what he was doing to her, but it was for the best. "It's at sea where I must face my pain.''

"You're not facing your pain, you're running from it.''

The words stung, but he knew she'd said them in anger.

"That's the difference between us, Becky,'' he said finally. His voice was a torn whisper. "And that's why we have no future together.''

Becky stared mindlessly at the ledger pages in front of her at the desk. The last entry in bold black script had been posted only yesterday: *To Molly about the house for cutting Baby Harry's hair...1s.0d.* Her hand closed the cover and she turned away as fresh tears blurred her vision. Since this morning when Nick said goodbye and she heard him ride away, she had locked herself away in the study, immersing herself in work. But everything reminded her of Nick...even the last entry for her brother's haircut. With all he had had on his mind, he had remembered the small gesture.

She closed her eyes and rubbed the back of her neck. The sound of heavy footsteps outside the door caused her to bolt upright. For the briefest of moments she thought that maybe...

There was a tap on the door and Finn called, "Mistress, may I have a word?''

She bit back the disappointment and cursed her foolishness to hope that Nick might change his mind and suddenly appear at the door. Dabbing her eyes, Becky answered, "Come in, Finn."

She rose and put the ledgers away in the desk.

"I came to tell ye that Ben was notified he'll be testifyin' at Keane's trial next week. Sally wondered if ye'd want to attend."

"Nay. I'll have too much to do with the fruit harvesters here." Besides, the very thought of what Keane had done sickened her. It was best to keep her energies on more productive things.

Finn shifted uncomfortably. "I—I also wanted to tell ye how sorry I am—"

"Thank you, Finn." Becky cut him off curtly. "We'll all miss Nick, but he's doing what he feels he must."

Finn shook his head and stared at her. "Most women would hate him for what he's done...."

Becky studied the older man who had been so like a father to Nick. "I love him, and I don't claim to understand why Nick feels he must avenge his crew, but I understand that he thinks he must."

She recognized Finn's need to understand Nick, as well, and although she found it painful, she knew that talking often helped ease the pain. Although Finn missed his friend, perhaps Finn was feeling guilty that he'd decided to give up the sea.

Finn shook his head. "The lad's made a mistake, and he'll live to regret it."

Becky sat down and motioned Finn to have a seat at the settle. "Nick was told his crew had died, but he never saw their bodies, or grieved with their families as I've done with my grief." She shook her head, her gaze in her lap. "I love him, and I only want him to be happy." She gazed back at Finn's angular face. "Hate would destroy this beautiful thing I have of him, and maybe I'm being selfish, but I cherish those beautiful memories, and I'll hold on to them.''

Finn said nothing for a long time. The wind brushed the leafy branches against the window. Far off, birds twittered in the mulberry tree. Becky listened to the sounds, all bringing back memories she and Nick had shared. She knew Finn's thoughts were of Nick, too.

Finally, Finn patted her hand, then rose and strode to the door. He turned and glanced at her over his shoulder, his face as dark and bleak as she felt.

Several days later, Becky glanced up from the basket of receipts she had been sorting when Sally ran into the hall. "Becky, come quickly. A—a magistrate just arrived, a-and he has a—a warrant for—'' Sally dissolved into tears. "Oh, Becky, he's here to arrest you."

Becky rose to her feet. "To arrest me?" She put her arm around Sally's shoulders. "Whatever for?"

Finn entered the room, his brow furrowed. "Mistress, the magistrate insists that he see ye—''

"Finn, stay with Sally while I see what this is about." Becky crossed the room, but Finn took her arm to stop her.

"The summons is for tax evasion against the crown, Becky. Apparently when Keane was captured and taken to the sheriff, he made his confession....'' Finn shifted uneasily as though unsure how to break the news.

"Keane? Out with it," Becky ordered. "Whatever you know, tell me."

Sally regained her composure and slipped her arm around Becky's shoulder.

Finn cleared his throat. "Keane gained leniency from his sentence by disclosin' that ye failed to pay the proper tax revenues, and that ye laid false claim to the unreported profits of Thornwood Hall."

Becky dropped into the chair, her mind fought to comprehend what Finn had said. *Of course, Keane had known. He had shared in the deceit, as well. But Keane had thought that in time, she might marry him and he'd one day share in the profits.*

"Finn," Sally said. "Go tell the crofters. They'll fight—"

"Nay, Sally. Say nothing to them. There isn't anything they can do and the news will only upset them." Becky sat back, thinking for a moment, then she glanced up at Sally. "Pack a small overnight bag for me, while I speak with the magistrate."

"Becky, you can't. Don't you understand? He's here to arrest you." Sally's hands shook as she put them on the back of Becky's chair.

"Dear Sally," Becky soothed, rising to her feet. "Be strong, my dear. The children will need you." She looked at Finn, his expression tight with frustration. Her heart went out to him. "Don't worry about me. Maybe if I explain—"

An angry knock on the study door interrupted Becky. Sally and Finn met Becky's gaze.

"Stay with the children, Sally, and don't worry," Becky whispered. "Finn, have Geer saddle a horse and go with me. He can bring my mare back to Thornwood Hall."

"Dear God, Becky, how can ye think of yer horse at a time like this?" Finn said, his face ruddy.

"Open up in there." The hammering on the door grew louder.

Becky strode to the door and opened it.

A grim-looking man dressed in a brown traveling cape and broad-brimmed hat stood before her. "Are you Lady Rebecca Sinclair?"

"Aye."

"I'm arresting you in the name of the Crown. Come with me."

* * *

"Nelda, keep the children in the house until Becky leaves," Sally said, shooing the children up the stairs.

"Aye, mistress," Nelda murmured, her eyes wide as she craned her neck to stare back at the drama unfolding in the courtyard.

"And be quick about it," Sally added, impatient to return to Becky before she left with the magistrate and his men.

After the children were safely above stairs, Sally hurried to join Molly and the small group of house servants who had assembled in time to watch as Becky rode between the magistrate and his men along the grassy slope and out of sight.

"How little an' brave our Becky looked," Molly said, sniffing.

"Dear God, Finn. What are we to do?" Sally murmured. When he didn't answer, she glanced up to see that he had left for the livery. "Where are you going?" Sally asked, hiking her skirts as she ran after him. When she reached the livery, Finn had already thrown a saddle blanket over his horse's back. He lifted the saddle from the rack and placed it on his mount.

"Finn?" she pleaded. "What do you think you're doing?"

"I'm goin' to London and try an' find Nick, what else?" he said, giving her an encouraging smile.

"But Nick's been gone almost a week. By the time you reach the docks, he'll have sailed."

"With a little Irish luck and a strong wind at me back, maybe I'll make it in time, love." He winked at her as he led the animal from the livery. In the paddock, he put his foot in the stirrup, then heaved himself onto the horse's back.

"A kiss for luck, darlin'." Finn swooped down and met her lips.

"Godspeed," she whispered, and he was gone before the tears welled in her eyes.

Lying quietly at anchor, the *Defiance* floated serenely among the other seafaring craft of every imaginable size and build. Men's curses and shouting rose from the crowded wharfs, the putrid odor from the city beyond mingled with the stench of the river.

From the quarterdeck, Nick watched the sentries post guard along the gangplank as men rolled barrels of flour and sugar into the massive hold. The ship creaked with the gentle motion of the wind. The new crew, their faces fresh and young, had already taken their places, eager to sail. So young.

He could hardly wait for high tide. Maybe when he was on open sea this terrible emptiness would leave him. In London, he felt landlocked. He'd never experienced such dissatisfaction while on a ship.

The ensign fluttered against the blue sky, and for a moment the image of Becky's blue skirts fluttering like a graceful bell came to mind.

He turned and leaned on the rail, his attention on the crowds milling about the wharf. A young girl, not much taller than Aphra, carried a basket of flowers for sale. Her sweet, high song reminded him of the children's voices when Becky sang with them.

A coach bounced along the crowded street. From the open window, a woman's bell-like laughter caught his ear. Nick turned, knowing it was not Becky, but hope and excitement welled inside him for that instant before reason jolted him back to reality. Of course the passenger wasn't Becky.

He cursed himself, squeezing his fists at his sides until his knuckles turned almost white. Would he spend the rest of his life hearing her laughter or seeing her in every lass with ebony hair? Would he ever be able to get her out of his mind?

Nick cursed himself again, then turned back toward the upper deck.

Chapter Twenty

Becky's thoughts whirled with the events since last night when she had been led to the cell in the common room at the shire's prison. She'd been glad the family hadn't been allowed to go with her. It would be easier to bear the humiliation, but not easier for her beloved family. Dear God, what had she brought on herself?

Just then, she heard the grating metal door of the peephole slide open, and the curious eye of the magistrate's wife peek in at her. The peephole door snapped shut, then Becky was alone again, with her thoughts.

She was being guarded like a common criminal. Yet that was exactly how society viewed her.

She sat down on the straw-filled cot on the floor and leaned her head against the stone wall. The only light came from a small barred window near the ceiling. Bright blue sky lay beyond. She glanced back at the dingy corner of the room. It became too painful to be reminded of the outside world she had no right to be a part of. She blinked back the unshed tears, struggling to keep her feelings in check.

She was guilty. Although she no longer disobeyed the

law and she would never cheat again, she had to pay for her past mistakes.

Nick has taught her the meaning of honor. She was guilty and she must pay for her crimes. She'd done the right thing in facing her misdeeds. Although she'd be sentenced to years in prison at her trial in a few days, at least the crofters would be saved from any involvement. Sally and Finn would care for her siblings as if the children were their own; Peter, Aphra and Baby Harry would always be surrounded by love—thank God for that.

Despite the horrifying events of the past night, Becky felt numb inside. It was as though she were walking through a dreamlike fog. None of this seemed real.

But it was real. She had been transported to a holding jail for the night. Any time now, the magistrate's wife would come and she'd be taken to London for sentencing.

She'd heard of what happened to tax evaders. If she was lucky, she'd be sent to the colonies as an indentured servant. If not, she might find herself imprisoned for life.

It was real that Nick had left, too. Just as he always said he would. She'd thought she tried to understand his need to return to sea, but now, she realized she had never truly tried—it had been too painful. She had foolishly thought that her love would be enough—love would heal his self-doubts and replace the emptiness he had for his crew's loss.

If only she could hate Nick, curse his name. But she couldn't. He'd always been honest with her. It was she who had been blind to believe she could change him.

Leaning against the bunk, she wrapped her arms about herself, her gaze back at the square of blue sky above her head.

It was she who had changed. A few months ago, she would never have faced what she'd done. Although she had no choice now, she knew Nick had taught her the meaning of courage and how to face the truth.

The truth was, she didn't want to remain at Thornwood Hall without Nick. She wasn't needed anymore. Instead of protecting the crofters as she had done, Nick had provided positions for them and given them back their pride. Another painful truth she could now face was that she had needed the crofters more than they had needed her.

Scraps of clouds drifted across the sky, and as she watched, she tried to imagine what Nick might be doing. In the dank cell, she pretended to smell the fresh sea breeze, envision Nick striding on deck of his magnificent ship, the wind furrowing his thick black hair. From his description, she visualized the ship's pristine beauty, brilliant white against the blue sky.

And Nick—as princely as he'd appeared at the Willoughby social—the first time she'd seen him in uniform. Her throat tightened as an indescribable sadness crushed her.

Nick had made his choice; that was the reality.

Without Nick, Thornwood Hall was just a warren filled with bittersweet memories. Becky's senses whirled, her heart ached with the image of the sultry afternoon when she braided chains of daisies, each flower a wish for their future. She squeezed her eyes shut against the memories. How foolish to believe in dreams.

She bit back the irony. The king had originally decreed the estate to Nick, and although in the end she had won it back, she had lost more than she'd ever known. For now she knew what real love was, and to live at Thornwood Hall with the memories of Nick haunting her at every turn, she would be in a virtual hell.

Seagulls cried in the distance as Finn jerked back on the reins and urged his horse among the fish vendors, cart sellers, and various townsfolk who made their living along the wharf. The gray Thames spirited the city's residents along its waters in every type of watercraft, from one-man rowboats to three-masted beauties.

Finn's gaze searched the assorted sailing vessels bobbing along the mighty river. His heart pounded with hope. Certainly Nick would be able to help if he knew Becky was in danger. But what could Finn do if he had arrived too late?

Making his way among the gangplanks toward a crowd of sailors, Finn asked no one in particular, "Have ye seen Captain Sinclair of the *Defiance?* She's a two-masted fire ship, outfitted with heavy cannon."

"I saw the cap'n yesterday mornin'," said a one-eyed man. "'E was signin' on the last of 'is crew, then preparin' to raise anchor."

"If ye want to sail with 'em, yer too late, mate," another man beside him said. "The *Defiance* sailed on this morn's high tide."

"Gone?" Finn swung around, his hopes dashed. If only he'd reached Nick in time. He felt as though someone had kicked him in the stomach. He turned and left.

"The *Lucky Fortune* is signin' on," the tall sailor called after him. But Finn didn't hear him. His mind was on how he'd explain to Sally that after all his efforts, he had failed to get word to Nick.

The next afternoon, two sentries stepped aside as the guards flanked Becky and led her up the Old Bailey steps and into one of the small rooms to await judgment. She felt calm and composed, already resigned to her fate.

A guard motioned for her to take a seat on the long bench beside the table, the only furnishings in the room. Earlier, a message had come that the Willoughbys had summoned a solicitor on her behalf, but she refused the offer. She didn't want them to see her like this.

The clank of the sentries' swords as they resumed their rest position at the door was the only sound she heard after the prison mistress had left her to wait to be called before the bailiff.

The trial would go swiftly, she thought. With a plea of guilty, with no convincing argument to the contrary, the charges would be read and then sentencing would begin.

She straightened her spine. When the guard glanced through the slit in the door, he wouldn't see a slouching figure. She'd never forget her dignity. Under the circumstances, she had done what she had to do for her family. But she was glad Nick was gone and that he'd never know of her humiliation.

Hours dragged by and she remained, for how long she didn't know. She had brushed back all sad thoughts and focused on Nick and their one night of lovemaking. If only they had had more time together.

It was too early to know if she was with child. But now, what would she do if their infant was born in prison? Would the authorities allow Sally and Finn to raise it, or would her baby be taken from her?

The sound of footsteps outside the door interrupted her terrifying thoughts. Her stomach clenched. She'd had no idea they would come for her so soon. She straightened her shoulders and hurriedly composed her face as the key grated in the lock and the guard creaked open the door.

"You've a visitor, mistress." The guard stood uneasily, his hand on his sword hilt.

Becky rose to her feet. "I told you earlier that I don't wish a solicitor. Now tell—"

"It's not the solicitor, mistress."

She felt suddenly apprehensive. She thought men of

the cloth only visited criminals when they were sent to the gallows. Who else could it be?

Before Becky had a chance to ask, the portal hinge squeaked and in the doorway loomed Nick.

She couldn't believe her eyes. Her voice faded as he rushed forward and swept her in his arms.

"Becky, thank God I found you." He crushed her to him.

"N-Nick!" Mesmerized, she could only stare as surprise and confusion rushed her senses. Was she dreaming? She drew back, her gaze riveted on the man she loved. "I—I thought—"

"I'm here, my love. I'll never leave you again."

"B-but, I don't understand. How—?"

"Let's leave this place. I'll explain on our way to Thornwood Hall."

"But I can't leave. Didn't they tell you, I'm—"

His strong arms lifted her off the ground and carried her through the door. "Everything has been taken care of, my love. The back taxes have been repaid, plus interest and penalties." He smiled at her, but he knew the idea hadn't sunk in yet.

"All of the money I owe?" She shook her head. "But how is that possible? Who paid my debt? Where did the money come from?"

Inside the corridor, heads turned and people gawked as Nick carried her through the hall. She curled her arms around his neck, breathing in his clean male scent. When they reached the main entrance, the damp wind from the streets carried the smell of coal smoke, and sewerage from the river. She buried her nose in his shoulder. She felt her face redden when the crowds along the road stared at them. She should insist he put her down, but she couldn't bear to be away from him. She must be dreaming, and she didn't want to waken just yet.

A coachman stood erect, then whirled around to open the door for them, and Nick helped her inside the vehicle. She recognized Nick's horse, Rex, tied to the back of the coach. "Where are we going?" she asked, unable to take in everything.

"We're going home, my darling. To Thornwood Hall."

He climbed beside her, then the coach jolted to a start. As the vehicle rocked along the busy London lane, Becky was torn between relief and dread. Any minute now, the king's soldiers might come chasing after her, swords drawn, ready to return her to jail. But for this moment, all she could think was how marvelous it was to feast her eyes on this man she loved.

The carriage careened around a corner and she leaned against Nick. The grin fled from his face. "Becky," he groaned, his voice hoarse. "How I've missed you." She buried her face into his chest, and she felt his fingers tighten the tangles of her hair.

"I love you, Becky," he muttered before he found her lips. He pulled her against him, devouring her with kisses.

Becky's mind whirled in sweet sensations, her body melting with his. When their lips parted, she asked in a shaky voice, "Are we...still married?"

"Aye, my darling. We're very much married." He touched her hair, tumbling it down around them. "Finn called me a madman, and I must have been to think of an annulment." He shook his head.

"B-but what made you change your mind?"

Nick kissed her again, a kiss that held promise more than passion. "Just before we were ready to sail, I knew I couldn't go through life without you. But I kept thinking of what you said before I left."

She cradled herself against him while she listened, unable to believe his words—that he loved her and he was truly beside her.

"You said my future was here, in my heart." He placed his hand on her breast. "On board, I knew you were right because that's where you were…here, within my heart, and that's where you'll always be, my darling."

Becky's breath caught on a sob. She lifted her head, his lips only inches from hers. "But how did you know I was in jail?"

"I didn't know until I went to Whitehall. You see, when I left the ship, I had an idea. I needed to explain to King Charles why I was returning to Thornwood Hall. While I was waiting for an audience with the monarch, I spoke to Barbara."

"Barbara. The king's mistress?"

"Aye. She had heard about Keane's confession and that you were arrested." Nick took a deep, shuddering breath. "God, how I wished I had been there for you."

She brushed a lock from his face. "You're here, now. That's what's important."

He sighed, then continued. "Barbara's motive for telling me was selfish. She feared that if the king discovered that you were being held in prison for evading taxes, he'd want to save you since you were my wife." He made a face. "Of course, Barbara's pride wouldn't allow her to admit it, but I think she feared Charles might make you his new mistress while I was at sea."

Becky sat up, offended. "How outrageous of her."

Nick nodded. "Aye, but consider the source, Becky."

Becky had heard of the king's many mistresses, and she could only feel sorry for him. For if he had found the one true love in his life, surely he would have had to look no farther. But Becky had far too many questions that needed answers.

"How did you answer Barbara?"

"Well…" He paused. "Do you remember me telling you that I thought Barbara had something to do with the robbery after Finn left the moneylender's office?"

"Aye, I remember."

"I reminded her of the incident. I knew if I could get back the gold, it would be more than enough to pay the past years' taxes on Thornwood Hall.

"When I explained this to her, and she realized that paying the back taxes would allow you to be free and that I'd safely keep you away from the king, Barbara agreed to help me."

He chuckled at the memory. "The witch. She refused to admit to being in league with the moneylender, but I didn't care, if she agreed to help me."

"So Barbara gave you the money for the estate's back taxes?"

"Not exactly." Nick paused to kiss the tip of her nose. "I suggested that Barbara bestow a gift to the king."

"A gift?"

"Aye. I offered to arrange for Barbara to buy the *Defiance,* the fully armed ship and crew. When she presents it to the king, Charles will be so delighted and overcome at her thoughtfulness—he's been desperate for a fighting vessel—that he'll be forever beholden to her."

"And she agreed to it?"

"Aye, she thought it a splendid idea."

Becky laid her head against his chest. "Are you certain, my love, that you won't regret selling the ship?"

"I'm certain." He hugged her, and he was overcome with a profound sense of pleasure at knowing they had a lifetime together.

"I only had to wait several hours before Barbara met me at the Old Bailey." Nick shook his head. "She arrived in a black veil, black cloak, completely in disguise.

She waited until I had finished all of the business and she was assured that you were free.'' He shook his head. ''Poor Barbara.''

Becky had only heard tales of the splendor of White-hall Palace, but she knew the simple pleasures of Thornwood Hall with Nick by her side were more precious than jewels or gold.

Nick pulled her completely on top of him. ''I'd never be whole without you, my darling. You've given me back my purpose, my soul, my passion. You've healed me, Becky.'' His voice sounded hoarse, and when she gazed into his passion-filled eyes, she knew he wanted her as much as she needed him.

His long legs were bent at an uncomfortable angle. Becky gave him a sidelong glance and chuckled. ''My love, you'll startle the coach driver if you get a cramp in your leg and yell out.''

Nick laughed, the rich sound filling her with happiness. ''If I cry out, wife, it won't be from a cramp.''

He pulled her to him, his hands cupping her hips as their bodies joined with the rocking of the coach.

When they arrived at Thornwood Hall, night had fallen. Utterly contented, Nick glanced down at his wife, nestled asleep in his arms. For the past few hours, he'd thought of the many times in his life that he had wished for something—longed for something. Yet at the time, he hadn't known what he sought.

Becky shifted against him, and he cradled her head under his chin as he had these past hours while she slept. God, he'd never get enough of her. And that was what he'd yearned for—this woman who was a song in his heart, his reason for being.

With her in his embrace, he knew the special reason he'd been saved when his ship sank. For she was his special reason, and he would spend his life making her happy.

Her head shifted on his shoulder. "Nick," she murmured sleepily. "Am I dreaming?"

He kissed her fingertips. God, how he loved her. "No, my darling, you and I are not dreaming," he whispered in her hair. "For our dreams have come true."

Epilogue

Christmas at Thornwood Hall
One Year Later

The Willoughbys' black-lacquered coach with the matched set of six white horses rumbled along the snow-dusted path of Thornwood Hall, the silver bells on the horses' reins jingling in merry rhythm.

"They're here," Aphra shouted from the evergreen-decked front window. Her hand shot to her mouth when she remembered that proper young ladies shouldn't raise their voices. "Shall I tell Molly to announce that the Willoughbys have arrived?" she asked softly, her voice a studied imitation of her sister's.

"Aye, do that, Aphra." Nick chuckled at the mercurial wonder of a little girl. One minute she was stitching a delicate pair of gloves for a Christmas gift for Becky; the next, she was trudging through the snowy woods, helping Geer and the men drag in the Yule log.

"Will you sit by the window and watch for Ol' Father Christmas until I get back?" Aphra asked, her face beaming with excitement.

Nick laughed. "Aye, I'll keep a watch." He smiled as she scurried off.

"Father Chris-chris," Baby Harry said, beginning to crawl up on Nick's lap. The youngster's rosy cheeks matched his satin suit, with his first pair of breeches.

"Ol' Father Christmas will be here soon, and he's bringing a good lad like you a shiny captain's whistle, I'd wager." Nick lifted Baby Harry onto his lap. "But first, you must help me greet our guests." Nick pointed outside where the footman helped Hazel and Willoughby from the coach. A servant, staggering under an armload of gaily wrapped presents, followed them to the front door.

"A very Merry Christmas," Nick offered, exchanging greetings with the couple.

"Oh, and a wonderful Christmas it is," Hazel added, allowing her husband to remove her fur wrap. "Now, when can I see that beautiful son of yours? Oh, it doesn't seem possible that he's three months old already."

"Becky and little Nicholas will be right down—"

"Merry Christmas," Becky called out from the top of the staircase.

Nick paused, his gaze lifted to his wife. His breath caught as Becky stood there, resplendent in a red velvet gown. In her arms was their son, Nicholas.

Nick swallowed back the lump in his throat.

Smiling, Becky glided down the steps, all eyes upon her, but her gaze never wandered from her husband's until she was at his side. Nick slipped an arm around her tiny waist, kissing her lightly on the cheek.

"So good of you to share Christmas with us," Becky said to the Willoughbys. "Cook and Molly were up all night baking mince pies, puddings, and preparing a great cake for Twelfth Night."

Becky lifted the blanket from the sleepy little face in

her arms. Beautiful violet eyes blinked back at them. Hazel sighed. "Oh, such a beautiful baby. Oh, Becky, he looks just like Baby Harry when he was a babe." She clasped her hands. "Oh, do you think I might hold him?"

Becky smiled, placing the precious babe into Hazel's waiting arms. "I'll sit here and wait for Sally," Hazel said, taking a chair by the blazing Yule log in the fireplace. "It will give me a chance to catch up on the news since her wedding."

"Finn and Sally are so happy," Becky added, taking Nick's hand. "Before you leave, Hazel, you must see the lovely cottage that Nick and Peter have helped Finn build."

"By the way, where is Finn?" Willoughby asked.

Nick winked. "I think he's looking for Ol' Father Christmas," he said, exchanging a knowing glance with the older man.

Just then, a chorus of voices could be heard from outside. Aphra and Baby Harry dashed to the window. "It's Ol' Father Christmas!" Aphra cried, helping her brother to the window seat.

Becky rested her head on Nick's chest as they watched the torchlight parade march past. Finn, dressed in the bright hood and robe of Ol' Father Christmas, led the singing. A huge bag swung from his shoulder, bulging with surprises for the children. Sally and Peter trudged beside Finn, then Nelda, arm in arm with Ben. Becky's distant relatives, the crofters and their children, paraded gaily in the rear, the men carrying torches, their strong voices blending in rich harmony.

Nick wrapped his arms around Becky and whispered into her ear. "Merry Christmas, my darling." She gazed up at him in that special way that said more to him than words.

Nick reached for a twig of mistletoe and snapped it off

in his fingers. "Remember what you told me about braiding a wreath of daisies and making a wish on each flower?"

"Of course." Becky smiled. "How could I forget?" She took the mistletoe blossom and twirled it in her fingers. "A circle of dreams, Mum called it." She closed her eyes, inhaling the fresh fragrance. When her gaze met his, her eyes were misty. "I was thinking of Mum and Da. How happy they'd be if they knew I'd found you and we have a son. But then...in my heart, I think they know."

Nick held her closer, his senses alive with the sounds of Christmas—the snapping of the burning Yule log, the aroma of holly, rosemary and bay garlands trimming the walls, the festive sights of white candles ablaze above red-velvet ribbons adorning the doors and windows.

Music, laughter and happiness filled his heart where nothing but darkness and isolation had been before he met Becky. God, he thought his heart might break with his love for her.

"Let's make a wish." Becky's violet eyes glistened.

"You make a wish. I have everything I could ever want," he said. "My greatest gift is knowing that you love me." His voice trembled with need.

Becky's eyes filled with tears. "Then let's wish something for our children." Nestling her head against his shoulder, she gazed at the mistletoe blossom. "I hope our children will have the courage to make wishes and the spirit to make them come true."

"If they have half of their mother's charming spirit," Nick teased, "there's no doubt they'll get whatever they want."

She made a face at him. "I love you, my husband."

He felt the immediate reaction she unintentionally gave

him. "While Hazel is watching our son, maybe we can leave and...pick another armful of mistletoe."

"To make a wreath?" she asked, feigning innocence.

"Mmm, we'll think of something." He pulled her to him, his heart full with the music of her laughter.

* * * * *

**Can the scholarly
Geoffrey de Burgh tame
the "wicked" Lady Elene,
who must become his wife?**

**Find out in Deborah Simmons's
terrific new medieval novel**

Coming in January
to your favorite paperback book outlet.

The deBurgh Bride

THE deBURGH BRIDE (ISBN 28999-5)

WELCOME TO *Love Inspired* ™

A brand-new series of contemporary inspirational love stories.

Join men and women as they learn valuable lessons about facing the challenges of today's world and about life, love and faith.

Look for the following January 1998
Love Inspired™ titles:

Night Music
by Sara Mitchell

A Wife Worth Waiting For
by Arlene James

Faithfully Yours
by Lois Richer

Available in retail outlets
in December 1997.

LIFT YOUR SPIRITS AND GLADDEN YOUR HEART with *Love Inspired*™!

Steeple
Hill™

LI198

Harlequin® Historical

"One of the top five historical trilogies
of the nineties." —*Affaire de Coeur*

Bestselling Harlequin Historical author

THERESA MICHAELS

presents the story of the second widow
in her heartwarming series

THE MERRY WIDOWS
Catherine

"Sensitivity, sensuality and a sense of humor are
hallmarks of Theresa Michaels' captivating storytelling."
—*Romantic Times*

Don't miss reading about Catherine in the second book in the
Merry Widows trilogy, coming to you in February 1998.

KEY TO MY HEART

Unlock the secrets of romance just in time for the most romantic day of the year— Valentine's Day!

Key to My Heart
features three of your favorite authors,

Kasey Michaels,
Rebecca York
and Muriel Jensen,

to bring you wonderful tales of romance and Valentine's Day dreams come true.

As an added bonus you can receive Harlequin's special Valentine's Day necklace. FREE with the purchase of every *Key to My Heart* collection.

Available in January, wherever Harlequin books are sold.

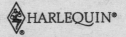

HARLEQUIN®

PHKEY349

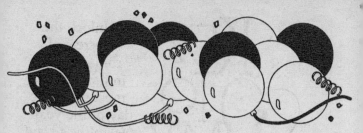

Ring in the New Year with

New Year's Resolution:

FAMILY

**This heartwarming collection of three
contemporary stories rings in the
New Year with babies, families and
the best of holiday romance.**

Add a dash of romance to your holiday celebrations
with this exciting new collection, featuring bestselling
authors **Barbara Bretton, Anne McAllister** and
Leandra Logan.

Available in December,
wherever Harlequin books are sold.

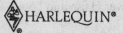

**Look for these titles—
available at your favorite retail outlet!**

January 1998
Renegade Son by Lisa Jackson

Danielle Summers had problems: a rebellious child
and unscrupulous enemies. In addition, her Montana
ranch was slowly being sabotaged. And then there was
Chase McEnroe—who admired her land and desired her
body. But Danielle feared he would invade more than just
her property—he'd trespass on her heart.

February 1998
The Heart's Yearning by Ginna Gray

Fourteen years ago Laura gave her baby up for adoption,
and not one day had passed that she didn't think about
him and agonize over her choice—so she finally followed
her heart to Texas to see her child. But the plan to watch
her son from afar doesn't quite happen that way, once the
boy's sexy—*single*—father takes a decided interest in *her*.

March 1998
First Things Last by Dixie Browning

One look into Chandler Harrington's dark eyes and
Belinda Massey could refuse the Virginia millionaire nothing.
So how could the no-nonsense nanny believe the rumors that
he had kidnapped his nephew—an adorable, healthy little boy
who crawled as easily into her heart as he did into her lap?

**BORN IN THE USA: Love, marriage—
and the pursuit of family!**